A passion from the past,
a love for the future. . . .

D0030116

The scent made him freeze in place.

He was held there by a scrap of a memory—one he'd thought forgotten years ago. A memory of exotic violet eyes fringed with thick, black lashes; of hair that slid through his greedy fingers like black silk; of creamy skin that held the sun's fragrant kiss; and of a lush mouth, ripe for kisses that—

"Hello, William."

The voice possessed a throaty resonance that made even a whisper clear. It was rich, deeper than usual for a woman, and yet still feminine and richly wanton. William knew it as well as his own . . . and it was the last voice he expected to hear in his own cabin.

"Aren't you going to return my greeting? Or are we still not speaking?" The lilting voice ran up and down his spine, as sensual as a warm hand.

William gritted his teeth against his traitorous body before turning.

There, sitting in a chair at the head of the captain's table, was the one woman he'd never wished to see again.

Turn the page for rave reviews of
Karen Hawkins's romantic storytelling . . .

Scandal in Scotland is also available as an eBook

Praise for KAREN HAWKINS

"Always funny and sexy, a Karen Hawkins book is a sure delight!"

—Victoria Alexander

"Karen Hawkins writes fast, fun, and sexy stories that are a perfect read for a rainy day, a sunny day, or any day at all!"

—Christina Dodd

"Karen Hawkins will make you laugh and touch your heart."

—Rachel Gibson

and her sparkling historical romances

One Night in Scotland

"Enticing repartee . . . charming and witty."

—*Publishers Weekly*

"Readers will be delighted by the perfect pacing, the humorous dialogue and the sizzling sensual romance."

—*Romantic Times* Top Pick

Much Ado About Marriage

"A delicious flirtation that pits a staid Englishman against a fey Scots woman. Humor, forklore, and sizzling love scenes lend this novel the perfect incentive for not wanting to put it down."

—*Winter Haven News Chief* (Florida)

"Delightful banter. . . . Colorful secondary characters . . . add humor and charm."

—*Publishers Weekly*

The Laird Who Loved Me

"Filled with biting reparté, humor, and sexual tension that will keep you turning the pages with glee."

—*Romantic Times* (4½ stars, Top Pick)

"Delightful in every way."

—Reader To Reader
Sleepless in Scotland

"Amusing yet profound. . . . Readers will be sleepless in America due to a one-sitting enjoyable time."

—Harriet Klausner

"Made me laugh, cry and fall out of bed. . . . Karen is an author who will transport you back in time [and] have you placing her on your must-buy list!"

—Night Owl Reviews (Top Pick)
To Catch a Highlander

"Love and laughter, poignancy and emotional intensity, endearing characters, and a charming plot are the ingredients in Hawkins's utterly delightful tale."

—*Romantic Times*

"Fast, sensual, and brilliant. . . . This is romance at its best!"

—Romance and More
To Scotland, With Love

"Another winner . . . there were so many charming bits in it, I can't even begin to describe them—but I found myself laughing a lot!"

—Rakehell Reviews
How to Abduct a Highland Lord

"Heated, exciting, and touching. Hawkins excels at taking tried-and-true plotlines and turning them into fresh, vibrant books."

—*Romantic Times*

"*How to Abduct a Highland Lord* is laced with passion and drama, and with its wonderfully romantic and thrilling ending, it's a story you don't want to miss!"

—JoyfullyReviewed

KAREN HAWKINS

Scandal in Scotland

Pocket Books

New York   London   Toronto   Sydney

Pocket Books
A Division of Simon & Schuster, Inc.
1230 Avenue of the Americas
New York, NY 10020

This book is a work of fiction. Names, characters, places, and incidents either are products of the author's imagination or are used fictitiously. Any resemblance to actual events or locales or persons, living or dead, is entirely coincidental.

Copyright © 2011 by Karen Hawkins

First Pocket Books paperback edition June 2011

POCKET BOOKS and colophon are registered trademarks of Simon & Schuster, Inc.

For information about special discounts for bulk purchases, please contact Simon & Schuster Special Sales at 1-866-506-1949 or business@simonandschuster.com

The Simon & Schuster Speakers Bureau can bring authors to your live event. For more information or to book an event contact the Simon & Schuster Speakers Bureau at 1-866-248-3049 or visit our website at www.simonspeakers.com.

Cover illustration by Craig White. Hand lettering by Ron Zinn.

Manufactured in the United States of America

10 9 8 7 6 5 4 3 2 1

ISBN 978-1-4391-7593-4
ISBN 978-1-4391-7601-6 (ebook)

To my husband, aka Hot Cop.
It's been a wonderful, crazy, divine seven years.
Or has it been eight? I don't remember. I only know
that however much time we've had, it's not enough.

$\mathscr{A}$ Note to My Readers

During the Regency period, a number of famous actors and actresses performed at Drury Lane theaters. One of the most notable was Sarah Siddons. Although Mrs. Siddons retired in 1812, near the beginning of the Regency period, she was the standard by which most actresses were judged for decades afterward.

Actresses occupied a very difficult position, as acting was only just becoming a respected profession. Famed actors and actresses mixed with the literary and social elites, and were often hired to perform scenes and even entire plays at various social gatherings. Unfortunately, actresses were also preyed upon by the wealthy and indolent for far more notorious purposes, and many younger actresses were lured from the stage for less than respectable reasons.

There are many stories about Sarah Siddons's

acting abilities, and one of my favorites is when she played Asphasia in *Tamburlaine*. After witnessing her stage lover strangled before her very eyes, Mrs. Siddons was supposed to fall lifeless upon the floor. Her performance was so gripping that members of the audience thought she'd really dropped dead, and raised a horrendous cry until the manager assured them that she'd only been acting and was, in fact, quite alive.

Scandal in Scotland

A letter from Michael Hurst, explorer and Egyptologist, to his brother Captain William Hurst.

William,

I doubt this will reach you before you set sail, but letter writing is one of my few diversions while locked in this godforsaken place. I shall endeavor to send this on the next English ship that arrives.

My captors are growing more impatient as the days pass. And while I'm perfectly capable of dealing with their rude treatment, being forced to remain in such close confines with my assistant, Miss Jane Smythe-Haughton, is making my captivity a living hell. She's removed all of my precious brandy and has implemented an exercise regime. I feel as if I've returned to boarding school.

William, as soon as you can, pray release me.

CHAPTER I

Dover, England
June 20, 1822

William Hurst strode onto the *Agile Witch*, the salty wind swirling his cape as he crossed the gangplank, his boots ringing with each step. He paused on the deck to look up at the rigging and gave a satisfied nod. Every brass hook and ring had been polished until they shone and every sail was freshly patched.

Good. An idle crew was a troublesome crew, and he had no time for such nonsense. He hadn't been captain for fifteen years without learning exactly how a ship should be run.

"Cap'n!" The first mate hurried over, saluting as he came to a halt. "Ye're early."

"Aye." William took another look about the ship. "She looks to be in fine fettle, MacDougal."

His first mate beamed. "Och, so she is. I put Halpurn in charge whilst I purchased supplies. He did a fine job keepin' the crew on task, except—" MacDougal hesitated. At William's pointed look, he continued, "There was a minor lapse in the watch, but I've taken care o' it. It won't happen again."

"Excellent." William lifted his face to the breeze. "Plan on sailing with the morning tide—our mission is urgent. And give Lawton a copy of the manifest. We make this journey at my brother's behest; he can damn well repay the expenses."

MacDougal chuckled. "Aye, Cap'n. Consider it done."

William headed belowdecks. Michael had gotten himself into quite a mess, all for the object now resting in William's coat pocket.

Entering his cabin, William removed the ancient Egyptian artifact from his pocket and placed it on his desk. Then he withdrew a chain from his neck and used the small golden key hanging on it to open the desk. He set the artifact inside and locked it away. It was a relief to have that damned thing under lock and key. His sister Mary had gone through hell getting her hands upon it, and now it was up to him to deliver it to the sulfi who held their brother prisoner.

"Soon," he murmured to the far-away Michael.

William returned the chain to his neck and tucked it out of sight before reaching for his map case. His fingers had just closed on the stiff leather tube when he caught a faint whiff of the purest essence of lily.

The scent made him freeze in place, held there by a scrap of memory he thought he'd forgotten years ago. A memory of exotic violet eyes fringed with thick, black lashes; of hair that slid through his greedy fingers like black silk; of creamy skin that held the sun's fragrant kiss; and of a lush mouth, ripe for kisses that—

"Hello, William."

The throaty voice yanked him from the memory. He closed his eyes, his hand still on the map case. Her voice possessed an unusual quality, a throaty resonance that made even a whisper clear. It was rich and low for a woman, feminine and wanton.

William knew the voice as well as his own. And it was the last voice he expected to hear inside his cabin.

"Aren't you going to return my greeting? Or are we still not speaking?" The lilting voice ran up and down his spine, as sensual as a warm hand.

He gritted his teeth against his traitorous body and released the map tube before turning.

Sitting in a chair at the head of the captain's table was the one woman he'd never wanted to see again. The woman whose gut-wrenching betrayal had left him hollow, causing him to set sail and keep from England's shores for more than two years.

He'd vowed to never, ever trust another

woman . . . especially this one. And he'd vowed to never trust her again—he'd promised himself he'd never again lay eyes upon her.

Yet here she was, sitting in his cabin, the fading sunlight caressing her creamy skin and limning her graceful neck. Her black cloak was tossed over the back of her chair, revealing a red gown as wanton as her nature.

Her gown was a perfect foil for her upswept black hair, the thin white ruffle at her décolletage pretending a modesty that was betrayed by the full breasts swelling above it. She was a master at looking innocent and wanton at the same time. It used to make him crazed for her. Fortunately, he now recognized artifice when he saw it, and it was written all over her beautiful face.

He removed his own cloak, turning away from her to break the spell of her beauty. As he hung the cloak on a brass hook by the door, he took a deep breath. Without turning he said, "Get out."

"You're not even going to ask why I'm here?"

"I don't care why you're here. Just leave."

A faint rustling told him she'd stood. "William, I must talk to you. I hoped you weren't still upset about us—"

"There was no 'us.' We were an illusion." He finally turned to face her, his icy gaze pinning her in place. "That's *all* we were and you know it."

She flushed, her skin pinkening as if he'd slapped her. "I'm sorry. I was wrong to have acted as I did and—"

"Leave." He had to grit his teeth. There was something about her that was simply breathtaking, mesmerizing, that made it almost impossible not to watch her. *Damn it, I should be over this! It's been years.*

Her hands fisted at her sides and she sank back into her chair. "I can't go. I came all the way here and I—" Her voice broke. "William, I am desperate."

Any other man would have been moved by her tears, but he ignored the obvious manipulation. "Find another fool, Marcail. This one isn't available."

She gripped the arms of her chair. "You *must* hear me out, William. No one else can help."

"What about your lover? Or has Colchester finally come to his senses and ended his protection?"

Her lips thinned. "Of course not. But this is a private matter."

"Private? Or 'secret?' Those are two very different words."

"It's both. I can't share this with Colchester."

"Don't you trust him?"

"Yes, but this could cause a scandal and I don't want him—or anyone else—hurt."

William examined her a moment. "Ah. You don't think Colchester *can* help you."

Her cheeks stained a deeper pink. "Whatever

you say about Colchester, he has helped me in ways no one else would."

"If by 'helped' you mean 'gave large sums of money,' I'm certain that's true. The earl is a wealthy man."

She shrugged indifferently, but her expression was strained and he took pleasure in knowing he was pushing the limits of her considerable acting skills.

That was how she earned her living, by treading upon the boards of Drury Lane. Marcail Beauchamp was beautiful, accomplished, and reportedly the finest actress England had ever produced.

His gaze flickered over her, noting that her elegant gown was a trifle too revealing for true modesty. *And that is the* other *way she makes her living,* he reminded himself harshly. *She gives herself to the highest bidder.* "Colchester can have you."

"William, please. Can't you put the past behind you long enough to hear me out? I—" She hesitated and he saw a flicker of uncertainty. But was it real? "William, I came to ask a favor."

He gave a bitter laugh. "No."

"You don't even know what I'm asking."

"I don't need to. If it has to do with you, I want nothing of it." *What was I thinking, to believe the words of an actress? I was besotted. Wildly, crazily, stupidly besotted.* He was older now, and knew her measure. His gaze flickered across her and he realized that she was just as beautiful as before, curse it—perhaps even more so. Her beauty had ripened, as had her body. Gone was her slender, almost coltish beauty; in its place was a seductive, mature woman who moved with an assurance that couldn't be faked.

"Please, William, this is important. And this is not easy for me, either."

He smiled coldly. "I don't care if this is easy for you." He pulled out a chair and dropped into it. "How did you get in here? The crew didn't alert me that I had a guest."

"I came onboard before it was light."

"There is always a guard by the gangway."

"He was asleep."

Ah. The watch lapse MacDougal mentioned. "I sense some trickery here. I know you, Marcail Beauchamp, and you cannot be trusted."

"You don't know me. You never did." She spoke with such quiet dignity that he was almost taken aback. And oddly unwilling to toss her out just yet.

He leaned back in his chair and crossed his arms over his chest. He could easily pick her up and throw her from his cabin, but he was loathe to touch her, unwilling to awaken memories that could be dredged back to the surface if his skin touched hers.

Some things were better left unexamined.

She stood as if restless, her lush figure on display

as she crossed to the port window. "So have I wasted my time in coming here?"

His jaw tightened. "Yes."

"I see." Her gaze fell to the floor and she bit her lip. Finally, she sighed and gestured gracefully toward the decanter and glasses on his sideboard. "Shall we at least drink to our brief reunion?"

"I'll drink to our final parting," he shot back.

Opening the decanter, she tossed him a rueful smile over her shoulder. "Still the same no-nonsense William, I see." She lifted the decanter and took a delicate sniff. "A very nice port."

"Thank you," he said shortly, watching as she poured out two glasses.

"You didn't use to be so discerning in your choice of drink," she said.

"I'm far more discerning in *all* of my pleasures now."

Her lips thinned, but she merely held one glass up to regard the color. "*Very* impressive."

"It's from Napoleon's private supply." William wasn't sure why he felt the need to mention that, but he had.

"I shall enjoy it all the more then." She replaced the stopper on the decanter and brought him a glass, then carried her own back to her seat. She sat and delicately swirled the liquid. "Is there any way to convince you to change your mind? If I told you what I need, you might reconsider."

"If there's one thing you taught me, it's to never trust an answer that's actually another question."

She paused from taking a sip. "I taught you that?"

"Oh, you taught me all sorts of things—none of them good." He took a deep drink of the port, the sharpness clearing his throat. "Enough of this. I have work to do; you have two minutes to tell me why you are here."

Her gaze narrowed and she pushed her glass away. "Fine. I came here because someone is blackmailing me."

"What does that have to do with me?"

Anger flashed across her face, so swift that he believed it real. "William, I am *desperate*. I don't know who is doing it or why, but it must stop."

"But you *do* know what information they hold over your head. Information you don't wish Colchester to know." William watched her closed expression as he drained his glass. "Did you stray, Marcail? Is that the secret? That you can no more be true to a man than a dog can stop himself from chasing a squirrel?"

Her eyes flashed fire. "It's nothing so tawdry, damn it! If my secret were revealed it wouldn't be I who would pay, but others."

"*What* others?"

"Their names don't matter." She folded her lips firmly.

"I am done with secrets and lies. I think you should go." William pushed his empty glass away, suddenly tired of it all. Tired by the deceptions that had left him so beaten all those years ago.

A regretful smile curved one side of her lovely mouth. "Ah, William. Life never gave us a chance, did it?"

What in hell did that mean? "Just go, Marcail." His mouth felt dry, and he wished his glass wasn't empty.

Marcail rose and came toward him. "Oh, I shall leave. But not until you've helped me."

"Damn you, I've already said I won't—won't help." Why was he slurring his words?

He looked at his fingers, cupped loosely around his empty glass. *I can't feel my hand.* The thought floated through his mind with an odd detachment.

But he'd had only one glass. It took far more than that to—

He looked up at Marcail to say, "You put something in my drink," but his mouth wouldn't form the words. His vision suddenly blurred, and a wave of weakness crashed through him.

No. He gathered every ounce of his strength and forced his numb arms to push him to his feet, where he swayed dangerously.

She frowned. "William, don't! You'll hurt yourself—"

He toppled forward. *Damn. She's poisoned me.*

A letter from Michael Hurst to his brother William, describing his first sight of Athens.

Upon arriving in this ancient metropolis, I felt as if I were perched upon the precipice of potential. This feeling was so powerful, I thought I had a fever. It is surprising how many times a good feeling can be confused with a bad one. Often one is unsure which feeling it really is until much later.

CHAPTER 2

William saw Marcail step forward, her slight body breaking his fall just before he landed on the floor.

Why has she drugged me? He was too numb to feel anything, his emotions as muted as his body. He watched with unemotional interest as she eased him to the floor and then made a pillow of his cloak and placed it under his head, her hands careful and sure.

Then, ever so gently, she slipped the chain from around his neck and went to his desk. The lowering sunlight cast her in a golden glow that made her seem ethereal, an angel of such purity, beauty, and exquisite grace that it pained him to watch her.

It was that grace that had won him in the first

place. Not her face nor her figure nor her rich voice, all of which had helped catapult her to fame. When she walked, she drew a man's attention and held it, almost as if she were dancing to music that only she could hear.

Her dark hair gleamed in the lingering light as she unlocked his desk and reached in.

How much gold was in the cubbyhole? Two hundred guineas? Three? I'll have to check the records once she leaves, the little thief. But why does she need it? Does she have debts she can't tell her protector about?

She straightened, and in her hand was the velvet bag holding the ancient artifact William needed to ransom his brother.

Even in his drugged state, fury trickled through. *I must have that artifact. I cannot free Michael without it!*

She tugged open the bag and glanced inside, her brows lowering as she slid the slender onyx box free. She traced the tip of a finger over the edge of the box, her expression perplexed. Uncertain, she glanced his way and met his gaze.

Her cheeks darkened as if she blushed, and she hurriedly tucked the artifact away.

William wanted to revile her, to cut her to shreds, but all he could do was glare at her with all of the force of his anger, which was burning through the drug's haze.

He tried with all of his strength to move and his

toes curled, which had been impossible just two moments ago. *The drug is already wearing off! Woe betide the wench soon.*

Even if he had to crawl on his hands and knees, he'd teach her a lesson she wouldn't forget.

She tied her cloak about her neck, then slid the box into a deep pocket. "I hate to leave you upon the floor, but I must."

He ground his teeth and glared.

She paused at his side and, with an almost regretful look, she stooped and placed a hand upon his cheek. Her gaze was bright, as if with unshed tears. "Don't try to follow me, William. You won't be able to reach me."

But he *would* reach her. Even if it took him the rest of his life, he'd exact a vengeance so harsh, so cold—

She bent over him, her long, silky hair sweeping over his cheek in a gossamer caress, the faint scent of her exotic perfume making his heart pound faster.

"I am sorry to do this, *mon cher,* but I have no choice." She brushed her soft lips over his, the kiss as gentle as sea mist. Then, in a voice tinged with remorse, she said, "To you, this is a trinket. To me, it is freedom."

With that cryptic statement, she rose and pulled her hood over her head, tucking her hair out of sight. "I knew you wouldn't help, so this was my only recourse. I did give you a chance beforehand."

She stepped toward the door, but William's fingers had closed about her hem. He held tightly to the skirt, his gaze blazing. Once he was free of this drug, he'd teach her the danger of crossing him.

"Good-bye, William." She yanked her skirt from his grasp and crossed to the doorway. There, she looked back. "I know you won't believe me, but I wish you well. I always have."

She left the cabin, quietly closing the door behind her, leaving William in the growing darkness.

A letter from Mary Hurst to her brother Michael as he prepared for his first expedition.

I hesitate to mention this, as I know you're quite busy with your preparations, but I am worried about William. Since he came back from sea he's so quiet, solemn, and—I think—sad. I asked him what was wrong, and he laughed bitterly and said he'd learned an important lesson.

I wonder if perhaps he fell in love and it didn't prosper?

Mother is certain he will overcome whatever is bothering him, though she has been taking special pains to tempt his appetite. I think that it will take much more than rabbit stew to heal a truly broken heart.

CHAPTER 3

"Tea, my lady?"

Lady MacToth closed her book and placed it on the overstuffed arm of her chair, the delicate wrinkles about her green eyes crinkling with her smile. "Briggs, you read my mind."

"As I do every day at four." Smiling gently, he held the silver tray a bit lower, noting how my lady's delicate, blue-veined hands shook slightly when she took her cup.

Her hands seemed to shake more each day, a fact that weighed upon his heart, though he was careful not to acknowledge it by so much as a blink. He had been with Lady MacToth since he was a lad of sixteen and she a newly married woman of twenty.

She was quite different then, a blazing actress feted by the world until she'd stunned society by marrying wealthy Lord MacToth, a man several decades older and far above her in social class. To the bride and groom it was the happiest day of their lives, but to some members of the ton, the marriage was a social disaster. Lord MacToth had married beneath his station and they would not soon forget it.

"More sugar, my lady?"

"Please!" Lady MacToth smiled like a child as he dropped two lumps of sugar into the steaming tea. His mistress took such joy in the simple things in life. It was unfortunate Lord MacToth hadn't been able to do the same.

He had been determined to prove to the world that his choice of a wife was no mistake, and he did so in grand fashion. He bought her the largest town house in Mayfair and filled it with enough fine furnishings and priceless art to earn it the nickname the Castle; dressed her as finely as any princess and draped her in enough jewels to win over a sultana. But try as he might, he could not buy society's cold approval.

Society did not forget, and it *never* forgave.

Briggs sighed to think of those early days. Lady MacToth had blithely ignored the slights and cuts, for her life had been filled with so many already that a few more were nothing to her. But Lord MacToth had been horribly hurt when people he'd considered his friends had turned their backs on his bride.

Briggs could have told them how Lord and Lady MacToth had fallen wildly, deeply, and passionately in love at very first sight, and it was that love that reconciled Lord MacToth to his new life. He avoided the society that had rejected his beloved and traveled to the Continent, where they were able to enjoy each other almost exclusively. Three years after the wedding came the birth of a daughter, who joined the couple in their solitary life of travel and luxurious pleasures.

Those were the Idyllic Years. Unfortunately, Lord MacToth's absence from English soil, where most of his investments were held, combined with a significant increase in spending as he attempted to shut out the ugliness of the world by dazzling his lovely young wife and new child with the finest of everything, caused a steady and unfortunate reversal in his fortune.

Worse, Lord MacToth turned a blind eye to every warning sign of his fortune's impending doom, including increasingly strident letters from his solicitors to return home to repair the situation.

Years passed, his fortune dwindled, and Lord MacToth found it harder and harder to shield his wife and daughter from the truth.

Briggs believed it was that strain which

ultimately led to my lord's blindingly sudden death. One day, his lordship complained of being tired and went to lie down for a nap. He never rose again.

Lady MacToth had been devastated, but she was made of sterner material than her husband. Upon being informed by his late lordship's solicitor of the estate's distressed situation, Lady MacToth faced reality without a flinch. She took her daughter out of the expensive boarding school in France and brought her home to England, placed the four largest of their five houses up for sale, dismissed unnecessary staff, and ruthlessly sold almost all of the famed MacToth treasures.

Lady MacToth oversaw each sale herself, and through her wily negotiations received top prices, too.

But when all was said and done and the mound of bills paid, Lady MacToth had only enough to continue to live very quietly and modestly in the remaining house on the edge of Mayfair.

Surrounded on all sides by up-and-coming tradesmen and their families, its location would not be satisfactory to a high stickler. But Lady MacToth had never wished to join society and she thought the small house lovely. She with her daughter, Lucinda lived there very simply until the child grew up, married, and moved into her own house.

As he lifted a small plate, Briggs repressed a sigh

at the thought of Miss Lucinda. "A tea cake, my lady?"

Lady MacToth chuckled, her self-conscious gurgle of laughter making her sound like a young girl. "Did you hear my stomach rumble?"

"No, indeed." Briggs picked up the tongs and placed a small cake upon a delicate Wedgewood plate and set it by her ladyship. "It's just that I know you so well, my lady."

"That you do." Lady MacToth took a nibble of the moist cake. "Briggs, it's lemon. My favorite! I don't know what I'd do without you."

Neither did Briggs—for with the exception of one of her granddaughters who visited often, Lady MacToth was quite alone in the world.

A deep gong sounded and my lady looked up. "Are we expecting a visitor?"

"No, my lady." Briggs stepped to the nearby window, lifted the edge of the curtain, and then smiled. "It's Miss Marcail."

"How lovely!" Lady MacToth took a sip of tea and carefully replaced her teacup, the bottom chattering against the saucer. "I wonder why she's come unannounced? She usually sends a note before—"

The door opened and a footman stood to one side as her ladyship's granddaughter entered the sitting room. Tall and slender, her delicate hourglass figure encased in a dashing pelisse of sea green set with navy blue ruches of ribbons, Miss Marcail Beauchamp was the picture of fashion. She tossed aside her veil, removed her fetching bonnet, and shook out the black curls that fell artfully about her face.

There was no denying her breathtaking beauty as she breezed across the room, a younger version of her once beautiful grandmother.

Briggs bowed. "Miss Marcail, what a pleasure."

She flashed a friendly smile. "Good afternoon, Briggs. How is your wife? I hope she's feeling better than when I was here last time. She had the toothache, I believe."

The Morning Post had once reported that a Russian prince had paid ten thousand pounds for the pleasure of having Miss Beauchamp sing a song at his birthday fete. Hearing that voice, Briggs could only imagine that the astronomical sum had been worth every penny. "My wife is feeling much improved, miss. Thank you."

Lady MacToth held out her hands to her granddaughter. "You are just in time for tea."

"That sounds lovely." Marcail gave her grandmother a swift hug. "Good afternoon, Grandmamma. I hope you're well."

Lady MacToth patted the space beside her on the settee. "I'm fine. Wondering, perhaps, why you've come in such haste that you didn't send a note as you usually do?"

Marcail cast a glance at Briggs.

The elderly butler immediately bowed and walked toward the door. "I shall bring tea and more cakes."

As soon as the door closed behind him, Marcail turned to her grandmother. "Yes, I'm fine. Yes, I'm eating well. And no, I'm not in love. Now that that's out of the way, we can talk."

Grandmamma's lips quirked, her eyes twinkling. "Am I so predictable that you can answer all of my questions before I even speak them?"

"Yes, but only in the dearest way possible."

Marcail was close to her grandmamma, which was a good thing for them both. Except for each other they were quite alone in the world, a state which was bearable when one was twenty-seven, but not as much so—Marcail suspected—at a more advanced age.

That was Mother's fault, for allowing Father's silly pretensions to define who she could and could not see. Marcail's father was Sir Mangus Ferguson, an impoverished Irish peer overly taken with his own lineage, and who did not approve of Grandmamma—though he was more than willing to accept her money until his profligate spending had forced her to cut him off.

Father had never forgiven her and he had forbidden his wife and five daughters to ever speak to Grandmamma again. It was a good thing Marcail never listened to Father. Even at fifteen, she'd already realized he was a braggart and a fool.

A soft knock announced Briggs, who appeared with a tray. Within seconds, she had a cup of hot tea and a plate with a tea cake, as a snowy white linen napkin settled across her lap. "Thank you, Briggs."

"My pleasure, miss." He turned to Grandmamma and asked in a gentle tone, "Would you like more tea before I retire, my lady?"

"Oh, no. I'm fine. Thank you, Briggs."

He bowed and quietly left.

Marcail waited for the door to close. "He is a gem. My butler is not nearly so circumspect."

"I don't know what I'd do without him," Grandmamma said honestly.

"I don't think you need to worry. Not only is he very fond of you, but you are a generous mistress."

"It pays to take care of the ones who take care of you."

"That's a good standard to live by." Marcail tried to hold on to her belief in the inherent kindness of mankind, which she'd learned from Grandmamma long ago, but the events of the last few weeks had stretched that belief to breaking. Her heart sank as she thought of the note in her reticule. She wasn't certain how, but she had to—

"Marcail, dear, you're staring at the teapot as if you think it might explode."

She looked up and forced a smile. "I'm sorry. I'm just a bit distracted."

With a soft, "Oh no!" Grandmamma set down her tea. "You've heard from that horrible black-mailer again."

Marcail grimaced. "I am quite the actress; I can't even fool my own grandmother."

"How did the note arrive this time?"

"I found it under my plate at breakfast this morning." Which had been a chilling discovery. It was one thing to find the notes inside her coach or tucked into some flowers in her dressing room, and quite another to find one placed in her own home. Marcail had never felt so unsafe before.

"I dislike that," Grandmamma said in her direct manner. "Did the servants see anything?"

"No, but they aren't really my servants, they're Colchester's."

Grandmamma shook her head. "I've been telling you these past two years that you should get your own house. It's the least that a—"

"Grandmamma!"

Grandmamma's parchment skin flushed, but she said in a stubborn tone, "The earl is using you to cover his own proclivities."

"And I'm using him to keep away the unwanted attentions that were making my life unbearable. We both benefit, and he has been most kind. I owe him more than I can ever repay."

"I know, I know. He saved you from the regent

when that arse was attempting to force himself upon you, hoping to press you into becoming his mistress. I'll forever be grateful to Colchester for his deft handling of that situation, but that doesn't mean you are indebted to him forever. You've served a purpose in his life, as well." Grandmamma raised an eyebrow. "I assume Colchester's tastes are the same as ever?"

"If you are asking if he's still wildly in love with George Aniston, then the answer is yes. They have been together for almost a year now."

"That's a long time for him."

"Yes, it is. While Colchester's 'tastes' are his own business, I don't care for Aniston. He is forever asking for funds and throwing tantrums over trivial things. I wish Colchester would be rid of him."

"He doesn't sound like a pleasant man."

"He's not when he's in a bad mood. However, when he's in a good mood he is very charming, and Colchester is mad about him. I don't think the relationship is good for Colchester with so many dramatic scenes—" Marcail shrugged helplessly. "I've told him what I think; that's all I can do. He just shrugs and says that sometimes life doesn't allow you to pick who you fall in love with, that it just happens."

"He's right about that; sometimes fate shoves you down a path you wouldn't normally take."

Marcail silently agreed. She loved Colchester

dearly as the brother she'd never had. To the ton, he was a sought-after bachelor, eluding matchmaking mamas and their daughters with a skill that had won him the admiration of his peers. No one had ever guessed his secret, and he'd lived a shadow life for so long that he wore the second skin as comfortably as the first.

She would be forever grateful for his assistance during those early difficult days. The near situation with the prince had terrified her, a brutal reminder of her vulnerability. She was an actress with no social standing to protect her, no family to ward off those with impure intentions.

Worse, at that time, she'd recently met—and straightaway fallen deeply in love with—William Hurst. After six months of a passionate whirlwind courtship, he'd been called back to sea for a three-week run to Dover. Even now, years later, her heart stuttered to a stop when she imagined how things might have turned out if hot, fiery William had heard about the prince's attentions. He lacked Colchester's understanding of the nuances of society. William's reaction would doubtless have resulted in a physical confrontation that would have left the prince bloodied and furious, which would have ended both William's career and her own. Thus her plan to save her sisters would have been ruined, and that fact had forced her to face the ugly hard cold

truth. As an actress she was a target for such impro-
prieties, and that left no possibility of a relationship
with William. She had to give him up, or risk causing both their ruins.

So it had seemed serendipitous when handsome,
dashing Colchester had offered his protection in exchange for one simple thing: to assist him in keeping
his secret from the eyes and ears of the ton.

Though it was the only answer to her dilemma,
Marcail had wrestled with it, desperate for some
way to keep her relationship with William intact.
But there was none. Her heart breaking, she wrote
William that she'd been mistaken in her love for
him and that she'd found another.

She'd hoped that the cold tone of the letter
would prevent him from ever wanting to see her
again, but immediately after he'd landed and received her letter, he'd stormed into her dressing
room at the theater, his beloved face set with anger
and hurt. Oh, the things he'd said— She winced.
The things *she'd* said, too. It had been a horrible,
painful time that even now made her eyes burn with
tears.

But that was the cost of the path she'd chosen.
She resolutely pushed away the old memory, wishing
her thoughts were as easy to control when she was
asleep. In her dreams, she and William were still together. She'd dreamed of him every night since last

week when she'd left him on the floor of his cabin, only in her dreams he wasn't angry. In her dreams he was tied to his bed, unable to move, naked as the day he was born as she caressed his—

"Marcail, you're flushed. Are you catching the ague?"

Marcail placed a hand to her heated cheek. "No. I was just thinking about the—the blackmailer, and it made me angry."

"It makes me angry, too. I wish you could ask Colchester for his help."

Marcail shook her head. "The fewer people who know the truth, the less likely it will be found out. As much as I love Colchester, he's a horrid gossip. He'll keep his own secrets to the grave, but cannot hold onto another's for longer than it takes to repeat it." She took Grandmamma's hand between her own. "I've worked so hard to get where I am, and have sacrificed so much. I can't stop now."

Grandmamma's face softened. "Your sisters owe you a great deal."

"They would do the same for me. *Someone* had to take control of our financial situation. If I'd left Father to run things, we'd all be in a paupers' prison by now, the house lost to creditors."

"He is a selfish man. I don't know why Lucinda wished to wed him. She was raised to be more forward thinking than that."

"I think he flattered her that she was better than everyone else."

"Better than *me*," Grandmamma said, her eyes flashing.

"Mother is wrong," Marcail said soothingly. "She is stubborn and won't admit her mistake, though I think she knows it. Father isn't easy to live with."

Grandmamma's shoulders slumped. "I wish your mother would just leave him, but I fear that will never happen."

"Don't look so glum. At least the debts have been paid and there's enough to fund a season for Elizabeth. And if all works out the way I've planned, by the time she's had a season or two I should have enough saved for Margot. And then Jane and—" Marcail sighed. "But none of that will happen if the ton discovers that they are related to a common actress."

Grandmamma's face fell. "I suppose I shan't see them when they're in town, either, then."

"Don't even think such a thing! They can claim the connection to you; our cases are quite different. Not only did you marry into the peerage, but it has been so long since you were on the stage that I doubt anyone would remember it."

"It would take only one person, my dear. People are not as forgiving as you think."

"Then that's their loss, for a more gracious and wonderful woman doesn't exist."

"La, but you are a fire-breather, aren't you? Unfortunately, that changes nothing. It would be better if I did not see your sisters."

"So long as no one guesses *my* connection to you, we will be fine. I've been careful when I come to visit; I always wear my veil and I take a hackney coach rather than use my own, which might be recognized."

"You're always protecting other people, my dear. But what about *you*, Marcail? What about *your* season?"

"I'm seven and twenty now, the time for my season has long passed." Marcail chuckled at her grandmother's expression. "Stop that! It's not as if I'm slaving in some coal mine. I have a wonderful career, I make an excellent wage, I'm able to provide for my family, and I have you to share dinner with whenever I wish. What more could I ask?"

Grandmamma frowned. "You may trick some people into believing that silliness, but not me. I know of the slights and the illicit proposals and the lack of regard for your art." She leaned forward. "I also know the personal price this charade has cost you."

Marcail wished she hadn't confided about William all those years ago, but there was no undoing it now. She'd been sick with the loss, which had hurt far worse than she'd expected. For a few weeks, she hadn't been able to leave her bed.

Grandmamma had sent Briggs to her home every day with notes and tureens of hot soup. Eventually, Grandmamma herself had threatened to come visit. The thought of her frail grandmother braving the rough streets and cold weather had forced Marcail to rise. Though her spirits remained low for months, she never returned to the sickbed.

Marcail waved a hand as if to banish that time. "I don't think of it very often." *Until last week.*

"Well, I do. You have enough on your shoulders. My child, we *must* stop this blackmailer. You can't keep giving him sums and sums of money as you've been doing."

"I would do something about it if I only knew who he was."

"I suppose this messenger, the red-haired woman, won't give you a clue?"

Marcail shook her head. "I get the distinct impression that Miss Challoner is afraid of the blackmailer. I've seen it in her eyes." And Marcail didn't get the impression that many things frightened Miss Challoner. The blackmailer's messenger was an interesting woman, quite tall and amazingly beautiful, with red hair and green eyes and a confident bearing that set her apart. There were times when Marcail got the distinct impression that Miss Challoner's hatred for the blackmailer quite equaled her own, but the woman refused to engage in conversation beyond the necessary, merely accepting with a bland expression whatever bundle Marcail handed over for delivery. *I wonder what the blackmailer holds over Miss Challoner's head? It must be something quite weighty. The next time I'm alone with her, I shall ask. It can't hurt matters.*

"I do hope you're being careful. I worry about your having commerce with these people. I also hate that you have to carry such large amounts of money to such horrid locations."

"I didn't have to go to a horrid part of town this time. Of course, he didn't ask for money, either." A flicker of regret flared and she resolutely tamped it down. It wasn't as if William had harbored tender thoughts of her before she'd stolen the artifact. If anything, she'd confirmed his already low opinion of her.

"What did the blackmailer want, if not money?" Grandmamma asked.

"He wanted me to fetch an ancient artifact."

"Fetch?" Grandmamma's eyes sharpened. "What do you mean by that?"

"I was told I must obtain an Egyptian artifact and—"

Grandmamma grasped Marcail's hand. "Please tell me that you haven't done something you'll be sorry for."

"Of course I haven't." Which was a complete and utter lie.

Grandmamma's thin brows rose.

Marcail sighed. "The artifact didn't belong to the person who held it, so it wasn't precisely stealing. I hoped the artifact might be a clue to my blackmailer's identity so I took it to someone who works with the British Museum. They examined it and said that, while ancient, it's not that rare."

"Perhaps the materials make it valuable?"

"No. It's made mainly of onyx, with very little gold, so . . . I just don't know."

"Stranger and stranger." Grandmamma shook her head and poured more tea into both cups.

Marcail noted how badly the older woman's hands now shook. *She's getting so fragile. I shouldn't be bothering her with my problems. I should—*

"Yes, you should bring your problems to me." Grandmamma sent Marcail a hard look before returning the teapot to the tray. "We are family, we two. Closer than most mothers and daughters."

Marcail smiled. "You read my mind."

"Hardly. Every time I wrest a problem from you, you tell me that it's really none of my concern and not to bother myself with it." Grandmamma's green eyes were grave. "We are strong, and we will overcome all adversity—including Miss Challoner and the blackmailer."

Marcail fidgeted with the edge of her cuff. "There is another thing about this situation that made it worse."

"What could possibly make it worse? I can't imagine—" Grandmamma's gaze narrowed. "*Whom* did they ask you to steal this artifact from?"

Marcail's cheeks heated.

"Allow me to guess. Captain Hurst, perhaps?"

"Yes."

"Then that's why you're so upset."

"No, I'm upset because I'm being blackmailed. It has nothing to do with William Hurst."

Grandmamma took a sip of her tea, her shrewd gaze never wavering.

"Honestly, it's been years since I saw him!"

Grandmamma listened politely.

"In fact, I wasn't even certain I'd remember what he looked like." He'd looked exactly as he had the last time she'd seen him—tall and powerful, his black hair framing his incredible dark blue eyes, and—

Grandmamma cleared her throat.

Marcail threw up her hands. "Oh, very well! He looked exactly the same, only older."

Grandmamma nodded. "I'm not surprised it was difficult to see him. You were most taken with him."

More than taken. She'd been wildly, passionately in love.

And when she'd seen him again, she'd felt like that mad, impulsive innocent all over again.

If she closed her eyes now, she could see his blue

eyes and dark hair, the cleft of his chin and the sparkle of his grin, and how his large hands had made her feel so—

"Your blackmailer must know of your past relationship with Hurst."

Marcail slanted a look at her grandmother. "How could he? It happened so long ago, and I was barely known then."

"I don't believe in coincidences."

"Well, if the blackmailer thought that our past history worked in my favor, then he was sadly mistaken."

"It's a pity you can't go to Bow Street. But I suppose you're right; the fewer involved, the better."

Marcail placed her hand on Grandmamma's knee. "We're already set on this course. There's no sense regretting it now."

"We all owe you so much, dear. Though Briggs never mentions it, I know that the coal bins are always full and we have much better cuts of meat since you arrived in London."

"That's not me, it's Briggs. He's an excellent bargainer."

"I've learned much from him over the years. I wish MacToth had done the same." Grandmamma looked at the portrait of a handsome man over the fireplace and her expression grew dreamy. "I wish you could have met him, Marcail. He would have liked you. He enjoyed women with spirit."

"I'm sure he did. He married you, didn't he?" Marcail chuckled. "One day, you and I will find a lovely house in the country where no one ever needs to know who or what we are."

Grandmamma's shrewd green gaze locked on Marcail. "You'd give up the stage? Just like that?"

Marcail hesitated. "Perhaps not completely. It's who I am, and I enjoy it."

"You are better than I ever was. I saw your Lady MacBeth last Wednesday, and you were magnificent. Better even than Mrs. Siddons."

Marcail threw up a hand. "Grandmamma, *no one* will ever be better than Mrs. Siddons. She may have retired from the stage a decade ago, but her presence is still keenly felt by all actresses."

"Sarah Siddons was a very good actress; I should know, for I worked with her myself. But last week, you outshone even her. While I wish you hadn't forsaken your birthright, I could not be prouder of your talent."

"Thank you. That means more to me than I can say." Marcail glanced at the clock over the mantel. "I wish I could stay longer, but I must go. The note I received this morning said that I'm to deliver the artifact to an inn in Southend. I have only three days before I'm due back onstage, so I must leave today."

"Southend? I don't like this at all. Please be careful."

"Don't worry, Grandmamma. I'll be fine. I always am." She stood and dropped a kiss on the snowy white forehead. "As soon as I return, we'll have dinner."

"I'll be waiting, so please send me word that all is well." Grandmamma waved her hand. "Off with you. Get this task done and over with."

Marcail gave her grandmother one last hug, then waited in the front hallway while Briggs called a hackney. When one pulled up to the stoop, she tucked her veil firmly in place and entered the carriage quickly, allowing Briggs to give her destination—a street corner several blocks from her home—to the driver.

With a wave to Briggs, Marcail settled back against the worn squabs and planned her coming journey. The coach rattled down the street, then rounded a corner and headed toward Hyde Park.

Not far away, a man dressed in the drab browns and grays of the working class watched, the thronging mill of people and carts swirling past him and his horse as if they were a rock in the middle of a swift stream.

Expressionless, he watched the hackney rumble past. Just before it turned at the end of the street, he murmured a word to his horse, jumped into the saddle and followed the hackney as it disappeared around the corner.

A letter from Michael Hurst to his brother William, from a ship rounding Gibraltar.

It pains me to admit it, but I'm a wretched sea traveler. I haven't left my bunk since we left port in Old Alexandria. If it weren't for Miss Smythe-Haughton and her infernal draughts, I would now be asleep.

But since I am able to sit up and write, I find myself wondering why you are able to go to sea for such lengths of time while my stomach protests if I merely set foot upon a ship. It makes me wonder which tendencies are decided by birth, and which by desire.

CHAPTER 4

$\mathcal{R}$ain pelted the cobblestones, pooled in the dips, and soaked every stocking and skirt hem it could reach. Through the downpour, a coach pulled up to a large classical building on St. James Street that let out quality bachelor apartments. The door of the coach opened and a man emerged waving the coach on as he dashed through sheets of rain. Wet in an instant, he paused under the portico to dump the collected rain from the stiff curled brim of his hat, then knocked it against his palm to dislodge more water. He removed his greatcoat and shook it vigorously before entering his apartment.

"Sir!" The butler was just reaching for the sitting

KAREN HAWKINS

room door when William appeared. Lippton set down a tray containing a decanter of whiskey, a smaller one of sherry, and five glasses to hurry forward and take William's coat.

Lippton grimaced at the weight of the wet wool. "It must be pouring."

"I practically had to swim here." The sky suited his mood, black and furious. He still had the bitter taste of defeat from Marcail's visit, even though it had been more than a week ago.

When he'd finally been able to drag himself to the door, he'd interrogated his men to no avail. She had blithely walked off his ship, waving good-bye to the unsuspecting crew. He'd sent crew members to search the inns near the dock, but she was nowhere to be found.

It was infuriating to be taken for a fool on his own ship, and even more galling that it had been *she* who'd done it.

As soon as day broke, he'd set sail for London. They'd run into a storm which had delayed their return and dissipated whatever good temper he'd had left.

When they'd finally docked two days behind schedule, he'd sent for his coach and gone directly to Marcail's residence in the heart of Mayfair. Four stories tall, the magnificent house possessed a portico flanked by twin lions set upon decorative pedestals. It was an ostentatious house, especially when one considered it had been purchased for the sole purpose of keeping a mistress.

The thought stirred William's anger with bitterness. He'd considered forcing his way in to demand the artifact, but the house was swarming with large, able-bodied footmen—and William was not prepared to fail again.

No, he had to find another way to deal with Marcail Beauchamp. One that involved him and her and no one else.

That decision made, he'd returned to his coach and had a few words with one of the footmen, whom he'd left standing watch under a sheltered area beside the street, a greatcoat now covering his livery. William then left for his own apartments on St. James Street.

Lippton shook out William's coat, water dripping on the marble floor and seeping toward the edge of the Persian rug. The white-haired servant tsked, hung the coat on a brass rack in the foyer, and then slid the umbrella stand beneath the dripping mess.

"I shall not be here long," William said. "I just need to clean up and pack some clothes."

Lippton lifted his brows. "You are leaving so soon?"

"Yes. I came to town to fetch something, and then I'm off to rescue Michael. Please send John

Poston to watch number twelve Grosvenor Square. I left a footman there temporarily. Tell him that the home belongs to the Earl of Colchester."

Lippton blinked. "We're watching an earl, sir?"

"No. I have no desire to know Colchester's comings and goings, but I *do* want to know the comings and goings of his mistress, Miss Marcail Beauchamp."

"The actress?" Lippton positively glowed with admiration. "I saw her perform a magnificent Lady MacBeth on Drury Lane. It was—" He placed a hand over his heart and closed his eyes in apparent ecstasy.

"You and every other man in London," William snapped. Damn it, did every man in England fawn over Marcail? No wonder the woman was impossible. "Tell Poston at once."

Lippton bowed. "Yes, sir."

William had turned to go up the stairs to his bedchamber when Lippton called after him, "Oh, sir! You have visitors; they are waiting for you in the sitting room."

Lippton's voice was one of doom. Which meant . . .

"Which of my family is here?"

"Five of them, sir. And we've little food in the cupboard as you did not inform us you would be returning to London so soon."

"Bloody hell."

"Yes, sir. Two of your sisters arrived an hour ago, along with the Earl of Erroll and your brother-in-law, Lord MacLean."

"That's four. Who's the fifth? Or need I ask?"

"It is Mr. Robert. He has been here since—" Lippton glanced at the tall clock that graced the entry "—a little over two hours. He's come every day for the last three days, sir, and he always stays at least an hour, sometimes more."

"And no doubt he's been drinking my whiskey every time he comes, damn him."

"Yes, sir." Lippton nodded toward the tray he'd set down when William had arrived. "That is the last decanter."

William sent a hard glance at the sitting room door. "While I send my family on their way, please pack my portmanteau. I shall need clothes for at least two weeks."

"Yes, sir. Oh, and yesterday an older person of rather low breeding called." Lippton couldn't have looked more put upon. "I wouldn't allow him beyond the vestibule, so he left you this." Lippton crossed to a small table beside the umbrella stand and picked up a dirty and crumpled envelope.

William ripped it open and scanned the missive, a grim smile appearing as the words sped by. "Excellent." It was the first good news he'd received in the last week. "This gentleman will return. When he does, tell me immediately. I must speak with him."

"Yes, sir." Lippton didn't look happy with those orders.

"Meanwhile, I shall face my family and explain how I managed to wreck our rescue plans for our brother, Michael."

"I'm sorry to hear that, sir. I'm quite fond of Mr. Michael. I shall miss his serial in *The Morning Post*."

"My sister Mary writes that, not Michael."

For the second time that afternoon, Lippton looked bitterly disappointed. Then he straightened his shoulders. "Shall I fetch refreshments for the ladies, sir? I can purchase some scones and—"

"Lord, no. That will just encourage them to stay. The fact that Robert has consumed all of my good Scottish whiskey is bad enough. Please have their carriages readied for their departure."

"Yes, sir."

William crossed to the sitting room door. He could hear the low murmur of voices inside, but they stopped the second he turned the knob and walked in. "Good afternoon." He closed the door and made his way toward the crackling fireplace, pausing to kiss his sisters' cheeks. "Caitlyn. Mary. Good to see you."

William had three sisters; the two older ones were twins, Triona and Caitlyn. He also had one younger sister, Mary. Caitlyn was the most beautiful; with golden hair and dark brown eyes, she drew the eye and held it. Mary was rounder but had a better sense of humor; her easy laugh encouraged one to join in and made her more approachable.

William glanced at Mary's hand. "Not yet married?"

She looked pleased as she slanted a glance at Lord Erroll. "Not yet. We've posted the banns, but Father won't arrive for another two weeks. We shall have to wait until then."

"Which will give us time to shop for a proper gown," Caitlyn added.

Robert, elegantly sprawled in a low chair, groaned. "William, *please* do not get them started. They've done nothing but chatter about flowers and rings and lace since they arrived."

Caitlyn's gaze narrowed. "*You* were the one who suggested lilies."

"An excellent suggestion that you both ignored," he said in a sharp tone. "Lilies would be perfect for—"

"I hate to interrupt," William said, "but I must leave very soon. Did you wish to speak to me, or did you just come to use my sitting room for your arguments?"

"We came to hear how you lost the artifact." Robert smoothed his lace cuff as if bored. "And to find out how you could be such a lumphead."

William shot his younger brother a hard look. "In a mood, are you?"

Noted for the quickness of his mind, Robert read social nuances and the emotions of those around him effortlessly. His skills had made him rise quickly at the Home Office where he worked for the home secretary.

William wasn't sure exactly what Robert's position was, but it seemed to afford him the right introductions since he moved in the highest circles of the ton with the ease of one born to it.

The funds for such high living didn't come from the Home Office, but from Michael's endeavors. Whenever Michael wished to sell something he sent it to Robert, who was adept at marketing precious items to the members of the ton, who were always looking for conversation pieces for their drawing rooms. Robert kept a portion of the funds from each sale and sent the bulk to Michael, who used the money to fund his explorations. It was a lucrative relationship for both.

But that was Robert; he'd always had a talent for making a silk purse out of a sow's ear and a desire to be something bigger and better.

Robert raised one eyebrow. "*I'm* in a mood? I'm not the one snapping at people."

"I'm wet, tired, and hungry. What do you want?"

"You're definitely wet; you're soaked through and through."

"It's raining, you fool," William retorted, going to the fireplace to warm himself.

"*I* didn't get wet," Robert returned smugly.

Mary pulled her skirts back so William's wet boots wouldn't brush her hem. "Robert, you arrived hours before the rain began and you know it. Stop being ugly to William."

Robert frowned at his practical-minded sister. "Our brother has lost the object we need to rescue Michael, and you say there's no need to be ugly?"

"No," she replied stoutly, "for I'm sure it was an accident, wasn't it, William?"

"It was more in the line of a theft."

Robert shrugged. "Whatever you wish to call it, it's a blasted shame that your carelessness will cause us more effort now. Mary had a hell of a time wresting the box from Erroll."

The Earl of Erroll, dressed as ever in head-to-toe black, slanted a cold gaze Robert's way. With his black hair and scarred jaw, he was a menacing sight. "Mary didn't work hard to regain the onyx box," he said with his soft Scottish burr. "She worked hard to prove her identity, for I'd no proof of who she was."

Mary nodded. "And any of us would have done the same after Michael wrote that letter saying he expected someone to steal the—"

"Michael was right," William interrupted.

"Someone *was* out to steal that damned box and they succeeded." It galled him to say the words aloud.

"Exactly how did the artifact get stolen?" Caitlyn demanded.

Caitlyn's husband, Alexander MacLean, the laird of his clan, placed a hand upon her shoulder. "Patience, my love. I'm sure William will tell us everything."

"Indeed I will." William had always liked Mac-Lean. The man had a dry wit and was able to curb Caitlyn's high spirits. Though perhaps her new-found temperance lay more in the fact that she was now a mother to her own set of twins, a boy and a girl who were as high spirited and impulsive as their mother.

William raked a hand through his hair, grimacing as water dripped down his neck. "I'm more than happy to explain what happened. After I got the artifact from Mary and Erroll, I took it straight to my ship. Someone was waiting for me in my cabin and they stole the blasted box."

Mary and Caitlyn exchanged worried glances.

"They knew you were coming," Mary said.

William nodded.

From where he lounged in the corner of the room, Robert pulled a monocle from his pocket, a thick black ribbon attaching it to his coat. He held it before one eye and examined William from head to toe. "You must not have put up much of a fight, for I don't see a bruise upon you."

"They drugged me." William had to almost spit the words, they tasted so ill upon his tongue.

Robert dropped the monocle, which swung from the ribbon and flashed in the firelight. "And how did they manage that?"

"My decanter of port was laced with it."

Mary looked shocked. "And they forced you to drink it?"

Damn it, must they know *everything*? "I didn't know the port was drugged, so I didn't hesitate when offered a glass." Besides, Marcail had poured herself a glass as well. It wasn't until later that he realized she'd never taken a sip.

"Then you must have known the person who drugged you fairly well," Robert said silkily.

William scowled at the five curious gazes locked upon him. "Yes, I knew her," he ground out.

Robert's gaze narrowed. *"Her?"*

"Yes, *her.*"

"Ah!" Robert said softly, leaning back in his chair. "I should have known."

Caitlyn blinked. "Who is this *her?*"

Robert tucked his monocle back into his pocket. "Sadly, there is only one 'her' for William: Marcail Beauchamp."

Caitlyn's eyes widened. "*The* Marcail Beauchamp, the Darling of Drury Lane?"

"None other." Robert looked so satisfied that William yearned to box his brother's ears.

Mary's gaze was fascinated. "I didn't even know you were acquainted with Miss Beauchamp. You've never said a word."

"He knew her years ago," Robert said.

"*Many* years ago. So many that I'd almost forgotten." William sent Robert a dour glare. "Here's what happened. When I arrived on ship she was already in my cabin. It never dawned on me that she wanted the artifact; I didn't know anyone other than ourselves was even aware of it."

"And she just demanded it?" Mary asked.

"No. She said she needed my help with something, and when I told her no and ordered her to leave, she asked for a drink, which she then poured. She'd doctored the port before I'd even arrived."

"I daresay she knew you wouldn't help her," Robert said.

"She was right." William ground his teeth. "While I was incapacitated, she stole the artifact."

Caitlyn shook her head. "Someone must have known of your connection and sent her to steal it."

"Perhaps," William said grimly. "She said something as she left—something about needing the artifact to win her freedom."

"What did she mean by that?" Caitlyn asked.

"I have no idea."

"She can't be in need of funds," Caitlyn said, pursing her lips. "Everyone knows she enjoys Colchester's protection."

"And he is as wealthy as Croesus," Mary added. "If I had a protector, I'd want one with that much money."

Robert's black brows snapped down. "That is not a proper subject for a lady." He shot a glare at MacLean and Erroll, who were both grinning. "I'm surprised you find that amusing."

MacLean placed a hand on Caitlyn's shoulder. "I find plain talking and forward thinking a joy in a spouse."

"It's one of Mary's best traits, too," Erroll added.

Mary sighed. "Please stay on the topic. We must figure this out." She turned to William. "What do you think Miss Beauchamp wanted with the artifact? She's not a known collector."

"We won't know until I catch up with her." He hesitated a moment. "I don't believe she did this for herself; she was sent by someone."

Robert leaned forward. "By whom?"

"More than likely, the person Michael warned Erroll about."

Everyone looked at the earl, who nodded thoughtfully. "The letter I received from Michael warned that I should be cautious with the object and trust no one, not even people I knew."

"Good God," Robert said with obvious disgust. "Trust Michael to make such a dramatic statement and not bother to explain it." He sighed and leaned back in his chair. "Not only have we lost the box, but only three of you have seen it—which means the rest of us cannot assist in any real way. We could stumble upon it and never even know it."

"I have a picture of it."

All eyes turned to Mary, who tugged the drawstring of the reticule hanging from her wrist. "I drew it when I was working with Erroll. I brought the drawing with me to show to a curator at the British Museum to see what he thought of it." She held out a drawing on high-quality paper.

William leaned forward but Caitlyn was quicker. "Is this the correct size?" she asked.

Mary nodded.

Robert leaned to the side so he could see the drawing. "Odd. I think I've seen that before, but it was a long, long time ago . . . No, it couldn't be." He flicked a glance at Mary. "How accurate is the detailing?"

William reached across to take the paper from Caitlyn. "This is exactly it. Well done, Mary."

She smiled, her face pink. "Thank you."

"You're welcome. And now I will bid you all adieu. I must pack my bags and leave."

Robert stood. "You plan to follow Miss Beauchamp?"

"Yes. I must find out who wanted that. I have it on good authority that Miss Beauchamp is leaving within the next few hours, and wherever she's going, she plans to stay overnight."

Robert looked skeptical. "How did you discover that? You just arrived."

"Oh, I have my methods."

Mary's gaze was bright with curiosity. "William, just how well *do* you know Miss Beauchamp?"

He shrugged. "Well enough."

"That's an understatement," Robert murmured. At William's sharp look, he continued, "I take it you're telling us you don't need our help?"

"Not yet. I will contact you as soon as I know more."

Robert nodded. "That's good. I've an errand of my own in Edinburgh."

MacLean quirked a brow at Robert. "Shall we expect the pleasure of your company after you finish your errand? You would be within a day's ride."

"Perhaps," Robert said, favoring them all with an odd smile.

William scowled. Damn Robert and his mysterious airs. "If you don't mind, I shall leave you all now. I must be off as soon as possible if I'm to retrieve that artifact."

Robert turned to his sisters. "Shall we retire to my house? Unlike William, I will offer you food and a very nice Madeira."

William added, "I've already ordered your coaches to be brought around."

A sudden knock sounded as Lippton stood in the doorway. "Sir, you asked that I inform you when your caller arrived. I escorted him to the library and he is awaiting you there."

"Very good. My family was just preparing to leave." He turned to them. "As soon as I know something more, I will write."

Robert stood and adjusted one of his French cuffs, his shrewd gaze locked upon William. "You know where this artifact—and Miss Beauchamp—have gone, don't you?"

"When I regained consciousness, I immediately sent word to my friend Fielding who oversees the Bow Street Runners. I asked him to have an agent keep an eye on the elusive Miss Beauchamp."

"Ah. That is your visitor, then."

"I believe so."

Robert turned to his sisters, who were standing ready to depart. "I suggest we leave this mess for William to sort out. He'll contact us if he has need of our help."

"William, please hurry," Caitlyn begged. "I worry about Michael."

"I don't," Erroll said.

Mary sighed. "Erroll says Michael is fine, and that in some foreign climes being held for ransom is almost an honor."

"It is until they cut off your head," Robert said blandly.

At the reproachful looks tossed his way, he shrugged. "I am merely repeating something Michael once said. I'm of the opinion that so long as our brother is under the protection of the indomitable Miss Smythe-Haughton, he will come to no harm."

Mary frowned. "She's just his secretary."

"She is his translator, curator, administrator, organizer—in a word, she is his everything. He just hasn't realized it yet."

"They don't even like one another," Caitlyn said. "Michael's said so in his letters."

"Exactly," Robert replied with a smug smile.

William made an impatient noise. "Whatever Miss Smythe-Haughton is or is not, I will get that artifact and deliver it as soon as possible. I will keep you all apprised of the situation as it develops."

He gave a quick bow and left the room, his mind focused on the man who awaited him in the breakfast room. *Michael, it won't be long now. Wherever I have to go, whatever I have to do, I will find that artifact and win your release.*

Letter from Michael Hurst to his sister Mary, from a rented room overlooking a busy bazaar in Turkey.

I am awaiting my new interpreter. He is to take my party on a two-week journey into the mountains, where the locals swear a number of ancient ruins are hidden. One of our contacts suggested that there is also treasure to be found, but finding just one ruin of a proper antiquity would be enough of a treasure for me. One never knows until one investigates. Never believe the ears until confirmed by the eyes.

CHAPTER 5

The young porter dropped Marcail's trunk to the floor, then pulled out a kerchief and wiped his brow. "I'll fetch yer portmanteau from the bottom of the steps next, miss."

"Thank you." Marcail unhooked her gray cloak of fine wool, trimmed with deep red satin, and hung it on a hook by the door. The room was a far cry from the luxurious house she occupied in London, but charming nonetheless. The bed's thick coverlet was decorated with yarn bows that matched the curtains, and the furniture was of good quality. As far as accommodations went, it was much better than she'd dared to hope.

The only difficulty had been finding a place for

her coach and six. This inn's stable was small, so she'd had to send her equipment down the street to a less genteel inn with a larger stable. All told, it was a relatively minor inconvenience.

The porter returned with her portmanteau and she pointed to a clear space beside the bed.

"Very good, miss. They's fresh water in yer pitcher and clean glasses, too."

"Thank you."

The porter's bright gaze locked on her veil and bonnet as if he wished he had the nerve to ask her to remove them. "Pardon me, miss, but I was surprised to see a genteel lady like yerself comin' into town, it not bein' ocean bathin' season no more."

The small town she'd been ordered to report to was eerily empty, as the weather had turned cold several weeks before. "I wish to enjoy the quiet."

"Ye'll still find plenty t' do if ye like walks upon the beach," the porter said helpfully. "'Tis a grand little town, fer all that it's not as popular as Brighton. Queen Charlotte herself stayed here one night twenty years ago! The day after she left, the lord mayor renamed two buildings and three streets after the royal family, hopin' more o' them might come."

"And did they?"

His face fell. "No. But we've grown all the same. Why, the town's twiced as big now as it was then."

Realizing she was about to receive an exhaustive

history of Southend-on-Sea, Marcail quickly pressed some coins into the porter's hand. "Thank you again for bringing up my luggage."

He backed toward the door, beaming. "It's my pleasure, miss. If'n ye need anything else, just ring the bell and someone will come t' see what ye need."

"Thank you." Smiling, Marcail herded him from the room.

"I'll be glad to brush yer shoes if ye leave them outside the door," the porter added as he crossed the threshold.

"I shall remember that, thank you." With that, she closed the door and turned the key in the lock.

After the porter's footsteps faded away, she hurried to her portmanteau. She removed all of the clothes from the bag and dislodged the false bottom, revealing the carefully wrapped artifact. "Good," she murmured, repacking the bag and returning it to the floor.

Now all she had to do was wait. If this was like her other exchanges, Miss Challoner would show up when she chose, which often left Marcail waiting for hours and sometimes days. The whole thing was most unnerving.

But the worst part was behind her. She'd procured the artifact; now she could deliver it and be done with it.

Yet she couldn't forget the blaze of William's

eyes as he watched her, condemning her every move. *Don't be silly; he was drugged. He probably wasn't fully aware of what occurred.*

The thought should have reassured her, but it just made her heart ache a little more. Blast it, she should be done with feeling bad about things that had happened, especially about things that *had* to happen. *Perhaps I should have just told him why I'd come, that I needed the artifact to protect my family.*

But even as she had the thought, she shook her head. He'd been too angry to listen to her. If she'd been on fire, he wouldn't have spared a glass of water to save her. *I had no choice; I did what I had to.*

Heart heavy, she removed her veil and bonnet and set them on the bed. She pulled out all of her hairpins and placed them on the nightstand, then threaded her fingers through the mass of waves that fell about her shoulders.

She was tired, worn, and ached from head to foot. Southend-on-Sea was almost a twelve-hour ride from London. Why had her blackmailer chosen this town? It was in the middle of nowhere, which made her uneasy.

She ruffled her hair and then went to look out one of the windows. The town sat on the North Sea at the mouth of the Thames, built upon a graceful slope that led to the sea's edge. The rainy street below was nearly empty, except for a man in dark clothing who appeared to be waiting for someone and a stray dog that was digging under a stoop.

Beyond the street, she could see a long pier jutting out into the water. Several boats were tied there, including a large ship. In the distance, two more ships slowly sailed toward the pier. It was a pretty scene, worth painting.

Sighing, she dropped the curtain and looked about the room, suddenly feeling very alone. "Just come and take the blasted thing," she murmured sourly. "I don't have all week to wait for you."

Not to mention that the longer Miss Challoner waited to claim the artifact, the longer William had to find her. She was safer here, away from London, but still . . . He had been so very, very angry. She would have to face him when she returned home. She'd been extremely careful that no one knew she was coming here. Except for three of her servants, everyone thought she was at home in bed, ill with the ague.

Still, she couldn't linger too long; she was due to begin rehearsal on a new melodrama entitled *Ali Pasha*. The script was in her portmanteau, as she'd planned to read it on the way, but the bouncing of the coach had prevented it.

Impatient, she went to the dresser and poured herself a glass of water, then sat in a chair and stretched out her legs.

It was as if the blackmailer was purposely trying to grind her spirit into dust. That was a silly thought, for it suggested that the person had a personal grudge against her, and she had no real enemies.

That is true, isn't it? Is there any reason someone would want my life disrupted in such a fashion?

She tapped her fingers on the arm of the chair, considering all the people she knew well enough for them to wish her either harm or true good, and realized that the list was short indeed. Over the years she'd become very private, only going to and from the theater, riding most mornings with Colchester to remind the world that they were supposedly a couple, and visiting Grandmamma. She simply didn't know anyone well enough to have an enemy.

She shifted restlessly. This whole situation reminded her of one of the mystery plays that the theater put on for the afternoon and early evening crowds for a penny ticket.

She rose to pull the script from her bag and then returned to her chair to read.

Two hours later, just as Marcail was beginning to doze, a knock sounded on the door, startling her. "Finally," she grumbled as she rose to her stockinged feet. She tossed her script on the bed, grabbed her boots, and stepped into them. Not bothering to lace them, she hurried to the dresser to repin her hair.

The knock sounded again, more insistent.

"One moment!" Miss Challoner certainly was anxious to get her hands on the artifact.

Marcail glanced at her portmanteau. *What is the value of that thing, anyway? I wish I knew.*

The knock sounded again, even louder this time, and she called out in an exasperated tone, "I'll be right there!"

She slipped in just enough hairpins to keep the hair off her shoulders and then went to the door. She undid the lock and swung it open. "Miss Challoner—"

William Hurst swooped her up like a sack of sand, tucking her under his arm, against his hip. Her hair immediately fell from its few pins as his drenched clothes soaked hers. "You're wet! Damn it, William, put me down!"

"Like hell." He crossed the room while she squirmed and kicked. "Hold still or you'll hurt yourself."

That made her madder and she squirmed even harder, kicking with all of her might. Her toes slammed into the dresser, one unlaced boot flying off. "Owww!" she yelled.

"I warned you."

"*Put me dooooooooown!* I swear to heaven, if you don't—"

He tightened his hold until she could only gasp,

no other sound fleeing her lips. She fisted her hands and pummeled his thigh as hard as she could.

"Stop that at once."

William's voice cracked the order and Marcail instinctively stopped. Perhaps it was just as well, for her toes throbbed. There was a time to fight and a time to scheme. Now was a good Scheming Time.

He reached the bed and tossed her onto the mattress, then returned to the door and locked it.

Marcail took the moment to sit up and scoot to the edge of the bed. Out of the corner of her eye, she saw the portmanteau on the floor, by her feet.

She quickly spread her skirts as if to shake them back into their intended folds. Hidden by this gesture, she shoved the portmanteau under the bed with her heel. It went partway but then stopped, blocked by some unseen object.

She'd just have to keep her skirts over it.

William tucked the key into his waistcoat pocket and leaned against the door, his arms crossed over his broad chest as he regarded her with a self-satisfied smile. "Well, here we are. I'd offer you some drugged port, but unfortunately I don't have any."

She pushed her hair from her face and pulled it all to one side. "So . . . here we are. We can't seem to stay away from each other lately."

"I'd be happy to stay away from you, if I could. I want that artifact."

"That's too bad. I already delivered it to its rightful owner."

"Who happens to be my brother. He purchased it in Egypt several months ago."

"He stole it, so he was not the rightful owner."

"Is that what you were told?"

She opened her mouth, and then closed it. "It's the truth . . . isn't it?"

He sent her a look of such disgust that her face warmed. "You don't even know for certain, do you? What in the hell is going on, Marcail?"

Her heart sank to her stomach as she read the truth in William's face. *It was a lie. It was all a lie.* She shouldn't have been surprised, for her blackmailer was anything but honorable. Feeling as if she might be ill, she smoothed her skirts and said in a tight voice, "I was told it was stolen and I should deliver it to the rightful owner."

"Who is that? Who is this 'rightful owner'?"

She shrugged, pretending indifference though she wondered the same. She'd accepted without question the story told to her simply because it had been easier not to ask questions.

William raked a hand through his wet hair, slicking it away from his face, his dark blue gaze locked upon her. Many men would look foolish with their hair plastered back, but the severe style worked for William, emphasizing the strong angles of his face.

He wasn't conventionally handsome like Colchester, who seemed soft compared to William. Bold lines drew William's jaw and brow, while his dark blue gaze, shadowed by a sensual sweep of lashes, was piercing and unflinching. He appeared exactly as he was—strong, determined, and indomitable. At one time, she'd loved to lie at his side in bed and trace his profile with the tip of her finger. Now he barely tolerated her presence.

"You're lying." His words were firm, spoken without question.

"I am not. I was told the artifact belonged to someone else."

"I don't think you believed that any more than I do."

"I believed it," she retorted. "I still do."

His gaze narrowed and he watched her for a long moment before he shook his head. "No. You're lying. You didn't believe it when you heard it, and you don't believe it now."

Marcail dropped her gaze to where her feet peeped out from beneath her skirts, one booted and one not as her heart tripped uncertainly. *He can't tell if I'm lying or not. He must be bluffing, too.*

Well, she knew how to deal with a bluffer. She raised her chin and met his gaze with calm certainty. "It doesn't matter what I think or don't think; the artifact is gone."

He looked around the room. "Where is it?"

She forced herself to laugh. "Still the same stubborn William."

"Still the same deceitful Marcail," he retorted, his gaze landing upon her trunk. He crossed to it and tried the lid. "It's locked?"

She shrugged.

His mouth tightened. "Fine. I'll open it in my own way." He lifted a foot and kicked the trunk.

She winced, biting back a protest.

He kicked again and again. Finally, the back hinges gave way and the trunk fell over on its side.

"That was a waste. Your artifact is not in there."

William reached down and upended the trunk. A rainbow of silk gowns and shoes tumbled onto the floor, twined about a handful of the finest lawn chemises.

She had to fight the urge to jump up and collect her belongings, but she couldn't do so without revealing the portmanteau. She was forced to settle for a tight, "You're going to pay for those."

"I already have." He stirred the clothes with one foot, his wet boot marring the silks.

"Oh, for the love of— William! Get your muddy boots out of my clothes! You're ruining them!"

He bent down and picked up an especially sheer lawn chemise. "Very nice. I suppose Colchester bought this for you."

"No, I bought it for myself. The gaslights are very hot in the theater and a lighter chemise is much cooler."

He threw it back on the floor and picked up a long silk night rail. He held it aloft, his blue eyes locked with hers. "Since when did you start wearing a night rail to bed?"

Her cheeks burned. "A gentleman wouldn't speak of the delicate details of a past relationship."

"And a lady wouldn't have such details in her past," he retorted.

She supposed she deserved that. He was right, anyway. She didn't used to wear a night rail to bed, but after she'd left him all those years ago, she'd been achingly lonely, especially at night. Wearing a night rail had made her feel less exposed and vulnerable. She shrugged. "A lot has changed since then."

He dropped the night rail beside the chemise. "I'm sure it has." He glanced around. "Did you bring any other luggage?"

"No, just the trunk."

He went to the dresser, and methodically removed each drawer, looking under and behind them as well as inside.

"You're wasting your time, Hurst."

He ignored her, searching the entire room before finally coming to stand before her with a frown.

While he'd been busy, so had she. Behind her skirts, she'd used her one booted heel to press hard against the portmanteau. It had shifted a tiny bit, then slid out of sight.

She shot a glance at the door. What if Miss Challoner arrived now? Both of them were intent on getting the onyx box. She had to get William out of here as soon as possible. Somehow, some way, she *had* to. "As you have seen for yourself, the artifact is gone."

He crossed his arms over his chest and rocked back on his heels as if readying himself for a gale. "I know you, Marcail Beauchamp, and I know you are lying."

The quiet, certain way he spoke gave her pause. She regarded him from beneath her lashes, annoyed by how he so easily dominated the room. He was so large and so *present*.

His gaze suddenly narrowed. "Stand."

She gripped the bedclothes on each side. "William, I don't—"

"Get up *now*."

"Why? You can see that I'm—"

"If you don't stand up I shall lift you—and there will be a price to pay."

She was so damned frustrated with being ordered about by everyone! The unknown blackmailer, the mysterious Miss Challoner, and now

William. She crossed her arms over her chest. "I am staying right where I am. You forced your way in here, tossed me about like a rag doll, threw all of my clothing upon the floor and stepped on it with your nasty boots, and now you think you can tell me what to do? I'm *done* with having no say in the matter. You can see that I don't have the artifact so there's nothing more to be said." She lifted her chin.

He watched her with a deadly calm. "Don't push me."

Her temper hot, she said haughtily, "Didn't you hear me? There is no reason for you to stay. You will leave *now*."

To her surprise and unease, he turned and grasped the chair she'd been sitting in earlier, and placed it beside the bed. He sat in it and gave it a not very gentle shake. "Seems firm enough."

"Firm enough for what?"

"For this." With that, he leaned forward and grasped her wrist. With a hard yank, he pulled her off the bed and toward him.

She wore only one boot and that one unlaced. She tried to keep her one shoe on, but as he propelled her forward, she stepped on her own lace, tripped, and fell toward him.

His other hand shot out as quickly as a snake, and he caught her easily, pulling her across his lap, facedown, her hair spilling over her so that her vision was obscured. In that instant, she knew what he intended to do and her hands went to cover her bottom, but he was too quick. He caught her wrists, gathered them in his hand, and easily held them to one side. "Oh no, my little liar. There is no getting out of this. You've deserved to be spanked since I first met you, and now I shall finally have my wish."

A letter from Michael Hurst to his brother William from old Alexandria.

While looking among some ancient texts located in the private library of a sulfi with whom she's become very familiar, Miss Smythe-Haughton found something very interesting last night. She has a tendency to become a "favorite" of men of power. While it has opened some doors, it is most annoying.

My assistant seems to think she's found a reference to an amulet that might be the Hurst Amulet. If she's right, it could mean that I've been looking for the blasted thing in the wrong country. Perhaps even the wrong continent.

It is very exasperating to expend so much effort trying to find something and then be told bluntly that you were "wrong, wrong, wrong." Why do I put up with that woman?

CHAPTER 6

For a moment, Marcail tried to catch her breath, intensely embarrassed by the way she'd landed. She put her hands on the edge of the chair and tried to right herself, but William's arms came to rest on her, one just below her bottom and the other over her back.

Marcail grasped William's calf and tried to push herself upright, but he held her tight. Had any other man held her thusly, she would be concerned for her safety, but while angry, no flicker of fear touched her. He would never purposefully hurt her. He was far too protective of his own sisters to ever cross that line.

Still, she wouldn't tamely accept being held in

such a ridiculous position. She twisted so she could see him.

"Let me up!" she demanded, pushing with all of her strength, but to no avail.

"I warned you there would be a cost if you made this difficult."

"William, don't you dare—"

His hand rested on her bottom, warm through her skirts.

She stilled, her heart beating an odd rhythm against her breastbone. She was a mish mosh of emotions, frightened by the ease with which he wielded power over her, angry with her own inability to dismiss him, and infused by an odd yearning at the feel of his hands on her.

At one time, she'd felt she would never get enough of his touch, an illness she thought she'd cured. But had she?

His hand cupped her bottom through her skirts, and then slid gently down her legs.

She tried to swallow, but couldn't. "William . . ." She clenched her teeth over the rest of the sentence, her ears burning with the husky yearning she'd heard in her own voice. She wished he'd . . . what? What did she want?

He reached her ankle and slowly caressed it, sending a shiver through her. Her body began to ache, craving that touch even as she flinched from it.

He flipped up her hem and she realized that his hold had slackened and she could rise if she wished to. But she remained where she was. Sheer, pure desire held her in place as she quivered for his touch.

He slowly slid his hand up the back of her leg, pausing to cup her calf.

She shivered as the air hit her bare leg. "William, I'm not going to—"

He pushed her skirt and chemise up, the cooler air tickling the skin on her now-exposed bottom. She was instantly aware of William's physical reaction as his cock pressed against her stomach.

She froze on the brink between frustration and fascination. It had been so long since a man had touched her—years. In fact, the last man who had touched her had also been the first, William Hurst.

Her cheeks burned as she realized her inclination was to squirm more, to entice him, to tease him until he satisfied her longings. Did she dare do it? Would it work? Or was he—

"You haven't changed much over the years."

Marcail closed her eyes, trying to force the waves of desire down. After a moment, she managed to grit out, "Neither have you." She indicated his stiff cock by rocking her hips.

William almost groaned at her motion. *Damn it, I'm supposed to be in charge here!* He'd lost his temper when he'd pulled her across his lap and he'd fully intended to spank her for her sins. But somehow, having her prone across his lap, her luscious form within reach, had completely wiped his mind of everything—why he was here, all the pain she'd caused in the past, everything except how exquisitely well she fitted to him.

How could he have forgotten how his body reacted to hers? How it had *always* reacted? How, even now, years later and many painful hurts ago, he couldn't stop his cock from yearning to sink into her softness.

It was weakness on his part that made him continue with his "punishment," though he was no longer sure which of them he was now torturing—himself or her?

His hand came to rest on her bare bottom, but this time he cupped her bared skin, sliding in slow circles as if to rub away the sting he'd once thought to inflict.

Marcail's heart leapt in her throat as she shivered through and through.

"Marcail, you stubborn woman." He continued to rub her bottom in slow circles and she caught herself holding her breath, wondering if he would move his hand lower to where she was beginning to ache for a touch. And oh, how she ached. She closed her eyes against an onslaught of pure, shivery need, wishing and wishing that he would reach for her. Unable to help herself, she pressed upward, arching her back so that her bottom pressed into his hand.

William took a deep breath, his heart thudding as hard as a mallet against his chest, his hand still cupped over her pink ass cheek. Smooth and rounded, it begged to be touched. He'd been so angry with her stubbornness, so furious to see the fine lawn chemises that Colchester had bought her, that there'd been no thinking.

He lowered his head at his own weakness. She'd squirmed in his lap in an attempt to free herself, unwittingly inciting his passion even more. She apparently hadn't noticed that he no longer held her in place.

A gentleman would put her skirts to rights and apologize. A gentleman would also feel regret for treating her thusly.

But to her, he was no gentleman, which was the reason why she'd spurned him all those years ago. It was also the reason why he no longer cared what she thought of him. Her actions of long ago burned still, though they did little to excuse his treatment of her today.

He noted that she'd stopped squirming and lay quietly across his lap and he wondered if she was fighting back tears. He'd seen her do that one time before—on the day he'd left after their final argument. The memory gripped him and he shook his head at his own impulsive temper. "Marcail?"

She shifted in his lap, her bottom pressing upward

as her hip grazed his cock. He gritted his teeth and forced his mind elsewhere, though it was difficult, especially with her rounded bottom within his line of sight. Unable to resist, he smoothed his hand over it once more, aware that she stilled at his touch and was lifting up to meet him even more. *She wants this.* The thought circled his mind, astonishing him.

He slid his hand off her ass to her thigh. Instantly, her legs parted just enough that, had he wished, he could touch her most private area.

He blinked. She wasn't angry but aroused, as was he.

As if to confirm his thoughts, she whispered, "William, please." Her voice shivered through him and left him thick with need.

William didn't think twice; he slipped his hand between her silken thighs, her dampness welcoming his touch. He stroked her carefully, slowly, each touch lingering on her hardened clitoris. She moaned and arched her back, her hips rubbing his cock with each move.

He was so aroused he couldn't think, couldn't move, couldn't do anything but continue to stroke her. She was wetter now, her movements more urgent.

Finally, he could take no more. He slipped an arm under her waist and flipped her over so that she was sitting, her head tucked under his chin, her bared bottom pressed into his lap. He lifted his hips and let her feel his thickened cock. "See what you've done to me?" he growled in her ear. "You are the most stubborn, challenging, unfaithful, scheming woman I've ever met."

She tilted back her head, her passion-bright eyes meeting his. "And you are the most intractable, rude, uncouth, arrogant—"

He kissed her, thrusting his tongue between her lips, and she melted against him. He deepened the kiss and she moaned into him, opening her mouth to his, pressing her chest to his.

Their passion, always just a red-hot ember away from full flames, burst into fire and for a heady moment, William wanted to throw himself into the seductive heat.

But only for a moment. This woman was a tantalizing armful, but there was a price for giving into this passion; there always was with women like Marcail. She also held something that belonged to him. Something worth far more than a romp between the sheets, even with such a delicious armful.

Pressing away a deep regret, he loosened his hold on her, pulled her arms from around his neck and then stood, setting her on her feet.

Her skirt fell about her ankles and she blinked up at him, her eyes smoky with passion, her expression uncomprehending. "William, I—"

An urgent knock sounded on the door, pulling

him out of the madness that had held him in his grip. *Good God, what in the hell had just happened?*

The knock sounded again, even more forceful, and William went to the door. "Right yourself," he ordered gruffly, not sparing her a second look.

Hands shaking, Marcail crossed to her dresser, located some hairpins, and made a deft job of securing her wayward hair. In the mirror, she watched as William replaced the chair before he unlocked the door. *Please don't let that be Miss Challoner.*

To her relief, the man she'd seen across the street stood in the doorway. "Cap'n, there's a fire at the docks!"

William swiftly went to the window, flipped open the sash, and leaned out. "Damn it!"

Marcail came to stand at his side. Seeing the bright glow, a sudden fear filled her. "Hurst, how did you get here?"

"By ship." He swiftly headed toward the door. "Get the coach," he told the messenger.

"I've already ordered it, sir."

"Good." William pulled her cloak off the peg by the door, then grabbed her wrist. "You're coming with me."

"But I—"

They were out of the room before she could gasp. "Put your cloak on." He locked the door and pocketed the key.

"But I—"

He tugged her cloak from her unresisting hands and tossed it about her shoulders, then grasped her wrist again and ran down the steps. When she stumbled on the bottom landing, he swooped her up with a curse and carried her out the door.

"Put me down!"

"No."

"But I can't leave!"

His gaze narrowed on her. "Why not?"

She couldn't tell him she was waiting to deliver the artifact she'd already sworn was gone. A swirl of wind made her toes tingle from the cold, and she said, "I have no shoes."

He gave her stockinged feet an impatient glance. "You won't need shoes; you'll be staying in the coach."

"William, just leave me here and—"

"No. I'll be damned if I let you out of my sight."

The coach pulled up and Hurst unceremoniously dumped her onto a seat, then sat opposite her, issuing terse instructions to the man who'd alerted him of the fire. He nodded at William's instructions, then shut the door. A moment later, she heard him climb onto the coach box and shout 'gee' at the team.

As the coach leapt forward, Marcail caught a glimpse out the window of another coach turning in. It was a dainty coach, trimmed in blue, and seemed oddly out of place in the yard. *Is that Miss Challoner?* Marcail had no way of knowing, but her heart sank when she thought of how angry her blackmailer would be if Miss Challoner returned empty-handed.

She twisted her hands in the ribbons of her cloak. "William, please release me. This is ridiculous. It's just an old box of little value."

"It's worth a lot to me. My brother Michael is being held prisoner by a sulfi who refuses to release him until that damned box is returned," he said grimly.

A sick weight pressed into her stomach. "I—I didn't know. William, I—"

The coach rounded a corner and the scent of smoke became thick, shouts and screams echoing ahead of them. William cursed and lifted the curtain.

She knew what he saw by the whiteness of his face. *Oh, no!* She looked past him and saw his ship tied to the dock, flaming as if lit from the furnaces of hell. The dark sky was alive as hungry red and orange flames licked at the blackening sails and mast.

The coach rocked to a stop and William thrust open the door. "You, madam, will stay here."

Marcail's gaze strayed to the flaming ship and she knew in an instant where he intended to go.

She grabbed his wrist. "William, I didn't know about your brother and the artifact. No one told me. They just said they wanted it and I *had* to give it to them—"

"So you'll return the box to me?"

She almost nodded, but the image of her young sisters' hopeful faces rose before Marcail's eyes. Her shoulders slumped under the weight of so many difficult decisions. "Damn it, it's not that easy. I *want* to return it to you, but I can't."

He yanked his arm free. "I don't have the time to discuss this. Poston!" he yelled up to his groom.

A second later, the man stood by the door. "Yes, Cap'n?"

William jerked his head toward Marcail. "She is not to leave the coach. Do what you must to keep her here."

The man eyed her up and down and, apparently satisfied that she would be no challenge, nodded. "Yes, sir."

A huge boom shook the air, the ground shaking as the ship rocked violently and then shuddered. Marcail gasped as wood and flames shot into the air and then landed in the water, hissing like snakes.

She couldn't look away, unable to take it all in: the ship burning brightly, the people running to and from the dock, the thick smoke billowing toward the sky, the cacophony of noise.

And William's broad back disappearing into the milling crowd on the dock.

Marcail turned toward Poston, her chest aching from the pounding of her own heart. "You must stop him!"

The square man shook his head regretfully. "There's no stoppin' the cap'n. The *Agile Witch* is his ship. He'll fight that fire with his bare hands if he has to."

Good God, he's going onboard! He can't do that; he could get killed!

Marcail gathered her skirts and started to jump down from the coach, but Poston was too fast. He set her firmly back onto the seat and shut the door.

"We have to stop him!" she cried. "If he goes onto the ship—"

"He'll be fine, miss."

"But it *exploded.* He could be in danger right now as we argue!"

Poston turned to look at the ship, the flames roaring into the sky, his expression increasingly dark.

A sail caught fire, making a distinctive *whoosh* as the flames raced across it. "No mere fire caused that," she pointed out. "What if there's another explosion while the captain's aboard ship?"

His jaw firmed. "Ye're right, miss. I need to see to him."

"I'll come with you—"

"Ye'll stay here, miss." The coachman pulled down the shutter and latched it, blocking sight of the burning ship and the mayhem about it.

"Poston, no!" In reply she heard the sound of something being drawn through the shutter handles. "What are you doing?"

She grabbed the door handle and tugged, but it was firmly tied in place. Heart sinking, she lunged across the coach for the other door but he got there first.

Desperate, she placed her hands on the window ledge. "You can't—" The shutters came whizzing down and she yanked her fingers out of the way just as they banged into place, leaving her in total darkness. "Poston, please don't—"

"I'm off to see to the cap'n. Ye'll be fine if ye stay quiet as a mouse."

"I won't keep quiet!"

"Then don't be surprised if'n ye attract some attention ye don't like. I don't know the people hereabouts, and I'll wager ye don't know 'em, either."

Blast it! She doubled her hands into fists and banged upon the door. "You can't leave me here! I demand that you—"

"Good-bye, miss." And with that, he was gone.

A letter from Michael Hurst to his brother William, from the deck of a cange as it set sail down the Nile.

After two false starts and endless paperwork, we're finally under way. You would be amazed by the bribery system here; it makes the thieves in Parliament look like amateurs. I must reluctantly admit that my intrepid assistant, Miss Smythe-Haughton, proved to be worth her weight in gold today. When the port authorities began to question our harmless cargo—digging tools, sifters, pickaxes, and such—her basilisk stare cowed them into speechlessness.

Never underestimate the power of a bossy woman.

CHAPTER 7

The gangplank from the *Agile Witch* was organized mayhem. Men were lined on one side passing up full buckets of water, and empty buckets back down the other. Another line of seamen hurried off the ship carrying casks and crates. The rest of the crew stacked them away from the dock and the smoldering ship.

William made his way up the gangplank and stepped onto the deck.

MacDougal, who'd been barking orders left and right, his gaze moving ceaselessly over the ship, caught sight of him and hurried forward.

"There ye be, Cap'n!" The first mate's face was black and grimy, and he had holes burned into his once white shirt.

"What happened?" William snapped.

"I dinna know yet. I was on the foredeck settin' the watch fer the night, and the next thing I knew, smoke was boilin' from the hold."

William frowned. "The fire started *belowdeck?*"

"Aye, in the storage hold, which was odd, fer there was no lantern aboot—nothin' t' spark a flame." The first mate rubbed his forehead, leaving a new streak of black. "But tha' is no' all of it, Cap'n. Whilst we were fightin' the fire in the hold, the deck went ablaze."

William shot his first mate a sharp look. "You're certain the fire on deck wasn't caused by the one in the hold?"

"They was on opposite ends o' the ship."

William balled his hands into fists. "Damn it."

"I said the same thing meself. One fire was enou', but two?" The first mate's gaze watched the scurrying crew. "In me forty years at sailin', I've never seen such."

"Neither have I. What caused the explosion?"

MacDougal's sooty white eyebrows snapped together. "Gunpowder, Cap'n. Two barrels hidden behind the main rail head. 'Twas a wonder no one was injured by the blast."

"Bloody hell, we've been sabotaged."

"Aye, Cap'n. Fer ye know I'd never allow gunpowder stored on deck, especially whilst we was at dock."

"I know you did all you could, MacDougal." William glanced around at the crew. "Is everyone accounted for?"

"Aye. Every last one."

"Injuries?"

"A few burns here and there, but no' so bad that a good pint won't set things to rights. And Jamie MacTosh broke his ankle jumpin' out o' the way o' a flamin' barrel when the kegs exploded. 'Tis a miracle, but no one else was seriously injured."

William scowled. "One is too many. Damn it, I wish I knew why someone set this fire."

MacDougal nodded to where some men surrounded the main mast. "I asked the bos'n t' drop the mizzenmast t' keep it from fallin' whilst we're working on deck. 'Twas torched well an' good, and could go down at any minute."

All around them, madness boiled. The smoldering sails had been tossed into the ocean, where they sizzled upon the waves. Water soaked the entire ship, making the wood wet and slick. Part of the mizzen deck was missing, broken timbers smoldering in place, while above, the blackened main mast stood like a grim warning.

Despite the severity of the situation, the fire was slowly being brought under control. There was a general cry of warning as, with a loud crack and a great shower of flames and sparks, the damaged mizzenmast was felled into the ocean, the flames instantly replaced with hissing smoke and steam.

So much damage and all from a small fire and a few barrels of gunpowder. Why would someone do such a thing?

He frowned. Whatever reason his invisible enemy had, he or she was deadly serious in their intent. He glanced around the deck, his gaze resting on the various places yet more gun powder might be hidden. There were several places, too many to safely search in a short period of time.

William made an instant decision. "MacDougal, get the men off the ship."

"But, Cap'n, the fire could flame back to life and—"

"It's too dangerous. If there was one cache of gunpowder, there might be another. Someone wanted to sink the *Witch*. Perhaps they've done their damnedest already and perhaps they haven't. I won't risk the men."

"Shall I form a crew to search and—"

"No. I'll do it. Just get the men a safe distance away."

"But, Cap'n—"

"Damn it, do it *now!*"

Looking none too happy, MacDougal reluctantly turned away and began bellowing orders. With startled glances at one another, the men put down their axes and buckets and filed down the gangplank.

"There's the last one, Cap'n," MacDougal announced. He joined William, who was already searching the ship. "Where do we start lookin'?"

"*We* don't start anywhere. You're going onshore to handle the crew."

"But, Cap'n—"

"Go."

MacDougal grimaced but did as he was told, glancing over his shoulder the entire way.

Soon William was alone on the smoldering deck, the acrid smell of smoke and burning tar making him cough. He pulled a kerchief from his pocket, dipped it in an abandoned water bucket, and held it over his mouth and nose as he continued his search.

He didn't know how he knew, but he was certain of what he would find.

And find it, he did . . .

Marcail ran down the slick wooden dock, her stockinged feet hidden by both the darkness and her long skirts. She paused at the end and looked up at the smoldering ship, hot winds lifting from the ashes to stir her hair and the clothing of every person crammed on the quay.

Smoke boiled from the ship as if she were a chimney, her sails gone, her burning ropes swinging like long fuses in the hot breeze. The still burning mast fell into the ocean with a loud *crack*, landing on the ragged and burned sails.

Along with the crackling roar of the fire, bellowed orders rang out over the commotion caused by the onlookers. Marcail covered her ears. No wonder no one had heard her beating on the side of the coach.

She'd finally taken matters into her own hands and escaped on her own. Her fists bruised, she'd managed to light one of the lamps and examine her prison, looking at the box seats (solidly constructed), the back panel (flanked by thick boards), the floor (iron framing with heavy oak planks, none of which was the slightest bit loose).

She had to find a way out; she couldn't bear thinking of what William might be facing.

Then her gaze had fallen on the door hinges.

Within seconds, she'd dropped to her knees to examine them. They were very sturdy. The metal plates were joined by an iron pin hammered through metal hoops.

She'd tried to loosen the pin with her hands, but it wouldn't budge. She needed a tool of some sort to pound the pin free. Almost able to taste her freedom, she tossed aside the seat cushions and opened the seat boxes. Coach blankets, small pillows, a foot warmer . . . No tools. Not a single one.

She'd rocked back on her heels, disappointed, but

then the foot warmer caught her eye again. Noting the thick handle, she picked it up.

Ten minutes later, the heavy iron pin had finally dropped to the floor. Marcail had braced herself against the seat box, placed her stockinged feet against the door, and given it a hard kick.

It had immediately opened, hanging at a broken, tilted angle, and she'd jumped out.

Now, she was free . . . and frightened by what she saw. It was madness here on the dock; people hurried here and there carrying buckets or just dashing about as if uncertain where to stand, while others stood staring up at the burning ship as if unable to believe the spectacle.

Marcail followed the horrified gaze of a young girl who clutched her mother's hand, seeing the smoldering mast and destroyed deck. *William loved that ship. He must be heartsick.* She turned her anxious gaze on the dock, but couldn't see him. *He must be here somewhere.* She hurried forward, her attention flickering here and there, trying to take in the unfolding situation.

She couldn't shake the feeling that all of this was somehow connected to her. It was beginning to appear that the onyx box carried far more importance than she'd thought, and not just to William.

From beginning to end, the entire situation had been a departure for her blackmailer. *Why does my blackmailer want that particular artifact?* she wondered as she stepped around two burly seamen carrying a large trunk to shore.

Something mysterious was going on. The box had to be wildly valuable. Perhaps she shouldn't hand it over to her blackmailer unless he promised to leave her and her sisters alone forever more. Or perhaps she should keep it until all of her sisters were settled, and *then* hand it over.

She paused, thinking of William's kipnapped brother. From what she'd read of Michael's adventures, chronicled every month in *The Morning Post,* he was quite capable of gaining his own release. He was an adventurer, after all. Dangerous situations were a daily occurrence for him . . . weren't they?

Perhaps and perhaps not. William must think his brother is in some danger, for he chased me all of the way here to regain the box. The artifact must belong to Michael. William was too certain of that for her to believe otherwise.

Which placed her in an intolerable situation. If the box belonged to Michael and he really needed it to win his freedom from his captors, then she couldn't keep it, no matter how much her blackmailer demanded that she should.

The thought made her sigh, which was a mistake as she gulped in a smoky plume of air that burned her throat and made her cough. She covered her mouth with her arm and pushed her way through the crowds, feeling as low as she'd ever felt. She'd lied to herself when she'd tamely accepted Miss Challoner's statement that the artifact didn't belong to William. Marcail should have known better.

After all, Miss Challoner was an instrument of a very evil man, one who was willing to harm Marcail's family without a flicker of remorse.

Why did I believe her? Yet Marcail knew. *Because it made it easier to do what I was asked.* She'd already sacrificed so much for her family that she hadn't hesitated when she was asked to sacrifice her honor. Grandmamma would be ashamed—as Marcail was herself.

She neared the gangplank, scanning anxiously for William, though she could barely see the figures on the ship through the smoke. Nearby, a line of men and women had formed a bucket brigade and were passing buckets of water to the ship. While there were plenty of people in line, the buckets weren't getting to them fast enough. Perhaps this was a small way she could redeem herself. Marcail dropped her cloak out of the way on the edge of the quay, grabbed an empty bucket, and carried it to the pump where two fresh-faced youths were pumping the water as fast as they could. One immediately set her bucket under the cold stream.

When it was full, she grasped the handle with both hands and hefted it. The large wooden bucket was amazingly heavy, and the rope handle hung upon her hands and squeezed them painfully together. Worse, water began seeping out of the bucket the instant it was filled.

Walking as quickly as she dared in her wet stockinged feet, she carried the water to the line, the bucket banging painfully against her shins. She gave the bucket to the end man, who quickly handed it off, then turned and handed her an empty bucket.

Marcail caught it and hurried back to the pumps, where two full buckets were waiting. She gave the boys the empty bucket and hefted a full one, this one larger and made of skin stretched over a frame. She staggered under the weight, gasping for air, which was heavy with smoke and the acrid scent of burning wood and tar.

Back and forth she went, carrying bucket after bucket, while the flames disappeared beneath billows of white smoke. The roiling smoke made her cough and stung her eyes; her shins ached from the painful bruises. Worse, her hands had been rubbed raw from the rope handles and she had to grit her teeth against the pain.

Still, she never stopped. Each time she approached the line, she would glance up at the ship, wondering where William might be and noting that the smoke was lessening bit by bit. It was working!

She wanted to jump for joy, but the call for more water was ceaseless.

Once again, she grasped the rough rope handle, blinking as her eyes watered from the pain. *We're winning. If we can just keep this up a little longer, the ship might be saved.*

Suddenly the man at the end of the water line held up his hand. "Wait, miss."

She set down her bucket and followed his gaze.

Men were pouring off the ship. Blackened by soot, they hurried down the gangplank, the row of water handlers following them. Smoke bellowed and obscured the gangplank as the last few men left the ship; soon it was empty and the dock packed even fuller.

She blinked in the thick smoke, seeing one last figure appearing through the gloom. Her heart quickened. Was it William? But no. The man was short and stocky. He came down the gangplank, ordering the men from the dock, his thick Scottish bellow clear over the loud hum of voices.

The man beside Marcail shook his head. "I wonder why he's orderin' th' men to th' shore? Shouldn't they be fightin' th' fire?"

"I should think so," Marcail said, noting that the burly Scotsman had succeeded in clearing the end of the dock nearest the ship. "I wish we knew what was goin' on. Why did they send away all of—"

BOOM! A terrific blast shook the dock and fire blew into the air in a huge ball, roaring over the quay. The air was rent with screams and the sound of pounding feet as everyone on the dock surged toward land.

Marcail had to fight her way to one side to keep from being carried away, her heart slamming against her chest as she stared at the ship in horror. Fire bellowed from the deck and crackled furiously, the flames now devouring the ship as if they'd been starved for this one, delicious second.

Where is William? Was he onboard? The question echoed numbly through her stilled brain. *Please God, no.* She tried to think clearly, but her heart was beating too furiously to allow her such a luxury. She found herself walking toward the ship, against the flow of people, her gaze locked on the shooting flames. She had to know. She had to go, to see— What?

Her mind refused to answer. She walked closer and closer to the burning hulk, men frantically chopping at the ropes that moored the ship to the dock. The heat was so great that her face felt burned, and she instinctively held up her hands to shield herself.

With a heaving cry, a bare-chested man near her slammed his hatchet through a thick rope and, with an almost human groan, the ship listed away from the dock. Then she slowly began to drift toward the sea, crackling loudly.

The voices on the dock grew quieter as the crowd of crew and townsmen watched the ship.

Marcail couldn't look away. Somewhere on that ship, dead or near it, was William. She knew it. Knew it for all she was worth. How had this happened? How could a ship just explode, and not once, but multiple times?

She turned to a sailor who stood nearby, his soot-blackened face a mask of sadness. "Sir?"

He looked at her, obviously surprised to be addressed. "Aye, miss?"

"What made it blow up like that?"

His face tightened in anger. "We was sabotaged, miss. Someone set gunpowder upon the deck and lit it. Thank God the cap'n figured it out or we'd all be dead."

"Captain Hurst? He knew?"

"Aye. That's why we all came runnin' off the deck just afore she went."

Had William made it? She had to clear her throat to continue. "Do you . . . do you know if the captain made it off the ship, too?"

The seaman blinked. "Why, o' course he did. He came running off like the devil hisself was chasin' him."

Relief shattered through her, as brilliant as any

light, and in the space of one second, she went from the lowest of lows to the highest of highs.

The sailor chuckled. "Did ye no' see him? He was only halfway down the gangplank when the *Witch* blew, and the explosion damn near threw him through the air, it did."

The sailor might have found it funny, but she could only feel relief. Smiling her thanks, Marcail wiped away a tear with her sleeve and began to make her way through the crowd to the coach. She was so filled with emotion that she didn't know what she thought, or why. She only knew that she needed some time alone before she faced William again.

A letter from Captain William Hurst to his sister Mary, after he landed in Bristol to restock before setting sail for a four-month journey.

Life aboard ship is simple and uncomplicated. There are rules much as we had at home—to be polite to one another, respect one another's property, and do your chores so they do not burden another.

There are differences, too, of course. For one, no one presses me to read the way Father was wont to. Yet I find myself doing it anyway to break the boredom, or out of curiosity and a desire to learn. Our father established reading as a habit and we're all beneficiaries of it.

CHAPTER 8

William watched grimly as the *Agile Witch* was slowly carried out to sea by the tide, listing sadly to one side. His ship was gone, burning like the blazes of Hades. She would sink soon, along with his favorite books, the paintings his sisters had made him, his new brass compass, and the maps he'd collected over the years.

Those were painful to lose, but they paled at the sight of the mighty *Witch* sailing her final few yards.

He pushed aside the weight of his thoughts. "That's the end to that."

MacDougal wiped his eyes with his ragged sleeve before he glanced around. After making certain that no crew members were nearby, he lowered his voice. "So ye found more gunpowder."

William shifted so that he was standing a bit closer to the first mate. "Aye," he said in a quiet tone. "Four barrels. Two large timbers had fallen across them and were smoldering, so there was nothing for it but to run."

"Och, what a crime!"

"Indeed. There was no saving the *Agile Witch*. We were fortunate the men were all clear of the deck when she blew."

They were quiet for a moment. Finally, Mac-Dougal heaved a deep sigh. "'Tis almost more than I can bear."

"Aye. The barrels weren't ours. They were marked in a way I've never seen before. A black circle with a red circle inside it."

The first mate's thick gray eyebrows were lowered. "How do ye think they got onboard? I'd have noticed them during the evening inspection, I'm sure, especially with such markings."

"I think someone slipped onboard and set the fire in the hold, knowing that all hands would report to fight it, including you."

"Which left the deck clear fer the devils to do their dirty work." MacDougal spat, his eyes wet with tears. "Damn them, whoe'er they are. Who would do such an evil thing?" His voice thickened. "It's hard to believe she's gone. She was right as rain one minute, and then the next—" He gulped back a sob.

William knew how the first mate felt, but he refused to give in to despair. Even now, his crew was watching, locked on his every move.

He slapped the first mate on the shoulder, forced a grim smile, and said in a voice that could be heard by all, "Don't take it so to heart, MacDougal. 'Tis but a ship. A damned fine one, but we'll have another one just as glorious as the *Agile Witch*." He glanced about the dock and nodded to the crew members who stood closest. "No lives were lost today, and we should be thankful for that."

The men nodded, their expressions slightly less bleak.

"Aye, Cap'n." MacDougal swiped his eyes with the tail of his soot-covered shirt, leaving a swipe of black across them until he looked like a masked thief.

William found himself chuckling, despite the sinking knowledge that he was now in even less of a position to rescue Michael. "MacDougal, collect the crew, find them a good night's lodging and a meal, and then assemble at the docks in Bristol. I shall write to London tonight and have my banker send you a letter of marquee for the purchase of a new ship."

MacDougal straightened. "Right away?"

"If I'm to rescue my brother I must have a ship, and I'd prefer not to commission one that I cannot do with as I will. See what ships are available once you reach the Bristol shipyards. And find a good, swift one."

"That'll cost ye a pretty penny."

"Expense be damned."

MacDougal brightened considerably. "Expense be damned?"

"You heard me. And while you're there, keep the crew out of trouble. When I arrive, I'll wish to set sail as quickly as possible."

MacDougal nodded, his composure regained. "Aye, Cap'n. A few days restin' in Bristol will be jus' the thing for the crew's morale."

William nodded as he watched the *Witch* tilt, slowly rolling to her side. He replied quietly, "I don't know why someone set that fire, but I intend on finding out. Meanwhile, keep an eye on the men. They're a superstitious lot and I won't have them saying we sail under an unlucky sign or any other drivel."

"If they thought that, then to a man they'd sign up fer some other crew."

"Indeed they would. Keep them happy in Bristol, and busy when you've the chance."

"Aye. And I'll put an end to any talk of ill luck, too."

"Good." William turned from the burning wreckage that had once been his ship. "It wasn't ill luck that sank the *Agile Witch*. It was a human, Mac-Dougal. A sneaky, conniving, evil human and when I find them—" He curled his hands into fists.

"Aye, Cap'n. I hope ye find 'em and crush 'em beneath yer boot heel, and then string 'em up on the yardarm fer the vultures to pick out their eyes, and then string 'em behind the ship so the shark can feast on their bones and—"

William had to laugh. "Stand down, MacDougal."

MacDougal gave a sheepish grin. "Sorry, Cap'n, but me blood is thirstin' fer revenge."

"As is mine." William could think of only one person who had ill intentions toward him. They'd sent the one woman he was susceptible to—Marcail—to steal from him, and now he suspected they knew he'd been within an Ames's ace of regaining the artifact, so they'd taken a drastic next step and torched his ship. Someone wanted that onyx box very, very badly.

"Will ye need a room tonight, too, Cap'n?" MacDougal asked.

William thought of Marcail, who waited for him in his coach, and he smiled coldly. "No. I will join you and the crew in Bristol in under a week's time."

MacDougal saluted smartly. "Very well, Cap'n. Ye

can count on me." He turned and began barking orders, the crew looking relieved at this sign of normalcy.

Passing by his crew, William stopped to congratulate them on their brave attempt to save the ship, then he strolled down the quickly emptying quay. A line of buckets marked the efforts of the townsmen and women who'd done their best to save his ship, and at the end of the line a burly barman, still wearing his apron, stared morosely toward the sea. William paused to clap the man on the shoulder. "Thank you for your help."

The barman stood a bit straighter. "Ye're welcome, sir. Was everyone on the ship saved?"

"All are accounted for, and other than one broken leg and some minor burns, the crew are fine."

"That's a miracle."

"Indeed it is. That wouldn't be true if it weren't for you and the rest of the town. I cannot thank you enough."

The man beamed. "'Tis the way o' Southend-on-Sea, Cap'n. When we see a need we don't ask questions, but do what needs to be done."

As William nodded and turned away, he saw Marcail's cloak pooled on the dock. He bent and picked it up, the softness of the brushed gray wool lingering on his fingertips as the red satin trim gleamed. There was no mistaking it; no other woman in Southend would own such a fine cloak.

The barman tsked. "The miss's cloak. She must have forgot it."

"You saw the woman who wore this?"

"Saw her? I *worked* beside her for nigh on an hour."

Worked? The man must be daft; Marcail wouldn't soil her hands with real work.

The barman's voice broke in, "Do ye know the miss, Cap'n?"

"Aye. She rode with me in my coach here to the quay."

Admiration showed in the man's eyes. "She's a good one, she is. Helped us with the bucket brigade, carrying buckets of water heavier than she was, and she ne'er complained a mite."

Why would Marcail help put out the fire on *his* ship? William couldn't think of a single reason. Until this moment, he'd been certain that she'd be pleased that he'd faced such a loss.

His gaze dropped to the large buckets and he rubbed his forehead wearily, struggling to make sense of it all.

Unaware of William's struggle, the barman continued, "Aye. She'll be sore tomorrow, that's fer certain." The man rubbed his back and grimaced. "I'll be sore meself, passin' all of those buckets onward. I wish we'd saved the ship."

"You did your best, and I'm eternally grateful," William replied automatically.

William couldn't imagine Marcail rolling up her silk sleeves and doing something as physical and dirty as carrying water buckets. It was completely at odds with his knowledge of her, knowledge written in her own hand years ago. In the letter she'd flatly told him that she was leaving him for a man who was wealthier and better placed socially than William would ever be.

Just thinking about it still had the power to make his stomach tighten. He'd been such a fool, such a blind, lovesick fool, that her letter—baring her ugly soul for the small-spirited, money-grabbing, social-climbing thing that it was—had nearly destroyed him.

It had been a brutal lesson to learn, but he was wiser for it. Though he'd shared his bed with a number of women and enjoyed his fair share of flirtations, never again had he succumbed to a woman's wiles.

He tossed Marcail's cloak over his shoulder, turned toward the street, and saw her picking her way up the crowded dock. Several men had paused to look back at her, struck by her beauty.

William simmered at their reactions. *Damn it, she should be in the coach.* How had she talked her way out of it? Somehow she'd managed to charm Poston, something William would have wagered couldn't be done.

Up ahead, Marcail turned to look down the street before crossing it, and he noticed that she was far from her usual cool, elegant self: her gown was dirty, her face shiny from her exertions, her hair clinging to her cheeks and neck.

She crossed the street, then turned to watch the final timbers of the *Agile Witch* sputter in flames upon the sea, her expression somber.

She looks genuinely sad. The realization made William's heart twist and he frowned, still struggling to reconcile his previous knowledge of her with her actions today. After a long moment, he shook his head and walked toward her.

She was still facing the ocean, but she blinked as if suddenly waking up, then turned away, stepping carefully, and he remembered that she wore no shoes. *Damn it, her feet must be cut and bruised.* His jaw tightened. *What are you trying to do, Marcail Beauchamp?*

He headed swiftly down the quay, his gaze locked on Marcail's dark head. He caught up to her as she stepped onto the small walk in front of the shops lining the dockside, and swooped her up into his arms. "Hello, my troublesome little—"

"William!" She buried her face in his neck, holding tight.

William stopped stock-still. *What the hell?* William scowled down at her, instantly aware of her lush curves clasped to his chest and the scent of lavender in her hair.

She looked up at him. "I was so worried—" Her voice caught as if tears choked the words from her lips.

She acts as if she cares for me, which I know to be a falsehood. Her seeming feelings are never real; I only wish I could say the same about mine. Truth be told, a decided amount of pleasure rose through him as he held her in his arms, which was a feeling best left unexamined.

Irritated with his own thoughts, he growled out, "Release my neck, woman! I've need of it myself."

She gave a watery laugh and loosened her hold. "I'm sorry. It's been a very trying hour. I-I was afraid that you were still on the ship when—" Her voice caught and she once again buried her face in his neck, her tears warm through his shirt.

He quickly headed toward the carriage. The "overcome innocent" was a useless charade; he knew her too well. He should simply drop her onto her stockinged feet and let her limp back to the carriage.

Instead, he found himself resting his cheek on her hair, the lavender scent tickling his nose.

Before he'd stopped believing in love he would have given the world for this moment, when he could hold her as if no one in the world mattered but the two of them.

But he was no longer that man. He forced himself to lift his cheek from her hair. "For God's sake, must I ask again? Loosen your hold."

She looked up at him, her nose and eyes red, her hair mussed, a smudge of dirt on her cheek, a hurt expression on her face.

"You look a fright," he said.

To his vast relief, she took instant umbrage and loosened her hold, her brow lowering. "Oh! You are *so*—" Her lips folded, then she snapped, "I'm sorry if I held you too tightly. I had no idea your neck was so weak."

That was more like it. William settled her more comfortably in his arms and turned toward the coach. He was certain people on the street were watching them with interest, but he didn't give a damn.

"You may release me now; I can walk the rest of the way," she demanded.

"Without shoes?"

"Without shoes." She didn't give an inch.

He never slowed. "I've too much to do to wait for you to mince your way to the coach."

"I don't want you to carry me."

"That is too bad."

"Damn you, put me *down*." Her furious voice tickled his ear. "I will scream if you don't."

"I believe I owe you a spanking from earlier in the evening. If you scream, I will deliver it now."

"You wouldn't spank me," she replied in far too smug a tone. "You didn't do it before and you won't do it now."

She was right, but he wouldn't admit it. Instead, he shrugged. "Fine. I'll prove it." He made as if to set her down, but she gripped him tighter.

"You can't do that *here.*"

"Oh, but I can." He lifted a brow. "Want to try me?"

She shook her head slowly, but her expression said something entirely different. Her lips were parted, her eyes dark, and he knew she was remembering the "spanking" she'd gotten before. His body hardened at the memory and he was glad her long skirts covered his reaction.

She sighed, suddenly looking as tired as he felt. "William, please . . . this is ridiculous."

He glanced down at her. Though she protested and kicked a little, her head was now wearily tucked against his shoulder.

His heart ached in an odd way and he held her tighter. "There's the coach now."

"You, sir, have a rude propensity for scooping me up as if I were a bag of flour."

"Bags of flour don't kick," he pointed out.

Her lips twitched. "They would if you handled them so roughly."

He frowned down at her. "Did Poston let you out of the coach?"

"No. He went to help you, leaving me trapped in the coach."

"You're free now."

"I worked at it," she replied huffily.

With her hair in a tangle, and dirt smudging her face, she looked like an outraged kitten. He hid an unexpected smile and replied in a milder tone, "I'm sorry I snapped at you for holding so tightly to my neck, but I couldn't see where I was walking."

She was silent a moment. To his surprise, she said, "I'm sorry, too. I was just worried. The ship was on fire and then there was the explosion and I kept picturing you broken and bruised, trapped by a burning beam with no one able to reach you, and the fire raging all around—"

"Good God, you have a vivid imagination!"

"I know. It's a burden."

"Tell your imagination that it will take more than that little explosion to rid the world of me."

She peeped up at him, her wet lashes radiating from her eyes, which looked darker than usual. "Invincible, are you?" she asked, a faint teasing note in her voice.

"Today, yes." They reached the coach. Despite his

intentions otherwise, he found himself oddly loath to release her.

He deserved this moment of peace, when he wasn't questioning her and she wasn't defying him. Soon enough, their relationship would return to its normal, abrasive path. And the more contentious their relationship, the better for them both, he decided. Despite all that had transpired between them, he was constantly aware of a tug of attraction that was far too strong. Once he had the artifact he'd never see her again, which was fine with him.

He suddenly noted how the coach door hung at an odd angle. "Interesting."

Marcail turned to see what had caught his attention. "Oh. That."

"Yes, that."

"Poston tied the shutters and doors closed. I had to find a way to open one from the inside."

"I didn't see Poston on the quay, but that's not surprising. Every person in town seems to be there." He set her on her feet, frowning at the dirt on her gown and her black stockings. He flicked a glance at her face and noted she was pale beneath the grime, her face streaked by her tears.

Too late he realized that he apparently had a weakness for emotional females, particularly ones with violet eyes and tear-streaked faces. The sooner she was back to being her usual composed, collected self, the sooner he could get the artifact and forget that this week had occurred.

He leaned back and regarded her from head to foot. "Good God, you're filthy."

Her tremulous smile disappeared as her chin snapped up. "So are you."

"Yes, but I was in the middle of the fire. You were not." Seeing her struggling for a witty retort, he hid his satisfaction and glanced at the door. "How did you open this door?"

"I used the handle of the foot warmer on the hinge pins." She reached inside and held up a pin, one end oddly flat. "See?"

"Bloody hell."

"I did what I had to." She tossed the pin onto the floorboard.

He could tell from the timber of her voice that her emotions were calmer now and not so raw. *Good. The last thing I want to deal with right now is a weepy woman.* He jerked his head toward the coach. "Get inside. I'll find Poston and we'll leave."

"Oh? Where are we going?"

"Back to your room, where you'll give me the artifact so I may save my brother."

"William, I must—"

"Hush." He picked her up and set her on the seat. "We'll discuss this later. Don't even *think* about leaving while I'm gone."

Her chin lifted. "If I'd wished to leave, I could have, and yet I stayed here. I was in plain sight the entire time and made no effort to return to the inn, though I could have done so."

"True. Just don't get any bright ideas now." He tossed her cloak at her.

She caught it, and as she did so, William caught a glimpse of one of her palms.

He grasped her wrist. She tugged, trying to free herself, but he ignored her and turned her palm upward.

A bright angry stripe of raw skin glared back up at him. "Damn it, how did you do that?"

She curled her fingers over the stripe. "It's nothing."

But it was. "You got that from carrying water buckets."

"I couldn't just sit by and not help. I knew how much your ship meant to you and I—I suppose I felt responsible, in some way."

He looked into her upturned face, noting the delicate rings beneath her eyes and how her shoulders slumped with exhaustion.

She brushed a stray strand of hair from her cheek, unwittingly exposing the angry red stripe across the palm of her other hand.

His gaze narrowed, his heart oddly twisted. *Damn it, don't begin imagining that her actions mean any more than her words. She's an actress—and a brilliant one, too.*

His gaze flickered over the delicate lines of her face and throat, obvious even through the fine coating of grime. "That does it," he said, straightening. "When we return to your hotel, I want to see every bruise, cut, and burn on your body."

She narrowed her gaze. "I'm not removing my clothing for you."

He shrugged. "Then strip for a maidservant. I don't care, so long as someone sees to your bruises and cuts."

"Why do you care?"

"I don't. But if you're patched and cleaned at least—ah, there's Poston now."

The groom hurried up. "There you are, sir! I was lookin' all over fer ye and I—" He leaned forward, frowning. "Why, the door is completely off its hinges!"

"Miss Beauchamp decided to take a walk."

"A walk, sir?"

"Yes," Marcail said in a bitter tone, "a *walk*." Why did they both seem surprised that she had wished for her freedom? She'd wager her last penny that neither of them would have accepted being locked in a coach.

"I found Miss Hurst wandering the pier and I convinced her to join us here."

"I was coming back on my own," she retorted. "If you'd been ten minutes later, you would have found me here."

Poston glanced from her to his master before saying in a quiet tone, "Pardon me, Cap'n, shall I fix the door so we can get under way? Or do you—"

"No, no. Fix the door." William climbed into the coach and sat across from Marcail. "Once you've secured that, drive us back to the hotel. Miss Beauchamp has something of mine that she would like to return."

Marcail sniffed.

"Yes, Cap'n. Right away."

Marcail lifted a hand to brush her hair from her face, caught sight of her filthy fingers, and winced. Her gown was streaked with soot and dirt from the buckets, her stockinged feet quite black. She was almost afraid to see how her face and hair had fared.

The coach dipped as John Poston replaced the hinge pins. Though it had taken her some time to undo them, he seemed to have no problem replacing them, though the final pin stuck out at an odd angle.

Upon seeing the sadly bashed pin, the groom had sent Marcail a concerned look, but he never said a word. He checked that the door would still work and, satisfied that it did, he closed and latched it. Soon, they were under way.

Suddenly weary beyond words, Marcail leaned back into her corner of the coach. When they arrived at her room in the inn, William would demand the artifact and she would give it to him. She had no choice, now that she knew what the stakes were for him and his family.

But what would she do about the blackmailer? Could she negotiate a settlement, exchange the artifact for another one, perhaps one that was worth more?

Whatever it took, she'd pay.

A letter from William Hurst to his brother Robert, written from the deck of his first ship.

I named my ship the *Agile Witch*. She's a wonder. She's swift and cuts the water like a cutlass. I wonder now why I hesitated so long to purchase her.

It's odd how often we face a change in our life that can only yield benefits, and yet we fight that change as if it carried poison and not opportunity.

CHAPTER 9

William broke the silence before the carriage had rounded the first corner. "I'm still astonished that you thought to steal the artifact from me to begin with. You had to know I wouldn't stand idly by and allow you to escape."

Marcail glanced at William from under her lashes. He seemed so calm, so controlled all of the time. *He didn't used to be that way. Life hasn't been kind to him.* A thought struck and she looked down at her hands, clasped loosely in her lap. *I hope he's not this way because of me. Surely our break was easier on him, for he had the benefit of being angry. All I had were regrets and—*

"Marcail?" He shot her a hard look. "We must talk about the artifact."

"You're right. It's time we dealt with this." She sighed. "I told you I'd handed it over already, but . . . I lied. I still have it."

"I know."

"How could you know?"

He appeared faintly amused. "Because you were still here in this town. Charming as it is, I can't see the great Marcail Beauchamp staying in Southend unless you were waiting to meet someone."

"I enjoy charming towns as much as I enjoy London," she said stiffly. "They're small and—and charming."

William lifted his eyebrows.

"I stayed in Brighton before—"

"Which is ten times the size of Southend."

"—and I enjoyed myself very much."

"I daresay you went with a houseful of guests."

Blast it, she hated it when he read her so well. She shrugged. "Perhaps."

"So you weren't alone . . . as you are here." His dark blue gaze flickered across her. "Suppose we begin again and you tell me why you're here and why you took that artifact. Only this time, tell me *everything.*"

She felt a deep flicker of anger. "I *am* trying to be honest with you, and you just—" She took a slow breath to calm herself. "William, we're facing a horrible conundrum. You need that artifact to free your brother, and I need it for—" Should she tell him? Could she afford *not* to?

She met his quizzical gaze. "William, it is as I told you before: I am being blackmailed."

The words hung between them like the light from a candle, flickering uncertainly, so weak that the faintest breath could extinguish it.

"Who?"

"I don't know. He sends—"

"He?"

"I think so. He sends a woman—a Miss Challoner—to deliver messages and to collect the funds."

"Miss Challoner. So the messenger has a name, at least."

"Yes. I don't know much about her. She says where to meet her, then when I arrive, she takes the money and disappears. I've tried to have her followed, but she always manages to slip away. She's very good at evasion."

"She's never been followed by John Poston."

"Your groom?"

"He's more than that. Poston was with Wellington's army in Spain and was the best tracker they had."

"Perhaps he could do better," Marcail said, though William thought she didn't sound very certain. "I must discover my blackmailer's identity."

She sighed. "I think Miss Challoner's afraid of him. She gets a look on her face and—it's fear. I know it is."

William studied Marcail. Her expression was earnest, but then it always was. Yet it was her voice that caught him and made him weigh her words more cautiously, tasting them for their truth. "How much has this person gotten from you thus far?" he asked.

"A lot. More than I can afford."

"What did you do, that you are willing to pay a stranger to hide it?"

She passed a hand over her forehead wearily, leaving a black smudge on her pale skin. "It's— It's complicated. I don't want to explain it all and— Just know that's what has happened and please, leave it there. I shouldn't say more."

He almost ground his teeth in frustration. "Marcail, I am not going to play games. I want the truth. *All* of it."

"It's not my secret to share."

His jaw tightened. "If you won't tell me what's happening, then don't expect my help."

"Oh! You are so— I've told you all that I could and— Damn you, William. I-I've had a horrid day." Her voice quavered, her eyes filling with tears. "I'm being *blackmailed* and they *forced* me to come to this tiny town and— Fine, it's *charming,* but there's *nothing* here for me, and then I had to *wait* and *wait* and then *you* showed up and then you threatened to *spank* me and then I find out that the artifact was really your *brother's* and now you want me to just *give* it back to you as if *nothing* else is of importance and—"

William held up a hand. "Stand fast!"

She stopped, her eyes wet and sparkling.

He lowered his hand. "Marcail, my brother's life is at stake. Surely that means something to you."

She leaned her head against the squabs, exposing the slender line of her throat. "Of course it means something, but I . . . this affects so many people other than myself."

"Let me put this in plainer terms, then. I must have that artifact back or Michael could be killed by the heathen devil who has taken him prisoner. To save his life, I must take this artifact to Egypt. What's at stake for you?"

She turned her head to look at him, her thick black lashes casting a shadow over her violet eyes. "I know you need the artifact. I-I can't forget that I took—no, I *stole* it from you." She swallowed, though it seemed to be difficult. "It's more rightfully yours than mine, but . . . I don't know what to do. The cost is so high, yet if I hand it over to Miss Challoner and something happened to Michael, I couldn't forgive myself and— Oh, I don't know what to do!"

There was such anguish in her voice that he

knew it must be real. "Marcail, you must tell me . . . what do you stand to lose if you face your black-mailer with empty hands?"

"Everything." The words were a broken whisper. "Everything I've ever worked for, and I've given so much. There are people who depend on me to protect them, and I can't—" Her voice broke. "Per-haps . . . perhaps there is another way. Maybe my blackmailer will understand if I explain things, con-vince Miss Challoner that I have no choice but to return the artifact to you. If she could see things our way, and then tell the person who is blackmailing me the truth about the artifact—"

"Do you really think this blackmailer doesn't know the importance of the artifact to me? They sent you to fetch it. Why would they have done so unless they were aware that I need it desperately?"

Her eyes darkened, a shadow passing over her face.

Is that fear?

She bit her lip. "Perhaps I can bribe him, give him enough funds that he doesn't care about the ar-tifact, or—or find something else he may want in its place." Her expression was desperate. "I have some funds set aside. I was hoping to save them for—" Her gaze flickered away. "But if this will solve the issue, it would be worth it."

William wished he didn't feel so damned guilty.

She'd stolen the artifact from him—she'd drugged him to do it, too, and he was foolish to forget it.

This was the trouble with her. He could overlook her beauty, ignore her intelligence and wit, but he was no match for the thing she possessed in the least amount, and yet used with such unconscious power—her vulnerability. It slayed him as surely as her potion-laced port had frozen him in place on the ship.

And that's why I cannot afford any weakness. I must never forget that my reasoning is flawed where she is concerned.

He shoved his uncertainty aside. "Unless you wish to tell me the specific reason you are being blackmailed, as well as justifying that the cost of it is the equivalent of a brother's life, then there is nothing more to say. I want that artifact and I'll have it this very night."

She closed her eyes and slumped against her seat. "Fine. I—I will give it you. I can't justify being the cause of anyone's physical harm. I just wish—" With the back of her hand, she pushed her hair from her forehead, unwittingly exposing the raw stripe on her palm. "But wishing is a waste of time."

The sight of her injured hand reminded him of her selfless actions on the dock. Now she was offering to return the artifact, as well. Somehow, he felt as if he'd misjudged her. But how? How could he be so wrong about her?

She crossed her arms as if cold. "The artifact is still in my room at the inn. You missed it when you searched."

"Where is it?"

"It's in my portmanteau. I stuffed it under my bed while you were searching my trunk."

"Blast it, someone could take it."

"They won't. It's hidden under a false bottom that's impossible to detect."

He supposed it was a safe enough place, then. "If I'd known that, I would have brought it with us. I don't like its being unprotected."

"Neither do I, but I hid it well. I know people cannot be trusted."

The faint bitterness in her tone hinted at numerous disappointments.

He suddenly realized that her reserved composure was no longer due to her overwhelming confidence. Now she used it as a shield against others. Somewhere along the way, she'd become aloof. No longer the innocent, fresh young woman who'd faced life with such cool fearlessness, she'd become a worldly, rather caustic, cautious woman.

He knew little of life on the stage, but he knew that it exposed one to unwanted aspects of life, like the advances of unwanted suitors. Some wealthy lordlings attempted to increase their apparent virility by hanging a beautiful woman on their arm, and those less well off thought it fashionable to fall violently in love with unsuitable women.

But she'd welcomed Colchester's attentions. She probably courted the fool until she'd secured his promise to provide her with the style of living she'd wanted.

She turned to him now, the lantern light playing across her silken cheek. "Where will you take the onyx box, once it's yours?"

Her voice was the husky ripple of black velvet, stroking him as surely as a hand. He shifted away, wishing he'd ridden up on top with Poston. "Michael is in Egypt. I shall set sail as soon as I can replace the *Agile Witch*."

Her brow lowered. "William, I'm genuinely sorry for the loss of your ship. I know you cared for her."

He had, of course. His ship was more than his way of making a living; she was his home. Or had been. A vision of the *Agile Witch* as she slowly sank, burning brightly in the moonless night, flashed into his mind. He instantly banished the memory; there would be time to mourn later.

He forced a shrug. "I shall purchase another ship."

"You can afford—" She caught his hard gaze and flushed.

Fury sharpened every word to a point. "I'm no longer a poor man, Marcail. I'm very well off."

Her rejection all those years ago had fanned his

ambition to new heights. He'd accepted the first and farthest assignment he could find, and had set sail.

Before their break, he'd been more taken with the adventure of an assignment. Afterward, he focused solely on profits. He pushed his crew as few others would, and had taken assignments no one else would or could. And he'd done it all to put funds into his account, and to prove to himself that Marcail Beauchamp had been wrong: he wasn't a hopeless failure "destined for nothingness." The words still burned his soul.

A temperate person would not dwell so much in the past, but would celebrate the benefits that her push had given him. He'd honed his skill and his crew to perfection, sailing dangerous shoals, through pirate-infested seas, and into storms others might avoid.

Over the years, his success had become the thing of legend, and the more success he'd had, the more influential people had sought him out—powerful, important people, people willing to pay generously for his services and his reputation for scrupulous integrity and astonishing good luck.

He was now a wealthy man. Though Colchester was rumored to be richer than Croesus, William knew he could hold his own.

Sadly, he found that his wealth now mattered

little. He had dreamed of confronting Marcail with a coffer of gold coins. In his imagination, she would have been overcome by the sight of so much wealth, and he would have sneered at her, laughed, and walked away.

But now, even that petty revenge seemed like too much effort. His soul was too tired to indulge in such mawkishness. All he wanted was his feet firmly planted on the deck of his own ship, and Marcail gone from his life.

He watched as she unconsciously began to smooth her silk skirts but winced when her wounded palms touched them. *Who is this woman who tossed her Bond Street cloak to the ground to carry dirty, heavy buckets until her hands were raw in an effort to save my ship? What does she have to do with the woman who sent me away, the man she'd claimed to love, because my income no longer suited her? Which is the real Marcail?*

She sighed now. "William, you deserve the truth. I thought to protect my family, but—" She took a deep breath. "I might as well confide in you."

"You're going to trust me with the secret your blackmailer holds over your head?"

She nodded.

"How do you know I won't use it to ruin you?"

"Because that's not your way." She spoke simply and with an assuredness that surprised him.

Marcail raised a brow. "Well? *Would* you tell my

secret if I shared it with you? Especially if you knew it could hurt others, far more innocent than I?"

He wouldn't, damn it. "Perhaps not," he replied grudgingly.

"I don't think you would. William, when I give you that box, my family will pay the ultimate price, not me."

"Your family? You told me you were an orphan. That your father was a blacksmith and—"

"I know what I told you," she interrupted. "It wasn't true. None of it was. My parents are very much alive."

Anger, hurt, and bitterness sat upon his shoulders and whispered into his ear. "Why would you deny them?"

"Because I wanted to protect them from what I'd become."

He frowned. "An actress?"

She nodded, her cheeks flushed. "I should have told you, of all people, but it wasn't my secret to share. My parents and my sisters need me and—"

"Sisters?"

"I have four."

"Damn it, was there *anything* you told me that wasn't a lie?"

Marcail looked down at her hands. She'd been truthful about a lot of things when she'd been with William. She'd shared her dreams, and her desires, and her love . . . the only thing she hadn't shared with him had been her past. "Before I came to London, I knew that I had to protect my family. The only way I could do that was to never mention them. Not even to you."

His dark eyes flashed. "It's no concern of mine." He leaned forward and said in a silky-soft voice, "I don't give a damn."

Tears stung her eyes. She'd known he would be angry, but she'd hoped that time would ease the pain for both of them. "William, I've told you what you need to know, so there's no sense in dredging up the past. It can't be changed. Besides, we have enough problems today."

"We wouldn't have these problems if you had been honest from the beginning. Once your blackmailer demanded the artifact, you should have come directly to me and explained what had happened. Then perhaps I would have helped you."

"I tried to do that!"

"When?"

"When I came to your cabin to fetch the artifact, I told you that I was being blackmailed. I-I'd hoped you would help me, but you were so cold." Her gaze locked with his. "You told me in no uncertain terms that you *wouldn't* help me."

"I didn't know what was at stake."

"That would have made a difference?" She

leaned forward. *"Really?* Because from where I sat, that wouldn't have mattered one iota. You were determined to get rid of me no matter the cost."

"At first, perhaps, but I could have been persuaded to assist—"

"I saw your expression, William. You didn't care what happened to me; you just wanted me gone."

She had a point; that was exactly how he'd felt. "Do you blame me?"

"No. I feared you wouldn't help, so I added the potion to the port before you returned. I gave you a chance to change your mind, but you refused to even listen."

Bloody hell, she is right. I didn't give her a chance. "I didn't trust you."

"So I drugged you." Her lashes flickered and she said in a quiet voice, "I'm very sorry for that."

He leaned back in his seat and crossed his arms over his chest. "So what will you do about this blackmailer now? Unless I assist you, you will be stuck with him for the rest of your life." William couldn't believe the direction of his thoughts; the last thing he should do was offer his help, and yet, she couldn't keep on paying funds to the blackguard; no matter what she paid, he would always ask for more.

Then and there, William decided he would help Marcail out of her predicament, and not just to keep her from being bled dry. He would help her because it pleased him that this was something she didn't wish to take to Colchester, but to him. It would also be a good idea to find out who ultimately wished for the onyx box and why. "I will help you bring this blackmailer to justice."

Marcail wasn't certain she'd heard William aright. "What could you do?" She caught herself holding her breath, waiting for his answer. She desperately wanted his help. She just couldn't bring herself to admit it aloud.

A smug smile touched his mouth. "There hasn't been a blackmailer yet who could withstand me."

He was so unabashedly certain he could manage the issue that for a wild, mad moment, the desire to put her problems into his large, capable hands was almost overwhelming.

The coach rumbled to a stop, and she realized with surprise that they were at the inn.

"We will finish this conversation inside." William opened the door and assisted her to the ground, holding her elbow instead of waiting for her to take his hand.

The wind whipped about them, and Marcail tugged the cloak closer against the cold night air.

William had turned to say something to Poston when a luxurious, blue-trimmed coach started forward and began to move through the inn yard, the same one Marcail had seen arriving at the inn earlier.

As the coach passed, a woman leaned forward to close the window, her green eyes meeting Marcail's.

Marcail suddenly couldn't breathe. *Miss Challoner.* The lady was no frail flower of womanhood, but an Amazon built on tall, statuesque lines, her beauty defined by her bold, sensual mouth.

Something about the woman—her regal bearing or her rich clothing—made one think of long lines of queens. Her red hair upswept and fastened with a diamond clip that mirrored the flash of her green eyes, she projected an almost unconscious power.

Marcail knew she should alert William but she couldn't move, her surprise and trepidation turning her into an ice statue.

Miss Challoner lifted a hand in a languid wave, then the window snapped closed.

That brought Marcail back to life, and she turned and clutched William's sleeve.

He looked down at her, frowning. "What?"

Marcail pointed to the road, where the faint clop of horses receded into the dark night. "Miss Challoner! She was in the coach that just left!"

He spoke to Poston and almost immediately, the groom jumped back into the coach and hied the horses.

William turned toward her. "I don't know if

John can find the coach in the darkness, but he will do his damnedest to discover her direction and then return for us. I hope he—"

But Marcail had already hiked her skirts and, oblivious to the danger of running on the uneven cobblestones in her stockinged feet, dashed toward the inn. *Please God, don't let it be gone. Please don't let it be gone!*

A letter from Michael Hurst to his sister Lady Caitlyn MacLean, written from a tent on an oasis in the Great Desert.

I've enclosed two wooden tops for my rowdy nephew and spirited niece. I trust they are doing well. Last week I saw two children playing in the Nile, both chubby in the way that children are, and laughing that deep belly laugh that only the innocent can.

I don't know which is more telling about a soul, their laughter or their tears. I suspect the latter, but hope for the former.

CHAPTER 10

William ran up the stairs after Marcail, his boots thudding on the plank steps. He found her bedchamber door ajar and Marcail kneeling beside the bed, digging underneath it.

He winced at the destruction in the bedchamber. Whoever had been here had been thorough. The chair had been overturned, the cushions ripped and the goose down stuffing tossed about. Every drawer in the dresser had been removed and left in a mishmash stack near the doorway. The mattress was flipped to one side, the sheets and blankets on the floor.

He scowled at the mess. "Bloody hell."

Marcail rocked back on her heels, her face pale.

"William, it's gone." She raised stricken eyes to his. "I thought it was safe under the false bottom."

Bitter disappointment rippled through him. "At least your worries are over. The artifact is on its way to the blackmailer."

She winced. "William, don't—"

"Don't what? Don't worry that once again that damned box has eluded my grasp? Damn it, Marcail, this is my brother's *life* we've been talking about."

"I understand that!" She sank upon the edge of the bed. "What do we do now?"

He wished he knew, his blood boiling at his lack of options.

Furious, he stalked about the room, kicking the goose down out of his way. It puffed into the air, then drifted back down to the floor. "I should have known not to trust you to put the damned thing in a safe place."

She stiffened. "This isn't about trust and you know it. It's about the artifact and who stole it. Maybe Poston will find out where she went, and we can catch up to her."

"This Miss Challoner." William stopped in front of Marcail. "Tell me everything you know about her."

"She's very tall, a good six inches taller than I am, with red hair."

"What else?"

"She's very regal appearing in the way she moves and dresses." Marcail grimaced. "I used her as my model when I played Lady MacBeth. It worked very well."

"How fortunate for you," William said drily. He raked a hand through his hair. "What else can you tell me?"

"Not much. She's uncannily good at making certain no one follows her."

"Perhaps it's not her, but her coachman."

"No, for she doesn't seem the type of woman to wait for someone else to save her."

Marcail expected William to sneer at her evaluation, but he nodded as if considering her words. "That's good to know." His gaze fastened on her. "There must be some reason behind all of this. When did your blackmailer first make contact with you?"

"I received the first letter a little over a year ago."

"Sent by post?"

"No. It was put inside a book I had left in my carriage."

"Your servants perhaps—"

"I thought of that, so I let them all go. Colchester was not happy about it."

"*All* of them?"

"Yes. It was difficult, but I had to protect my family and it was the only way to make certain the blackmailer wasn't inside my own residence."

"But the demands didn't stop after you changed the household staff?"

"If anything, they increased. The letters just show up; sometimes they're in the mirror frame in my dressing room, sometimes they're tucked into my reticule, or left on the seat of my carriage. The last one was under a plate on my breakfast tray."

"Inside your own house?"

"Yes. That frightened me."

"It should have. You said that until now, all of the demands had been for money."

"Yes." Her gaze darkened. "And I paid it all."

William noted the steely note in her voice. "This family of yours must be something indeed, that you'd protect them even though it costs you so much."

She met his gaze directly. "My career has cost me more than you could ever know."

He wondered briefly if she meant that her career had cost her their relationship, then decided that couldn't be it. Her greed alone had done that.

He waited, but she didn't offer any more information. Though it was irrational, it hurt that she still refused to share her past without prodding.

The noise of an arriving coach sent him to the window. He pushed aside the curtain. "John Poston is back."

Her shoulders slumped as if she bore the weight of the world. "He couldn't find her."

"Care to wager on that?" William lifted the window and leaned out. "Poston!"

The groom, who had already climbed down and was yelling for the postboys, looked up. "Aye, Cap'n! She took the North Road. She has a light coach and four. While our coach is heavier, we have a six-horse harness."

"We could catch her, then."

"Yes, Cap'n. She may be faster in the short term, but if we have a stronger team we can wear hers down. The only problem is finding a fresh team. Ours is already worn."

"Are there any horses to be had?"

"The stable here is too small to be of much help, but the innkeeper says most people lodge their horses down the street at the Bull and Bush."

Marcail bit her lip. Her carriage, horses, and coachman were at the Bull and Bush. She owned a prime set of horses, too. She had to do *something* to help. She pushed beside William and leaned out the window. "Poston, I have six excellent horses at the Bush and Bull. Tell my coachman, Burghman, that I sent you and that he is to assist you in any way possible. If he questions you, send him here and I'll explain things to him."

Poston's gaze flickered to William, who nodded.

Marcail withdrew from the window and looked around the room. "It will only take me a few minutes to pack and be ready to leave. I'll need some—"

"Stand down. I'm not taking you with me." William shut the window as if that settled everything. "I will travel faster without you."

"Nonsense." It felt right; she was certain that this was the proper direction for her to take.

She began picking up her garments, shaking the goose down off of each one. "I have only the trunk, my portmanteau, and a smaller case. It will all fit on the coach roof."

"Marcail, you are not going."

"You have to take me with you; *I'm* the only person who can identify Miss Challoner."

"There can't be that many tall redheads in England."

"No, but she headed north. Once she gets to Scotland, redheads will be plentiful." She tossed some of her gowns and chemises onto the bed.

William crossed his arms over his chest. "I thought you had to return to London."

"I do, but surely we'll catch up to her within hours."

"I'm not so certain. She has the benefit of knowing where she's heading. We could be chasing this woman for several days."

"Then I shall write and inform the theater that I will be late returning. They'll wait for me." She gave him a calm smile. "They have to; *I'm* the leading lady."

She expected him to be pleased by her support, but he appeared annoyed. "Why in the hell are you doing this?"

"I suppose I feel responsible, since I stole the artifact to begin with." Somewhere along the way, she'd gotten so focused on her goals for her family that she'd lost her moral compass. "Furthermore, I can't keep paying this blackmailer. He is obviously far more unscrupulous and dangerous than I realized, as evidenced by his attack on your ship. He must be stopped."

William's jaw tightened. "You think that's who set the fire?"

"Who else had anything to gain?" She began to sort through an assortment of shoes the thief had dumped in a pile. "I think Miss Challoner and her minions knew you were here trying to regain possession of the artifact, and she used the fire to draw you away and give her time to recover it herself. If she waited until you were onboard, you could have sailed away with it."

He didn't agree but he didn't disagree, and she was encouraged by that.

She placed her last pair of shoes in the bottom of the empty trunk. "The time has come for me to confront Miss Challoner and whoever she takes her orders from, and I'd rather do that with you than alone."

Before he could object, she added, "Come, William. Admit that having me along would be beneficial. I've allowed you to use my team. Surely that shows you how sincere I am in this venture."

"They are Colchester's, not yours."

"No," she said sharply. "I purchased that team myself." She paid for many of her own possessions. It wasn't necessary and it made Colchester grouse, but it allowed her some independence.

She shook out her best pelisse, a sage wool trimmed with bronze silk ribbons, and frowned when she noticed a footprint on the hem. She brushed it and then hung it on a peg by the door. "Well, William, what do you say? Will you take me with you or do you prefer to chase every red-haired woman in Scotland?"

He scowled. With his dark look, his arms crossed over his broad chest, and tattered clothes, his feet planted as if he stood upon a ship, he could have been any handsome pirate from a Drury Lane play. "You're a foolishly stubborn woman."

Her chin lifted, but before she could reply he threw up a hand. "I don't want you to go, but . . . damn it, you make a good point." He let out a sigh that was more of a growl. "Pack your bags. I'll give you twenty minutes, less if Poston returns sooner with that team."

She sent him a glowing look that made his breath catch.

William hated that she could still ignite such heat in his traitorous body.

Anger edged his voice as he replied coldly, "It makes sense that you should come along. You started this and you'll finish it."

He stalked toward the door. "Pack. I'll send someone for your things."

She nodded and started to turn away, her shoulder brushing his sleeve.

William didn't know what made him reach for her. Perhaps it was the way her loose hair revealed the delicate line of her neck; or perhaps it was how her lips turned down in faint disappointment, a sight that tugged at him though he tried to deny it.

Whatever it was, he pulled her firmly against him, surprising her.

She tilted her head back to see his face, her eyes wide. "William?"

"Just a word of warning, my little liar: I am in charge of this expedition and what I say goes."

She arched a brow, but shrugged. "Fine. You can be in charge if it makes you feel better."

"It does. And when we recover the artifact, it is mine and you are not to get grandiose ideas of stealing it for your own benefit. Are we clear on that fact?"

She jerked free of his hold, her eyes flashing with indignation. "I would never do such a thing."

"We shall see." He turned toward the door and left.

Marcail fought a very unladylike urge to stomp her foot. With a low growl, she marched to the door and slammed it. She went to turn the key, but it was gone.

Muttering under her breath, she turned back to her things. In a satisfyingly short time, the small trunk and portmanteau were neatly stacked in the center of the room.

A soft knock sounded on the door. At her call, the door opened and the porter stood in the doorway holding a bucket of steaming water.

"I was asked t' bring ye some fresh water, miss. Is the washbowl broken?"

She glanced to one side of the dresser where large pieces of glass announced the broken pitcher, but the washbowl was intact.

The porter set down the bucket and fetched the bowl and replaced it upon the stand, finding the cake of soap and some towels in the process. He tsked as he rearranged the items on the stand. "It's a heavy bowl, miss. I daresay whoever ransacked yer room couldn't break it, though he tried." He poured the hot water into the bowl. "I'm sorry this happened, miss. We've ne'er had such behavior here at the Royal Hotel before."

"I'm sure you haven't. Please thank the inn-keeper for the water."

The porter headed for the door. "Oh, 'twasn't Mr. Clabber who ordered the water, but the cap-tain. He said ye helped fight the fire at the quay and would want to wash. Do ye need anythin' else, miss?"

"No, thank you. That will be all."

The porter closed the door and Marcail swiftly removed her gown, chemise, and stockings. She washed as well as she could. The warm water was blissful, the feeling of once again being clean making her sigh with happiness. Though the water and soap stung her raw hands, she staunchly hurried through it.

It was so kind of William to send her the water. She didn't understand the man at all.

Shouting arose in the courtyard along with the tramping of horses' hooves. She hurriedly pulled on new stockings and slipped her chemise over her head. She'd just tied it when she heard William's voice at the bottom of the stairs.

She quickly twisted her hair into a knot and pinned it in place, then reached for her gown. She yanked it over her head and was attempting to lace it up when a sharp knock echoed on the door. Be-fore she could answer, William stalked in.

She spun around, her ties forgotten. "Blast you,

William! What's the point of knocking if you're just going to storm in?"

He gave her a wolfish grin, his dark hair damp, water droplets sprinkled on a multicaped overcoat that was susprisingly fashionable.

"It's raining?" she asked, reaching back for her ties and hoping he wouldn't notice that the neck of her gown wasn't as secure as it should be.

"Aye. We're taking your coach instead of mine since it's lighter and faster."

"Fine, I—*ow!*" The ties had rubbed her raw palms and she maneuvered them so that only her fingers made contact.

His dark gaze took in her struggles. "That's not working; you're going to have to actually hold the laces."

"I know, but they hurt my hands."

He muttered a curse and crossed to her, turned her around, and laced her up with an expertise that made her face flame.

Each time his hand brushed her skin, a jolt shot through her, making her skin prickle and her nipples tingle as if he'd touched them.

Finally, he was done. "There." He stepped away from her and went to her stacked luggage. "Is this all?"

"Yes."

"Good. Then I'll send the porter up for the rest."

He hefted the trunk to one shoulder, his expression inscrutable, though his jaw was tight. "Poston is impressed with your coach. Colchester spares no expense, does he?"

"He tends to be an excessive gift giver, but as I told you before, I purchased the team myself." She threw her cloak over her arm and swept out of the room.

He joined her at the bottom of the stairs, looking dark and—damn it, *delectable*. Even after all these years, after all the pain and trouble, he still appealed to her—a fact that she'd best forget.

She glanced at him from under her lashes as she walked past, noting the sensual line of his mouth and the strong set of his jaw. His dark hair fell over his forehead and made his dark blue eyes seem all the more brilliant.

She tugged her bonnet on and stepped outside into the light rain.

William sent the porter after her remaining luggage, bustled her out of the rain and into the ready coach, and then spoke with John Poston about their journey.

Marcail removed her bonnet, shook off the raindrops, and placed it on the seat beside her, watching William through the carriage window.

There was one other issue that was bothering her, itching her thoughts like a gnat bite, and that was how efficiently he'd tied her laces. He'd obviously spent the past few years tying many, many sets of laces. *Of course he had. What else did you expect?*

She'd known he wouldn't become a monk after she'd sent him away, he was too passionate for that. She'd known he would enjoy the favors of many other women. Yet it hurt, facing the evidence of those missing years.

Those years should have been mine. Had my life been different and my obligations less, we might have— But I can't think that way.

There was no sense in wishing for what was gone; it would never return. She pulled her cloak over her, tucking it about her legs, then she closed her eyes and rested her head against the high squabs. It had been a long day and she was exhausted beyond thought.

Soon, the coach rocked as William climbed inside. Feeling sad and alone, Marcail kept her eyes shut, hoping he'd think she was asleep.

He shut the door and banged the flat of his hand upon the coach ceiling. Then they were under way, the coach rolling out of the inn yard and onto the road leading out of town.

A letter from the Earl of Colchester to his mistress, Miss Marcail Beauchamp, upon the occasion of their first anniversary.

By now I trust you will have seen your present. I know what you're going to say, that it's too grand or big or what have you. But it's mine to give and give it I shall.

So please take this small gift—'tis naught but a coach, after all. I am regarded as a leader of fashion, therefore you must be in fashion, too. A lamentable burden, but there it is.

CHAPTER II

Marcail awoke to a blindingly bright light that made her immediately close her eyes again. "Good God," she muttered, putting a hand on her bed to lever herself upright. As she did so, a rather violent jolt almost sent her tumbling. She grabbed the closest solid object—her pillow—and hung on for dear life.

In that instant, it dawned on her that pillows were neither *this* firm nor *this* attached. It also dawned on her that beds didn't go lurching about.

She blinked herself awake and realized that she was lying on the seat of her coach, her arms wrapped about a man's thigh.

And not just any man's thigh, but a very firm,

very muscular thigh. *William. Oh, good God, how did I get here?*

Heart pounding, she peeked up at him and saw that he was sound asleep, his hat tipped down over his eyes, his arms crossed over his broad chest.

She cautiously unwrapped her arms and tried to rise, but he stirred restlessly, his arm coming to rest on her shoulders.

Marcail immediately replaced her cheek upon his thigh and waited with bated breath, aware of the warmth of his arm as it rested on her. Perhaps she should just stay where she was, considering the rocking of the coach.

Somehow during the night, she'd curled up on the coach seat, her feet tucked under her, her head resting in William's lap. Her cloak must have fallen while she was still sitting, for it was bunched over her hip. Not that she was cold, for she was far too snug with William's arm over her.

It was odd and—if she allowed herself a moment of complete honesty—heavenly.

She listened to his slow, even breathing, remembering the events of the day before. If anyone had a reason to sleep like the dead, it was William. Despite his stoic expression, she was certain the loss of his ship had hurt deeply. She snuggled a bit closer to him and sighed.

Damn that stoic expression. He's gotten far too comfortable hiding behind it. Yet another difference from the man she'd fallen in love with years ago. Back then he had been expressive, open, sharing. She'd loved his genuine interest in a variety of things, his curiosity about life and all it brought. Now he seemed far older than his years, and harsher than he should be.

Is that because of me? She hoped not. *I never meant to hurt him—but it was a matter of doing it then, or waiting for something bad to befall us both.*

She turned her head and looked at him again. His chin was buried in the muffler around his neck, his hat casting a shadow over his eyes. The sound of his breathing was deliciously comforting.

Marcail knew she should move, but part of her wanted to savor this moment. There was something so very intimate about waking up encircled by another person. The warmth of the moment, the softness of his woolen breeches, the firm thigh beneath that, the scent of his sandalwood cologne, all held her in place.

Marcail closed her eyes. Colchester had his own apartments on another floor. Though he made a show of coming to visit her suite for appearance's sake, he rarely stayed more than an hour or two, at most.

They'd sit by the fire and talk about their day's events; sometimes he'd help her with her lines. He was a talented thespian and she'd always thought it a pity that he'd never been able to use his gifts.

She treasured those times with Colchester, who'd become the brother she'd never had. As his relationship with George Aniston had blossomed she saw much less of him, of course, and she was often home alone for days on end.

For someone who grew up with four sisters, the solitude was difficult; there were times when she was achingly lonely.

The coach turned a corner and Marcail noticed that the road seemed much smoother. Were they nearing a town?

She glanced out the uncovered window. The storm clouds had disappeared and the brilliant blue sky of an early spring day filled the windowpane. She lifted her head a little to see if the view provided any clue to the temperature.

As she shifted, William stirred, his hand moving from her shoulder to settle directly on her breast.

Marcail froze, instantly aware of the curve of that large hand as it intimately warmed her breast. Shivers traveled over her and she silently grasped his wrist and lifted his hand, hoping to move it away.

He murmured something in his sleep and replaced his hand exactly where it had been before.

Startled, she peeped back up at him, but his deep breathing never faltered. Perhaps she should wake him?

But then she'd have to rise, and she didn't wish to. Perhaps she could just ignore his hand—yet she found herself fighting a most unladylike urge to arch into the embrace.

Stop that! It's an accident; random contact. Don't overreact. She'd be better off thinking of a way to set their new partnership on a better footing.

Yesterday they'd spent the entire time at each other's throats. She wanted this day to be different, and the wonderful feel of his hand loosely cupped about her breast seemed to promise that. They were no longer at odds, but partners.

It would only be for a day or so, but she couldn't ignore the opportunity. This was her chance to get William to see her in a new light.

But what did one say to a man one had recently drugged, tied up, and robbed? *That sounds bad even to me.*

She'd attempted to apologize, which hadn't been very well received, so what could she say? Perhaps—

She gasped. William's thumb was now rubbing her nipple though her clothing. Her nipple peaked, sending sensations rippling all of the way to her now curled toes.

Marcail grasped his wrist and twisted to look up at him. "You, sir, are awake!"

His hat was still pulled down over his eyes, but

his lips curved into a crooked grin that was masculinely wicked. "Am I?"

"Oh! You—" She tried to sit up but found her hair was trapped beneath his leg. "I'm caught. Move, Hurst."

He chuckled and tipped his hat back, his blue eyes warm with laughter. "Perhaps I like having you at my mercy."

Her heart leapt at his teasing tone. She'd wanted to start on a new note, but not one with her at such a disadvantage. "William, please move."

"And if I don't?"

She made a fist and let it hover over his unprotected nether regions, then smiled sweetly.

He instantly complied. "Touché." He lifted his leg and she was freed.

Marcail pushed herself upright and scooted to the far end of the seat. Without his arm about her, the air was uncomfortably cold. She shivered as she wrapped her cloak around her and buttoned it. "I was trying to lie very still so that you wouldn't awaken. Had I known you were pretending to sleep, I could have been much more comfortable."

"Hmm. Perhaps you enjoyed it."

"You flatter yourself," she replied loftily. "I was merely being considerate."

He raised his brows.

"At first, I thought you didn't realize you were doing it—"

"Uhm-hmm."

"—but then I realized you knew *exactly* what you were doing."

He leaned forward, his eyes sparkling. "Admit you enjoyed it—at least a little."

A lot, yes. Never a little. "Especially not a little. You, sir, owe me an apology."

He didn't look the least bit sorry. "I rather enjoyed having you asleep in my lap. You must have been comfortable, for you slept for a long time."

"I was exhausted; I could have slept on a rock." She searched the seat for her missing hairpins, still feeling flustered. "How did I come to be sleeping on your lap? When I went to sleep, you were on the opposite seat."

"You slept for a short time sitting up, but then we went through a rough section of road and you started to slip to one side, so I stopped you from falling and hitting your head."

She had an instant, faint memory of William's warm hands as he gently settled her head onto his lap, but it was gone so quickly that she wasn't certain if she'd actually remembered it, or if her imagination had enjoyed the scenario so much that it had just adopted the idea.

He regarded her with mock seriousness. "It was a very dangerous moment. You could have lost an eye."

Her lips twitched. "That would have ended my career, for there are no parts for women with only one eye."

He seemed to consider this. "You could play one of the witches in MacBeth."

"Well . . . that's the *only* part."

"And having only one eye would make it very difficult for you to choose such ravishing bonnets." He reached for her bonnet on the opposite seat and held it up. "Even I like this one, and I'm not much of a bonnet admirer."

She eyed the bonnet with satisfaction. It was a flat-crowned velvet confection with jaunty red sashing to match her pelisse. "I do have a fondness for hats."

William tossed the bonnet back onto the seat. "So I remember."

Her good humor fled. Every time he mentioned their past, she had to fight a wave of guilt. She knew from experience that of all the emotions, guilt was one of the most destructive, which was why it was so prominently featured on the stage.

As she pinned the last few strands of her hair back into place, the coach slowed down and she leaned forward and watched as they pulled into an inn yard.

As soon as the coach halted, William opened the door, stepped out, and pulled down the steps. He held out his hand. "Would you care to alight?"

A low-slung, squarish inn made of gray stone sat beside a narrow country road. Six other small houses and a church with a graveyard were the rest of the small village.

"Poston!" William called as Marcail alighted.

The coachman was just swinging down from his perch. "Aye, sir?"

"Make inquiries about a tall, red-haired woman. She may have stopped here; I haven't seen many inns on this road."

"There have been remarkably few, which is good fer us, Cap'n. If a lady, redheaded or no', stopped, she'd be remembered. That will be different once we come to the North Road, though." Poston's thick gray eyebrows lowered. "'Tis very busy and it will be harder to track 'er."

"*And,*" Marcail added, "she's notoriously difficult to follow, so we must make haste and use every advantage we have."

Poston nodded. "She's keepin' up the devil's own pace. I expected to catch her before now."

William turned to look at the horses. "You're having them changed here?"

"Yes. The ostler at the Bull and Bush said 'tis run by his cousin, and the cattle are all bang up to the mark. He said we could pick up a horse fer an outrider, too, if ye wish."

"We could send a footman ahead to scout."

"That's what I was thinkin', too."

"Do so, then." He turned to Marcail. "You should avail yourself of the accommodations, for we won't be here long. The weather is going to turn so we need to hurry."

Marcail looked doubtfully up at the clear sky.

"Yes. The sunrise was red; we'll see a squall before nightfall. With any luck, we'll catch up to Miss Challoner before then."

"Very well; I shall be swift. I'll need my portmanteau, if you please."

He turned and yelled for one of the footmen, who fetched her portmanteau into the inn.

Marcail followed him inside and requested a room and a pail of water. Since there was no time to have the water heated, she took a very cold and shivery sponge bath. The maid who attended her oohed and aahed over the gown Marcail selected to replace her crushed one, a deep blue dress with ruched violet trim that matched her eyes. Then the maid put up Marcail's hair, twisting it into a smooth knot.

Marcail stepped back and surveyed her reflection with satisfaction as the maid repacked the portmanteau, and then they went downstairs and out to the inn yard.

Marcail tucked her gloves into her pelisse pocket; she still couldn't bear the touch of gloves stretched across her hands. "Betsy, please ask one of the footmen to tie the portmanteau back onto the coach."

The maid didn't move.

Marcail turned. "Betsy?"

The maid's gaze seemed frozen on something over Marcail's shoulder.

She looked—and froze also.

William stood by the pump, stripped down to his breeches and boots. He reached into a bucket, removed a large soapy sponge, and lathered his broad, powerful arms and chest. Marcail's fascinated gaze followed every stroke. His body was solid muscle, that rippled with every move he made.

"Gor'!" Betsy cooed.

Marcail could only nod, her heart pounding. Seeing him shirtless and bronzed brought back a flood of memories—of his warm hands caressing her, of the feel of his lips tracing a line from her shoulder to her breast, of the strength of his muscular arm as he slipped it about her waist and pulled her close—

She had to close her eyes to keep from moaning aloud, her body aching for what it had once welcomed. *It has been so long. So very, very long.*

The jingling sound of a harness announced the arrival of Poston and the coach. Two saddled mares were now tied to the back, and someone had attempted to clean the muddy exterior of the coach.

Her hands shaking, Marcail opened her reticule,

found a coin and held it out to Betsy. "Thank you for your assistance."

The girl forced her attention away from William and brightened on seeing that it was a shilling, not a penny. "Thank 'ee, miss!"

"Of course. Just be sure to give that portmanteau to a footman." And with that, Marcail gathered her skirts and hurried to the safety of the waiting coach.

William caught sight of Marcail as she stepped into the bright sunshine that filled the inn yard. Under her silky gray pelisse she now wore a blue gown that made her violet eyes darker. But it was her exotic coloring—her black hair, violet eyes, and pink skin—so sensually offset by her prim clothing and neatly pinned hair that made his breath catch.

She never failed to fascinate, this tempting, tasty armful of pure trouble.

As she neared the coach she sent him a quick look, then flushed.

For the love of God, she'd seen him naked plenty of times! Still, something about her unease made him feel as daring as a pirate. He threw a towel over his shoulder and gave her a mocking bow.

She dipped into a jerky curtsy, but just before she turned away he caught her expression. The pure lust he read in her eyes almost sent him reeling.

He knew that look and reacted to it immediately. *Perhaps not everything has changed, after all.*

As if she knew his thoughts, she whipped away and climbed into the coach, barely waiting for the footman to open the door.

William grinned, watching her trim figure and how her skirts clung in a manner unlike other ladies of society.

Bloody hell, she was a hot little piece. Somehow he'd pushed aside all memories of her provocative nature. "Probably because you didn't want to go mad dreaming of her, you fool," he murmured to himself.

A sane man would avoid her at all costs. A sane man would ride up on top with the coachman, or ride one of the extra mounts. A brisk ride would clear the lust from his brain.

But William couldn't forget the stark longing he'd seen in Marcail's eyes.

The fresh team pawed the ground, ready to go.

William swiftly rubbed his hair dry with the towel, yanked a clean shirt over his head, and pulled on his coat. He tossed two clean cravats over one shoulder, fastened his portmanteau, and tossed it to the footman who was tying Marcail's bag on the roof of the coach. "Tie that down, too," William ordered.

Poston, who'd been talking to the postboys, came forward. "Almost ready, Cap'n?"

"Almost. Let's find that woman and end this.

Don't stop until you see her coach." With that, William climbed inside the coach and shut the door.

In no time, the coach started forward with a jolt that made Marcail clutch the edge of her seat. "Goodness, we're in a hurry."

"Oh yes. We're in a great hurry now." William latched a curtain over one window, blocking out much of the sun. Somewhere between the moment he'd looked up to catch Marcail crossing the inn yard looking like an angelic seductress and the moment he'd climbed into the coach, he had made a decision.

Marcail placed her bonnet and cloak on the seat opposite hers, looking curious as he latched the other curtain, casting the coach into near darkness.

Then William reached for her and her eyes widened with a flare of pure passion. "William, we shouldn't—"

"Hush." He slipped an arm around her waist and pulled her onto his lap.

She came easily, her arms slipping around his neck. "Oh, God, *yes*." And then she kissed him eagerly. Her intoxicating lips were warm, her freshly washed skin fragrant against his.

God, how he wanted her. After all these years, he desired her as he'd never desired a woman before. As if she were the last woman on earth and he the last man.

He bent to kiss the delicate hollows of her neck

and the slender line of her shoulder, all of the places that a proper lady showed in an attempt to drive a man wild with desire.

She moaned throatily and clutched his shoulders, her fingers grasping for purchase. Hot lust consumed him. He was aflame with her, the feel of her, the scent of her, the warmth of her. He wanted to dive into her, sink into her heat and sweetness, and never again arise. She was perfection and beauty, graceful flesh and silken softness.

She stirred him with her words, tempted him with her passion, and enslaved him with her wit and beauty. He'd tried to fight it, but couldn't. All he could do was succumb to his desire, and protect his heart as best he could, holding tight to the old hurts and memories.

This is just a physical moment and means nothing to either of us. Marcail was no naïve innocent. And so long as he remembered exactly who and what she was, his heart would be spared the pain he'd experienced the last time he'd opened himself to her.

She sighed, her sweet breath brushing his neck, and suddenly nothing mattered except his desire to feel all of her, taste all of her, possess all of her.

He cupped her ass through her skirts and swung her around so that she was straddling him. She moved with him as easily as if they'd made love in a coach a hundred times before, anticipating each other's movements, enjoying each second of passion.

They'd always had this instant, instinctive connection. It had been one of the many things that had tied them together. Even when they'd first met and the awkwardness of newness had been a barrier, *this* part of their relationship had been amazingly easy and rewarding.

At the time, William had thought it a sign that he was truly in love. Now he realized it was something more primal, a recognition of a kindred sensuality. Emotion had nothing to do with this perfection of body, rhythm, and passion.

She positioned her knees on either side of his hips, lifting her tempting breasts to just the right level. The coach hit a bump and William moved his hands to her lower back to steady her, then she held his shoulders as he worshipped her breasts with kisses.

He loved her breasts. They were delightfully full but not too much, filling his hands but not spilling over them, their pink-and-white perfection begging for his attention. He untied the lacing at her neck and tugged her gown loose to reveal a thin chemise that barely concealed her luscious nipples.

He slipped a hand inside her chemise to free one of her breasts. She had the most perfect nipples he'd ever seen; large and dusky pink, they beckoned and tempted. He pressed his mouth over her nipple and teased it to a peak, just as he'd dreamed of doing when he'd awoken to find her snuggled in his lap.

He flicked her nipple with his tongue, then blew lightly across the moistened skin. Marcail gasped his name and arched against him, driving his passion higher still.

The coach hit a rut in the road and Marcail gripped his shoulders tighter, pressing her breast into his mouth, demanding more.

He obliged her, pulling her farther down so that he could tease her with his knee beneath her skirts.

Outside, the world sped by in cold daylight, but here, nothing existed except her deliciously labored breathing, perfect breasts, and warm, pearl pink skin. He brushed her chemise aside and unhooked her skirts. "Take them off," he growled.

She chuckled, the sound warm and inviting as she did as he suggested. It took both of them to divest her of all of the layers society had bound her with, but soon she was naked, straddling his lap, glowing and ready, and all his.

He pulled back to admire her. She was lithe, her breasts set high, the nipples thrusting upward as if pertly demanding a kiss. Her body was a symphony of graceful curves and mysterious shadows, and he ached to taste every inch.

He drew his fingers down her neck, across a

delicately hollowed shoulder, over her breast and proud nipple, to the flat planes of her stomach.

Marcail moaned, closing her eyes and allowing his callused fingers to roam where they would. William traced a line from her navel to her gently rounded hip and then stopped there, meeting her pleading gaze.

Her eyes were like smoky velvet as she whispered, "I've missed you."

Those weren't the words he'd expected to hear, and they took him aback. "You *missed* me? Then perhaps you shouldn't have sent me away." He bent forward to trace a kiss along her shoulder, noting with satisfaction how her skin goose-bumped under his touch. "*This* is what you've missed—what *we've* missed all of these years because of your foolishness."

"And your pride," she added in a breathless voice.

"Perhaps." He raked his teeth over her collarbone and she moaned, writhing in his lap.

"I know. Oh God, I know." She threaded her fingers through his hair, holding him as she nipped at his bottom lip and pressed against him in a way that made him mad with lust.

"Hold still, damn you," he growled and captured her by cupping her bared ass. She gasped and shivered at his touch, her nipples puckering as if he'd touched them.

God, he loved the firm curve of her ass. He'd

forgotten how perfect it was, how it filled his hands and made him instantly hard with lust. "Why did you end this?" he whispered as he kissed his way up her neck to the soft, responsive spot behind her ear. "Why did you send me away?"

She clutched him closer, her voice husky. "I had to. You cared so much, as did I, and—and it never would have worked. We were doomed from the beginning."

He kissed her, stopping the words he didn't want to hear. Words he already knew in the heart of his heart, but hadn't wanted to admit.

He held her face between his hands and thrust his tongue into her mouth, stoking her passion until she writhed anew.

She tugged on his lapels and then broke the kiss. "Undress. I want to see everything." She rocked back on her heels and began tugging fiercely at his clothing. She looked like a naughty sylph with her hair primly pinned upon her head, her body unabashedly naked.

Soon his jacket and waistcoat were on the floor, his breeches undone.

She tugged his shirt over his head, and his breeches hit the floor next. Then he was as naked as she, the cool air teasing his cock, which was at full sail and battle ready.

Marcail pressed him against the seat and

straddled him once more, her thighs deliciously warm against his.

He lifted his hips and stroked her with his erect cock.

She closed her eyes, a deep, rich moan rising in her throat. "William."

The word, low and soft and sweetly urgent, set him afire and he grasped her by the waist, lifted her, and positioned her over his cock. Slowly, he pressed into her.

It took a moment, for he was at full mast and she was a tight fit. But she wiggled her way into place, gasping as she did so, and causing him to moan with pleasure when she finally slipped over him.

He couldn't look away. Her eyes were closed, pure ecstasy on her face. "It's been so long," she murmured. "So, so long . . ."

He knew that truth before she'd even said the words. Her breathtaking tightness wasn't that of a woman well loved. He tried to focus on that and why it mattered, but the feel of her, so right and inviting, overwhelmed him. She wriggled against him, sending a bolt of lust through him that stole his breath.

William held her tight and allowed the sway of the coach to do its magic, each bump an exquisite tease, each rocking sway a delicious agony. Marcail gripped his shoulders tighter and tighter . . . then gasped his name, and he held her shuddering body as pleasure overtook her. Afterward she lay panting against his shoulder, trembling from head to toe.

It was all William could do not to give in to his own release; her slick heat was so perfect, so *his*. After she'd regained her breath, he feathered kisses over her face, slowly moving his hips against her. Soon she was moving, too, rocking against him, the intensity building. His passion answered hers, and he grasped her waist, lifting his hips to meet hers.

God, but she was a tight piece, warm and already wet with wanting. His body surged toward hers as he firmly planted himself in her.

She moaned, her white, even teeth biting down on her bottom lip as she looked straight into his eyes and met him thrust for thrust. Each upward stroke stole his breath, and every downward stroke threatened to force him over the edge of his control. But he refused to give in, tightening his hold and bringing her down more and more firmly.

He captured her, possessed her, dominated her, just as she enthralled him with her every move. Damn it, she was *his* and his alone, and he was afire to brand her so.

Almost too afire. "Hold," he ground out, pressing her down upon his cock as deeply as he could.

She gasped and arched back as he held her there, his body burning.

She moaned and began to rock restlessly, her urgency growing. "William, *please*. It has been so long."

William stilled. That was the second time she'd said it. *So long? But what about Colchester?* Suddenly her urgency and tightness held new meaning.

She moved against him, her breasts swaying erotically, and all thought left William's brain. He relentlessly tamped down his own desire, slipped his hands under her rounded ass and lifted her again and again, directing her in when and how and how fast—

She moaned as he lifted her up and down, thrusting into her. He increased the pace to match her breath and she gasped his name and then rocked wildly on him as she came with a gasp of wild abandon.

He was no match for her passion; his own had built uncontrollably. At the last possible moment, he lifted her off his cock and exploded in waves of blinding passion that shook him to his core.

For several minutes they leaned against each other, damp skin to damp skin, their mingled breaths fast and loud. Slowly their rapidly pounding hearts returned to normal, and William gradually became aware of his surroundings—of the rocking of the coach, of the creak of the leather straps, of the feel of the rug beneath his bare feet. Yet even more than those things, he was aware of the silky smoothness of Marcail's hair beneath his cheek, her warm breath on his neck, of the way she fit against his chest, her warm thighs embracing his own.

They sat there in the chilled carriage, their skin warmed by each other, his arms about her, her face buried in his neck, savoring and hoping . . . both afraid to move.

A letter dated two years ago from Michael Hurst to his brother William, regarding a meeting.

I fear I will not be arriving in Paris by the fourteenth as I had hoped. To my shock, my assistant, Miss Smythe-Haughton, has decided that the care of a small thief was our—which apparently means my—concern. As you know, I do not enjoy children, and I would think a bluestocking like Miss Smythe-Haughton would feel the same. But upon being faced with the choice of an informative trip to Paris or undertaking to correct the ill-bred activities of a troublesome waif, Miss Smythe-Haughton has inexplicably chosen the latter. I would leave without her, but she has our tickets and refuses to part with them until the present situation is resolved to her satisfaction.

My dear brother, never allow a woman to hold all of the cards. You will regret it every time.

CHAPTER 12

*I*n the months following the end of their relationship William had dreamed of these moments: of the warmth of her in his arms, her head upon his shoulder, of her sensual scent. Everywhere he went, he saw things that reminded him of her—the way a woman might tilt her head, or a random playbill tumbled down the street by a playful wind. It had seemed the universe was conspiring against his determination to forget her.

Oh, he'd been a lovesick fool, one of the worst, longing for lost moments.

It was difficult to realize that those moments were his again—his to live and to savor. *But not for long,* cold reality whispered in his ear.

A prudent man would take this gift of unexpected passion for what it was, a moment's impulse for them both. But with Marcail, he was never prudent. He couldn't be.

Marcail stirred and lifted her head, meeting his gaze with a faint blush, an awkward smile touching her soft, swollen lips. "That was . . . surprising."

"So it was. But it was always that way between us. One spark, instant flame."

She winced as if that thought pained her and he frowned. "Marcail, are you well? You winced—"

She flushed. "I'm fine. I wasn't expecting—" Her color deepened even more as if embarrassed by her own words. She gave an uncertain laugh. "I'm sorry. I-I'm just overwhelmed. That was lovely." Her gaze met his and he could see the sincerity in her violet eyes. "It was perfectly lovely."

With an awkward smile, she turned away and began to gather her clothes, her movements jerky and unsure.

Now that some of William's blood had returned to his head, he remembered how she'd gasped that it had been "so long" since she'd experienced a man's touch. How could that be if her relationship with Colchester was what it seemed?

And her urgency was not the response of a sated woman. It was the reaction of a woman long denied.

She'd hidden so much about her private life from

him. Could the real nature of her relationship with Colchester be one of her secrets?

He caught her wrist as she lifted her gown from the seat opposite.

Her surprised gaze found his. "Yes?"

William sensed the hope and the multitude of questions contained in that one word. "Marcail, don't—" A flood of "don'ts" fought for expression. *Don't be so protective. Don't pretend things are as they are not. Don't hide yourself from me.* He didn't know which to say first.

"Don't what?" she asked. When he didn't answer immediately, her expression closed and she tugged her wrist free and continued to collect her things.

He knew then that the moment was lost.

"I know what you meant to say. Don't count this interlude as more than the whim of the moment? I shan't, I promise you."

"No. That's not what I was going to say."

"It should have been." She started to slip from his side, but he held her there.

"Stand down, woman. We must discuss this. We've spent too many years with words left unsaid between us, which hasn't done either of us any favors."

She opened her mouth as if to argue, but as she looked at his expression, she sighed. "Very well, but I'm cold. I must at least dress."

He allowed her to slip away, fighting the urge to drag her back onto his lap.

She set aside her clothing, found her reticule, and pulled out a handkerchief before pinning him with a cool gaze. "Please turn away a moment."

Blast it all to hell, he didn't want to turn away. He wanted her to—

Damn it, what *did* he want? He frowned and did as she'd asked, using his extra cravat to clean himself before he tugged on his breeches and shirt. As he slipped back into his waistcoat and coat he heard the rustling of Marcail's skirts as she put herself to rights.

The silence seemed heavy and awkward, exacerbating his already irritated spirits. He wasn't used to people questioning his orders or asking him to explain himself, damn it. He wanted what he wanted, the way he wanted it. What could be simpler than that?

And yet, though he had no problem ordering his crew about, he found himself uncertain in the presence of Marcail—a feeling he distinctly disliked. He was a man of action, of decision, not some maudlin mock-shirt like his brother Robert, who thought it amusing to feign being in love and utter flowery phrases as if words were free.

With Marcail, William became entangled between what he wanted and what he felt, which seemed destined to be at odds. At this very moment, he was torn by three disparate, distinct, and conflicting emotions. First, release at their heated coupling; followed by frustration at the realization that somehow even that wasn't enough; and then last, pure irritation because, damn it, he had no idea what he really wanted, either from her or himself.

Well, he knew *one* thing he wanted, which was to bed her again. And again. And several hundred more times after that. Judging by her eager response, she felt the same. *I think.*

And there he was again, uncertain about—about everything, damn it.

"I'm finished if you wish to turn around now." Her rich voice broke the silence and washed over him. He wrapped the clean cravat about his neck and turned to face her.

In a remarkably few minutes, she'd managed to put herself back together neatly and perfectly. Her black hair was smoothly wrapped about her head, her gown seemingly uncreased, her color returned to normal. If anyone had opened the door of the coach, they'd have seen a cool, calm, and collected Marcail Beauchamp and a mussed, heated, and irritable William Hurst.

She deftly arranged her skirts so they fell in delicate folds about her feet. "William, I feel that I must thank you."

He scowled. "What for?"

"For the—" She waved her hand, the gesture so graceful it could have been a part of a dance. "You know."

He did know. He'd expected many things, but a dismissive "thank you" wasn't one of them.

She was so damned contained and unbothered by their passion while his body still hummed with it; his cock still pulsed as if she held him now.

She chuckled, inflaming him more. "It was excellent fun, wasn't it? I wonder why we didn't tear each other's clothes off last night."

"Indeed. We wasted nearly twenty-four hours."

She flushed at his mocking tone, but lifted her chin. "It was a surprise, but I am glad it happened. I was just—"

"—hungry for a real man," William finished.

She stiffened. "I wouldn't put it like that."

"Wouldn't you? It is becoming more and more apparent that Colchester isn't the perfect peer he so likes to pretend. What's wrong, Marcail? Why has it been so long since a man has touched you?"

"I don't know what you're talking about."

"In the throes of passion, you said you hadn't been touched in a long time."

"I-I said that?"

"Yes. Twice. And I could feel the truth—you haven't been with a man in a *very* long time."

Marcail didn't know where to look; her cheeks

felt as if they were afire. "I don't recall saying that. Perhaps you are mistaken."

He slanted her a disbelieving look as he tied his cravat and tucked it into his waistcoat. "What else could you have meant?"

She sent him a resentful glance. "It doesn't matter what was said. That part of my life is private, thank you."

He flicked a half smile her way. "I know that you don't love Colchester."

"I never claimed to. My relationship with Colchester is purely business. I wrote that in the letter I sent you."

"You don't need to remind me; I remember every damned word. The trouble is, I'm beginning to doubt it is true. In the last few days I've begun to realize that much of what you said and did at that time makes very little sense."

"The part about Colchester was true then, and it is true now. Our relationship has been beneficial for us both."

He smiled and leaned back in his seat. "And that's all you want. *Beneficial.*"

She flashed him a look. "It's all I'm allowed to have."

"The trouble with that is, as coldly and calculatingly as you've arranged your life, you're as hot natured as am I. You can't stop yourself where I'm concerned any more than I can stop myself."

He was right. She couldn't even sit in the same coach without constantly being aware of him and yearning to touch him. But admitting that would just encourage him, and she'd encouraged him enough today already. "You're exaggerating our situation. We succumbed for a moment; don't make more of it than it is."

"You can deny it when we're not touching. But once I do this—" He reached out and grabbed her wrist, his large hand encircling it easily. "I can feel the flutter of your pulse beneath that delicate skin of yours. How can you deny that?" his deep voice rumbled.

She jerked her wrist free. "Stop that! What happened in this coach is a result of the passion that we share—that much is correct. The rest of it—that I'm not satisfied with Colchester—is mere drivel."

He settled back in his corner, a faint smile curving the hard line of his mouth. "We'll see about that, my little liar."

She shrugged and undid one of the curtains, tucking it aside and allowing the morning light to flood across them. "I hope we stop soon; I am famished."

"Of course you are, after . . ."

Her cheeks flamed, but she said no more, merely picking up her cloak and spreading it over her lap.

When she'd first sent William away, she'd thought she'd known what she was giving up. It

hadn't taken her long to realize she'd grossly un-
derestimated the cost of her decision. She'd missed
him an agonizing amount. Though Colchester had
attempted to comfort her, she'd been inconsolable.

She'd expected to miss William's love, but she
hadn't expected how much she would miss their
physical relationship. In the months after his departure she'd ached with loneliness and the desire to be
held once more, a longing that only William could
have assuaged.

Now, having experienced their passion anew and
discovering to her astonishment that it flared even
more brightly than before, she wondered how she
would find the strength to turn her back on it once
again.

With a careless finger, William flicked a tassel
that hung from one of the curtains. "This is quite a
coach. It makes mine look positively meager."

She glanced around the interior and shrugged.
"It's well sprung. That's all I really care about."

"I must commend Colchester on his taste, both
in coaches"—his gaze flickered across her—"and in
other areas, as well."

"I'll be sure to tell him when I next see him."

"Please do. I'm sure Colchester pays a good deal
for his luxuries, though I daresay you are the most
expensive."

Her gaze narrowed. "Actually, I ask him for very

little. He just likes to give extravagant gifts. It is a failing of his."

"A failing? So he's not the paragon of perfection you once thought him."

"I am even more fond of Colchester now than when I agreed to be his mistress. People say he is a fribble and worse, but they don't know him. Few people really do."

"Except you."

She hesitated. "No matter what you think, Colchester's been nothing but kind to me. He has supported me in my career as no one else could have."

William heard the gratitude in her voice and the taste of jealousy was bitter in his mouth. "I am surprised that Colchester allows you to still tread the boards."

She raised her brows. "Allow? Colchester doesn't 'allow' me anything."

"He has no say in your career?"

"Why should he? It is *my* career. "

William frowned. "Your relationship with the earl is rather odd."

"It works well for us."

He shrugged and looked out the window, amazed by his seeming determination to hurt himself as much as possible. He was a complete and total fool if he'd thought to go on this journey with Marcail and not relive the past.

He couldn't seem to stop digging, as if he hoped to find a key that would unlock some understanding of those events. He'd thought they'd been happy. And now, after their passionate lovemaking, she couldn't deny they still shared an attraction.

The whole thing was beyond William's comprehension. But nothing had been normal from the first time he'd seen her. He wasn't the sort to fall instantly, deeply, madly in love with a beautiful, exotic actress whose past was shrouded in more mysteries than the Egyptian pyramids. Yet he'd done so the instant Marcail's beautiful violet eyes had met his across a crowded room.

He picked up his hat and settled the brim so that it shadowed his eyes.

Marcail was looking out the window, a pensive expression on her face. She looked achingly beautiful.

He remembered the first night he'd seen her. He'd known who she was, of course, who hadn't? Even a new captain with six months left in his navy commission knew that one didn't visit London without attending four much discussed events: Astley's Amphitheater to see the wild animals, Vauxhall Gardens for the fireworks and evening concerts, Madame Tussauds to view the famous wax displays, and Drury Lane to see a performance by London's newest star, Miss Marcail Beauchamp.

So he'd gone, not expecting to be impressed. From the moment Marcail had placed her delicate slippered foot upon the stage, she'd possessed it—and him.

Their relationship had happened so quickly that neither of them had had time to evaluate it. His determination to remain aloof had quickly melted in the hot burn of passion. They'd been swept along by their feelings, helpless and vulnerable. Now that he was older and able to look at things with the wisdom of distance, he realized that he hadn't really known her.

As real as it had seemed, the love affair had been doomed from the second it had begun. That didn't make its end any less painful. He didn't love often, but when he did . . . Now, he was more cautious. Far too cautious, perhaps.

And so was she. Her face had changed over the years; she looked wary, protective now.

William knew he hadn't been the cause; their relationship had meant the world to him, while it had meant nothing to her.

Who hurt you after we parted, Marcail? Was it Colchester? You say you never loved him; is that true? Or is it an attempt to cover the failings of that relationship? "I wonder what Colchester will think of this venture of ours. Does he know you've come with me?"

"No one does, though I plan to send word once we reach the North Road. A letter will find its way faster from a coach house there than one of these isolated inns." She hesitated and then said, "Whatever you may think of him, Colchester is a very good and gentle person. I wish you had the chance to get to know him as I do."

"I don't think it would be proper for me to get to know your lover the way you do," William said drily.

She blushed. "Don't be ridiculous! I've always thought you two would like each other, given the chance. He's always been there when I needed him."

The sincerity in her voice hit William like a blow to the stomach. "Then why isn't *he* the one chasing down your blackmailer?"

Her chin raised. "I've already explained that I don't wish him to know of this problem."

"What you *haven't* explained is why."

She pressed her lips together for a moment, then said, "We don't burden each other with our personal problems."

"How do you know he's so good if you don't share your problems with him? How is that a fair measure of a man's character?"

She replied stiffly, "You don't understand."

"I understand plenty. You've convinced yourself that Colchester is a fine fellow without expecting him to prove it."

"The earl and I are very satisfied with our relationship."

"I know *he* must be; he has a mistress who asks for nothing and adds to his consequence. How many men have that?"

"I take pride in providing for myself. I haven't told Colchester about the blackmailer because, as kind as he is, he cannot keep a secret."

The coach hit a rut, jolting them both and sending the curtain swinging. The sunlight flickered over her face, making her violet eyes appear smoky.

William crossed his arms over his chest and lifted an eyebrow. "I'm listening."

She sighed. "I became an actress because my family needed the money. It was the only way I could earn a decent wage."

"I'm sure many young women come to London thinking the same thing."

"Yes, but none of them is the granddaughter of Lady MacToth."

William frowned. "MacToth. I know that name."

"My grandmother was a famous actress until she married my grandfather. It was thought that he married far below his station and she was never accepted by the ton, so they chose to live abroad."

"I remember that story. They were shunned by society."

"It was difficult for them both, but they were deeply in love. She was devastated when he died some years later. She had one daughter, my mother."

"I still don't hear anything worth being black-mailed over."

"My mother also married a peer of the realm, and my father is not an easy man. He is very conscious of his status and he convinced my mother to abandon my grandmother, accusing her of being 'too low' for their company."

"Lovely."

"Yes. Worse, he ran the family fortune into the ground with senseless investments and expenditures. He believes he deserves the best of everything, regardless of the cost." She looked down at her clasped hands. "Things became very difficult. The creditors were threatening to take the house and everything in it. Father refused to admit things were so dire, and Mother isn't one to take action. So I did."

He frowned. "How old were you when this happened?"

"Seventeen. I used my grandmother's connections to gain entry into the theater. She didn't wish to do it, but I explained how desperate things were. It was our only choice. And I had some advantages beyond her sponsorship. My voice carries very well and—" Her cheeks heated. "It worked well for me. I became successful very, very quickly."

"How did your father feel about that?"

"He was furious."

"I can imagine he would be."

"Not for the reasons you might imagine—he wasn't concerned for my welfare. He was concerned for his own reputation."

The fool. "Would I know him?"

"You might; he is a member of White's. He is Sir Mangus Ferguson." Marcail hated saying the name aloud, since she'd spent so much time protecting it. "If you met him, you'd remember him as a proud, rude, ill-suited—" She clamped her lips shut.

William was silent a moment, his gaze considering. "Your last name isn't Beauchamp. So this is the secret you've been hiding—that your family has a place among the gentry."

"I'm not protecting my father," she returned sharply. "If the world knew of my connection to the Fergusons, it would ruin my sisters' chances in society. I've saved my money and made certain they were safe, and they will have what they rightly deserve."

He shook his head. "And you once told me you were the sole daughter of a lowly, long-deceased blacksmith."

"I sometimes tell people that," she agreed. "It keeps them from asking more questions."

"But we were lovers, for God's sake!"

The anger in his voice made her close her eyes. "I couldn't tell anyone. I had to protect them." She opened her eyes and regarded him evenly. "I'm an *actress,* William. Do you know what that means to most people? Do you know the insults I have to bear, the insinuations, how men think I'm—" She pressed her lips into a straight line and tried to swallow a groundswell of tears.

William didn't know what to say. The anger and hurt in her voice surprised him. "I thought you loved the attention."

"No. I love acting, but I could do without being an actress." Her rich voice was tinged with bitterness. "Don't tell me my career didn't give you pause when we first met, for I know you were very jealous of it. It's one of the reasons I knew we had to part."

He frowned. *"One* of the reasons?"

"There was so much against us. When we first met I wasn't honest with anyone, including myself."

She sighed and leaned back against the squab as if too tired to hold her head upright. "I was so naïve. I thought that if I loved you enough we could surmount any obstacle, but then you left and that gave me time to see life the way it really was. Reason returned and . . . I knew we had to part."

"So it was never about my lack of funds."

"No. It was about success and security. Colchester is well known in the ton. No one would dare make improper advances to me so long as he and I are together."

William's jaw tightened. "Who dared to be improper toward you?"

"It doesn't matter. You were at sea, but Colchester was there. And I realized that had you been there, things would have been worse, not better."

William's chest ached, as if someone were sitting on it. "I should have been there."

"No," she returned sharply. "Colchester didn't care for me the way you did. He dealt with the situation in a very calm, satisfactory manner, and I was left with my career intact and no one's life was changed for the worse. Had you been there, all hell would have broken loose. I would have been left without a job, and you would have lost your commission and your future—"

"Hold. What does my commission have to do with—" Realization dawned. "Damn it, it was the prince, wasn't it?"

She flushed. "It doesn't matter who it was; that was almost eight years ago. And since I've been under Colchester's protection, no one has dared treat me with anything other than respect."

William hated to admit it, but there was some truth in what she said. He'd been a hot-blooded youth, quick to anger and quicker to charge. Life had taught him much since then, including prudence.

William looked at her now, noting how the

sunlight caressed her black hair and lit her creamy skin, making it glow as if dusted with pearl. Her large eyes were outlined by a thick fringe of lashes, while her mouth—which was a bit wide for common beauty—bespoke a deep passion and sensuality. She was fascinating to watch; it was difficult to tear one's eyes from her. It was no wonder the prince—and other men—were tempted.

"William, I must face this blackmailer and stop him. I must continue to protect my sisters from my lost reputation. I've saved enough for them to have dowries, and my oldest sister is set to be launched this coming season. I can't sit by and allow someone to wreck the one thing I've worked so hard for."

"So the cares of your family are upon your shoulders."

She nodded, an oddly lost yet regal nod, like a child at a tea party trying to maintain a dignity she didn't yet possess.

"Do you see your sisters often?"

A shadow passed over her face. "I see them when I can. They can't acknowledge me in public, of course, so I visit when Father is not home."

William thought of his own family, of how close they all were and how they always supported one another. This journey for Michael was no sacrifice, but a loving duty.

That was the call Marcail had answered, the call

that had fallen on the deaf ears of her vain father. It would be a pleasure to tell that damned ass a thing or two about the importance of family over society.

"So now you know," Marcail said in a defiant tone.

He realized she'd taken his silence as reprimand. "I wish you'd told me all of this years ago. Why didn't you?"

"The secret of my life isn't mine to tell."

He leaned forward then, his dark blue eyes almost blazing. "I wasn't just a passerby, Marcail. I wasn't a-a stranger who admired you upon the stage. I *loved* you. For that alone, I *deserved* the truth."

"It was my burden, not anyone else's."

"Damn it, Marcail. When you love someone, you share everything—the good, the bad, the awkward, the scary. It's all part of who you are. If you don't, then—" He shook his head. "I am realizing how unready we *both* were for our relationship."

That hurt, but she forced herself to shrug. "We were very young. What did we know of life?"

His expression darkened and she had the impression that he disagreed with her, but he didn't comment. Instead, he reached up and hit his fist on the ceiling. Almost immediately, the coach began to slow.

William gathered his hat and overcoat. "I am

going to ride ahead and see if I can discover any information about the elusive Miss Challoner."

"Of course." She felt a deep flicker of regret. She'd told him the truth at last, and she could almost feel his palpable disappointment. "I believe I shall nap. I haven't had the sleep I'm used to."

The coach halted and William climbed out, pausing to pull a wooden case from the seat box. He flipped it open, revealing two pistols.

"What are those for?" Her voice wavered just a bit. She'd never considered that he might be in danger.

He checked to see if the pistols were loaded and, apparently satisfied, tucked them into his waistband and covered them with his overcoat. "Hopefully they'll never be used, but I'd be a fool if I didn't prepare for the worst."

"You—you are taking Poston with you, aren't you?"

William lifted a brow. "Afraid I'll get lost?"

"No, I just thought he would be the one to go; you said he was an excellent tracker."

"He is, but I want him here, to watch over the coach." *And you.*

William hadn't said the words, but she heard them, so she snapped back, "And I want him with you, to watch over your *horse.*"

William looked surprised, but then chuckled.

"It's a good thing he's *my* groom, then." He replaced the empty case and closed the seat box. "I'll meet with you when we stop to water the horses." Without a glance back, he closed the door.

She heard low talking and then the sound of a horse cantering past the coach. With a shudder, the coach rocked back into motion.

For the rest of the day, she saw him no more.

Letter from Michael Hurst to his brother Robert, stationed at the London Home Office.

Once again, I am astonished by the prices you acquired for the last few artifacts I sent. I shall be able to fund at least two more expeditions from the proceeds.

Yet I've been thinking less about monetary issues lately. Studying these ancient civilizations has made me more aware of my mortality. There comes a time in every man's life when he looks back with regret at some point—a day, a decision, a hesitation to act—that allowed a precious opportunity to slip away. Regretting is an exercise in futility.

The past cannot be relived—but the future is the place for atonement.

CHAPTER 13

The coach traveled at breakneck speed, stopping late in the afternoon at a small village. William had left a note there for Poston at the one and only inn.

Marcail watched eagerly as Poston scanned the scrawled writing. "Well?" she asked when he tucked it in his pocket.

"The captain received word of Miss Challoner."

"Thank goodness!"

"Aye, she stopped here only"—Poston pulled out his pocketwatch and glanced at it—"an hour ago."

"Then he's catching up!"

"I don't know, miss. His horse was winded and the inn had no mounts left to trade."

"Still, even a winded horse could catch up to a coach."

"She's no longer in a coach, miss."

Marcail's heart sank. "No?"

"She and her men are on horseback. They hired every horse from the stables here, which is why the captain couldn't change his own." Poston's brow lowered. "They took every last one, three more than they had riders for."

Just when she'd thought they might be making some progress. She rubbed her lower back, which ached from the jouncing coach. She'd been riding for so long that even though she was standing upon the firm earth, it felt as if she were still rocking inside the coach.

"Are there fresh coach horses in the stables? It sounds as if Miss Challoner only took the riding stock."

"I'll check, miss."

"Good. Change ours if you can. Then ask the innkeeper if anyone nearby might have a good, fresh horse they would be willing to sell us."

"Sell?"

"Yes." She removed her reticule from her cloak pocket, and poured a stream of coins into his hand. "Find a horse and go after the captain. I won't have him facing Miss Challoner and her men alone."

Poston's hand closed over the coins. "Yes, miss! I'll see to it right away."

Marcail nodded and entered the inn. No one came to greet her, so she searched through the rooms, finally finding the innkeeper's wife frantically putting together several bowls of stew for her unexpected guests. Marcail had immediately assisted the harassed woman, who sent the inn's lone maid to deliver the bowls of steaming stew to Marcail's men who were waiting in the inn yard.

Since Marcail had traveled every summer to various genteel locations with a summer troupe, she knew how to avail herself of the best the inn had to offer. In addition to some cheese and bread for her own lunch, Marcail took an inventory of the larder and issued some rapid instructions to the innkeeper's wife, placing a heavy silver coin into the woman's eager palm.

Taking an apple with her, Marcail wandered into the empty common room, her mind racing after William. *And to think we once believed we might catch up to the elusive Miss Challoner in one day. I warned him that she was elusive.*

She paused by the window and saw Poston overseeing the changing of the team for a set of lively ones. Good. At least she wouldn't be too far behind.

She bit into her apple and looked up at the sky.

As William had predicted, heavy gray clouds hung overhead, a stiff chilly breeze waving the trees and shrubberies. The single lane was lined on each side with merry, thatched-roof houses separated by verdant greenery, patches of colorful flowers, and a bubbling brook . . . and yet she felt like the village idiot.

Though she'd fumed for an hour after William had left her alone in the coach, her sense of fairness wouldn't allow her to ignore the harsh truth in his words.

He was right; their relationship had been doomed from the beginning—and not from his overprotectiveness, the excuse she'd told herself through the years. No, the fault was hers for not fully sharing herself.

At the time, she'd told herself that she couldn't afford to trust her secret to anyone . . . but perhaps the truth was something different. Perhaps she'd been afraid to ask William to share her burdens because she'd believed they would drive him away.

So, faced with the belief that he would eventually leave, she'd found a convenient excuse to send him away on her terms. Perhaps she'd thought that small measure of control would make the separation easier.

Her heart heavy, she paced until a movement outside the window caught her eye. William was riding into the yard, his greatcoat flapping behind him, his horse limping noticeably. She spun on her heel and headed for the door.

"Miss?"

Marcail turned to find the innkeeper's wife standing with a youth who held a large, obviously heavy basket. The woman curtsied. "The food ye ordered, miss. James here will carry it fer ye."

"Thank you. Just in time, too." Marcail nodded to the youth. "Follow me, please." She emerged from the inn to find William standing beside the coach, an impatient look on his face. "What happened?" she asked.

"My horse drew up lame. I had to return to change her, which will cost me too much time."

Marcail turned to the youth. "James, you may give the basket to Captain Hurst, if you please."

The gawky lad handed the heavy basket to William.

"Thank you, James," Marcail said.

The lad turned a fiery red. "Y-ye're welcome, m-miss." He hurried back into the inn.

William looked at the basket as if it held large rocks. "What in hell is this?"

"Food for the men." She climbed into the waiting coach, arranging her skirts about her. "You may place the basket on the floor. It is very heavy and shouldn't slide."

"I've noticed how heavy it is," he grumbled, but placed the basket on the floor and slid it to the other side of the coach. "There must be more than food in here."

"I also purchased several bottles of ale in case we find ourselves without an inn."

"That's very resourceful," he said grudgingly. "Ah!" He looked down the road. "Poston's found us some new mounts—several, in fact."

Marcail leaned forward to see one of the footmen riding toward them leading three prancing geldings.

"Where did he get the funds for—" William's gaze narrowed on Marcail. "You gave it to him?"

"He told me that Miss Challoner was on horseback now, and I thought it would be best if he joined you. We knew from your note that she took all of the fresh horses with her, so I sent him to see what he could find."

"I will pay you back," William said stiffly.

"Nonsense. This is my chase, too. Just catch that blasted woman, please."

"Very well. This inn is the last one until we reach the North Road."

"How far is that?"

"Only three hours away, which is why we must press on. With a fresh mount and some luck, I'll find her before this storm breaks and retrieve that damned artifact myself."

"I wish I could come with you."

"The weather is going to make this difficult enough. Miss Challoner will rue the decision to leave her coach behind."

Marcail frowned. "I wonder why she did that?"

"She must know we're close on her heels. She may be sending someone back to scout the road behind her." William glanced up at the sky. "But she may have made a mistake with this one." He undid his muffler and then rewrapped it more thickly around his neck. "We'll meet you at the first large inn on the North Road, the Pelican."

"William, be careful. Miss Challoner and her men might be armed, and you could get injured or—"

William stepped up into the coach, slipped a hand behind her head, and kissed her. Surprised, Marcail melted into him, welcoming his tongue when he slipped it between her lips. Instantly, she was afire with wanting him, restless with desire.

He broke the embrace as abruptly as he'd begun it, though he kept his hand cupped around the back of her head. "That is half of a kiss. I will claim the other half this evening at the Pelican, so don't tarry."

Her heart did an odd little dance. "I-I shall look forward to it." Her voice was husky with passion.

"Do that." He pressed a quick kiss to her forehead and, with a wink and a heart-stopping crooked grin, he was gone.

Marcail leaned forward to watch out the window as he leapt upon a sturdy mare. He and Poston rode swiftly away, the gray sky above rumbling the protest that she felt in her heart.

William was a constant surprise. When he'd left the coach before he'd been irritated and angry, and with reason. But the ride seemed to have done him a world of good; his mood was now much improved. Of course, some of that might be because they were closing in on their quarry, but Marcail dared to hope that some of William's good mood was because of her.

It was a silly hope, but she couldn't banish it, try as she might. She settled back against the seat, a silly smile on her lips, which still tingled from his kiss.

Soon the coach jerked into motion and they were once again under way.

They reached the Pelican many hours later. Immediately after William disappeared down the road, the heavens had opened, causing them to slow their travel to a crawl.

Marcail hated to think of William riding in such a downpour, but could do nothing about it. She could, however, help the footmen who were left in the weather. She knocked on the ceiling and asked her new groom—a very correct young man by the name of Charles Robbins—to order some of the footmen to ride inside the coach with her, but Robbins stoically refused.

She tried to argue, but he merely stood in the drenching rain and repeated, "No, miss. It wouldn't be proper," until she was ready to scream. Since arguing was doing her no good and was only making them go more slowly, she finally gave up. They splashed on, creeping through increasingly thick mud and slicker roads. Several times she felt the back of the coach slide, only to catch at the last possible moment.

They stopped only once, when one of the back wheels bogged down in a thick patch of muck. While the footmen dug the wheel free, Marcail pulled out the basket and made certain that everyone had a good afternoon meal and some ale.

They were soon on their way again and Marcail was left to her own devices in the lonely coach. It was a long and excruciating afternoon, with nothing to do but think about what William had said to her.

His comments about Colchester had made her angry, but now she wondered about her evaluation of the man she'd long considered her best friend. When she had a problem, she never thought of going to him. And it was true that she saw less and less of him as time passed, so they didn't even have the ease of companionship to decorate the sham that was their relationship.

Had she placed Colchester on some sort of pedestal, even as she'd denied William a fair place in her life? Had she allowed her judgment to get so bent?

She didn't know. She only knew that after talking to William, she was beginning to question many aspects of the decisions upon which she'd based her life. She wished with all of her heart that she could talk to Grandmamma about these revelations. In fact, Marcail needed to send a post to Grandmamma from the Pelican or she might worry.

The rain finally eased to a steady drizzle, the gray sky darkening further as evening arrived. They turned onto the great North Road just as it grew almost too dark to travel and reached the Pelican after a harrowingly slow ride through a very slick section of road. A number of other coaches were pulling into the Pelican as they did; the place bustled, a very different sight from their previous stops.

Robbins waited in line to pull the coach to a halt at the walkway that led into the inn. Soon he opened her door and set down the steps.

Marcail tugged her cloak hood over her bonnet and took his hand, stepping onto the flagstone walk that was raised above the mud. "Robbins, have you seen Poston or the captain?"

"Nay, miss. If they're not inside, then perhaps they've taken refuge from the weather."

She nodded and allowed him to hand her off to a footman. "If you hear of anything, please let me know."

The groom nodded. "Aye, miss. As soon as we know something."

"Thank you." She shouldn't be worried, she knew. William and Poston were a force to be reckoned with.

She reached the portico in front of the inn and released her footman's arm. "Pray have my portmanteau and trunk delivered to my room. I shall bespeak one immediately."

"Yes, miss. I'll fetch yer luggage now." He bowed and left.

Marcail pushed back her hood and looked about her with approval. The Pelican was a large, rambling, two-story structure, the windows filled with warm lamplight and cheery red curtains. The sound of voices laughing and talking was welcome after two days of very little company.

Better yet, the scent of savory bakery goods and roasting meat made Marcail almost weak-kneed with longing for a hot meal.

Inside, she found the innkeeper and his plump wife scurrying to and fro from the common room to the back hallway, ordering a handful of servants to fetch this and that. From the laughter bursting from the common room, it was obvious that the Pelican was enjoying a bountiful night.

Marcail went to the wide doorway that led to the common room and looked inside, her gaze scanning the sea of masculine faces, but William was not among the crowd.

Disappointment flashed through her. Where was he?

The innkeeper noticed her standing inside the doorway and hurried to meet her, introducing himself and his wife. He'd no sooner done so than a call from the common room sent him hurrying off, and Marcail was left in the capable-appearing hands of Mrs. MacClannahan.

The woman looked Marcail up and down and sent an evaluating glance at her Bond Street bonnet.

Marcail inclined her head. "Mrs. MacClannahan, I would like a room and a hot bath."

"Ye're fortunate, fer we've only one room left. I'll have it readied and a tub sent up." She took Marcail's cloak and whisked a gaze over the pelisse and gown now revealed.

Marcail had the instant feeling that if anyone were to ask, Mrs. MacClannahan could correctly tell them the exact value of her gown, pelisse, and bonnet. It was most disconcerting.

"Here, now, miss. Don't ye be goin' into the common room. There's an untoward amount o' men who apparently cannot handle a little weather, so we're nigh full up fer the night."

"Ah. I see." Poor William would have to bed down in the stables. "Mrs. MacClannahan, in the last hour, you haven't perchance seen a tall red-haired woman, have you?"

"Nay, just a few farmers, a squire and his son, a Frenchman who reeks of cologne but can tell a whopping good tale, two gentlemen on their way to London to see a boxing match, and two ladies who are sitting in the small parlor."

Marcail hid her disappointment. "If you see such a woman—very tall, very pretty, with red hair—please let me know. She's my cousin. We were traveling together, but we've gotten separated."

"Very good, miss. I'll keep me eyes peeled fer yer cousin."

"Thank you. Is there a place I could sit while my room is being readied?"

"Aye, we have a parlor, we do. Fer proper 'uns like yerself. Ye can join the other ladies there."

"That sounds lovely."

"Excellent, miss. It'll only cost ye two pence."

Marcail paid the small fee and followed Mrs. MacClannahan to a large door opposite the raucous common room.

Two elegantly dressed older ladies occupied the chairs placed before a crackling fire. They were sipping tea, their bright blue eyes amazingly similar as they fixed upon Marcail.

The plumper, shorter of the two put down her cup and stood. She gave a quick curtsy, bobbing her gray head, her blue eyes owlishly framed by a pair of spectacles, her lace mobcap perilously close to falling off her curls. "How do you do? I'm Lady Durham and this"—she indicated her companion, who'd just put down her teacup but had remained in her chair—"is my sister, Lady Loughton."

Lady Durham's sister seemed to be much of the same age, her hair just as white but contained in a neat bun instead of her sister's wilder curls. Whereas Lady Durham was plump, Lady Loughton was angular and wrenlike.

Lady Loughton inclined her head. "I hope you'll forgive me for not standing, but I've hurt my knee."

"Of course." Marcail curtsied. "I am Miss Marcail Beauchamp. I hope your knee isn't too badly injured."

"Well, it is. I fell when coming into the front hallway and my knee is very sore. The entryway is quite slick." She sent a hard glance at Mrs. MacClannahan. "*Someone* should see to keeping it dry."

"Which I've done," Mrs. MacClannahan said in a testy voice. "Ask Miss Beauchamp if 'tis not so. Ye didn't find it slick, did ye, miss?"

"Not at all, though my feet weren't covered in mud." She nodded toward the two pairs of shoes that were drying by the fire, both crusted heavily.

Lady Durham blinked at the shoes as if seeing them for the first time. "Oh. Well. We had to exit the coach on the other side, due to our box of tonic. It was blocking the door."

"Tonic?"

"Oh, yes," Lady Durham said, her expression earnest. "We're on our way to London to deliver some of our very best shee—"

Lady Loughton kicked Lady Durham in the shin.

"Ow!" Lady Durham grabbed her leg through her gown. "Jane! Why did you do that?"

Jane, apparently made of stern stuff indeed, merely said, "What we're doing is our own business."

Marcail spread her hands before her. "Please, I've no wish to intrude but there doesn't seem to be any other room I could purchase just now and my own bedchamber is being readied."

Lady Durham was instantly contrite. "Oh, my dear, no one is suggesting that you must go elsewhere."

"Unless you ask too many questions," Lady Loughton qualified. "I don't have patience for questions."

Mrs. MacClannahan sniffed. "This is me only lady's parlor and ye'll all have to share it. The common room is full o' men."

"That's true," Lady Durham said, blinking owlishly behind her spectacles. She leaned toward

Marcail and said in a low voice, "I know, for I listened in when I went to fetch my dear sister some medicine for her poor knee. But then the French are always so *improper.*" She turned to her sister. "Jane, isn't it pleasant to have a visitor?"

"I suppose," Lady Loughton grumbled, rubbing her knee and wincing.

Lady Durham added in a bracing tone. "She's quite thin and doesn't look as if she'll eat many tea cakes."

Lady Loughton sniffed. "I suppose she won't. But just *don't* expect us to entertain you with tales of what's in our coach."

"Of course not," Marcail said, quelling a smile.

Lady Loughton pinned the innkeeper's wife with an intent look. "I hope you're not charging poor Miss Beauchamp for the use of this parlor when we've already paid for it."

Mrs. MacClannahan flushed. "I charge by the person, I do."

Lady Loughton lifted her brows. "Miss Beauchamp, if I were you, I would demand the return of my money. It was unfairly charged."

Mrs. MacClannahan stomped to the door. "I'm leaving. And don't be askin' fer more tea, neither, for I won't bring it to ye!"

"Good," said Lady Loughton. "It's wretched. Pray tell your kitchen maids to leave it on to steep at least five more minutes. This pot of tea is so weak, you could read through it."

The door snapped shut behind Mrs. MacClannahan.

Marcail sighed. She would have loved a cup of hot tea.

Lady Durham clapped her hands. "Miss Beauchamp, come and sit by me." She indicated the chair to the side of her own. "I shall pour you some tea. There are two extra cups and it is really not as bad as Jane says."

Marcail removed her bonnet, unbuttoned her pelisse, and hung them on a hook near the fireplace. A hot bath *and* hot tea? Her lips almost quivered from the excitement. "That would be lovely, thank you."

Within moments she was ensconced in a chair, a lap blanket spread over her, a cup of delicious warm tea in her hands. She breathed in the scent of bergamot and orange pekoe.

"Excellent tea, isn't it?" Lady Durham said, nodding so hard her cap flopped on her head. "It's a bit weak, as Jane pointed out, so I added a little something to mine." She glanced at the closed door and then slipped a hand into her pocket and withdrew a small brown bottle. "Just a bit of this and the tea tastes—here, would you like some?" She uncorked the bottle and the distinctive scent of cognac wafted through the air.

"Emma!" Lady Loughton snapped, looking thoroughly put out. "You can't go around giving people your medicine."

"I was only going to give her a small bit, just to liven up her tea."

"I'm sure it's lively enough for Miss—" Lady Loughton's bright blue gaze narrowed. "What did you say your name was?"

"Miss Beauchamp, but you may call me Marcail."

"Marcail, what an unusual name!" Lady Durham said brightly, sipping her tea, which was now half cognac. She scanned Marcail with interest. "I think I might have heard that name somewhere."

"As have I," Lady Loughton said, tilting her head to one side. "You look familiar, too . . . Hmmm-mmm."

Marcail took a sip of tea, hoping that neither of them knew who she was.

Lady Durham held up her brown bottle. "Are you certain you don't want—"

"Emma, leave the child be."

Lady Durham's smile faded. "Very well. I was just trying to be polite." She slurped her drink and then replaced it on the table. "So, Miss Beauchamp, what brings you to the Pelican? Oh, and do call me Emma. We're all cozy here in the parlor. No need to stand on formality."

Lady Loughton dipped her head. "You may call

me Jane, if you wish. I'm not one for formalities, either."

Marcail had to smile. "Emma and Jane, then. I'm waiting for someone."

Jane's bird-bright gaze fastened on Marcail. "Oh, is it a *romantic* meeting? Those are the best."

"I'm looking for my cousin. If you happen to see a very tall, red-haired lady, would you let me know? We were separated."

"Oh dear, how dreadful for you." Emma tsked. "We haven't seen many women travelers today, have we, Jane?"

"Not today, though that Frenchman in the common room could be female. He's covered with lace and minces when he walks."

"I think he's rather handsome," Emma said. "He's certainly tall. Of course he wears far too much cologne. I had to put some of my medicine under my nose so I could breathe after he passed us in the hallway."

"He must have bathed with the stuff, acting as if—" Jane set down her cup with a click. "That's it! I *knew* I'd seen you before. Your eyes and coloring are so unusual that I couldn't forget them. You're that *actress*!"

Marcail's throat tightened painfully. *Here it comes.*

Emma gaped through her glasses. "Why, Jane, I do believe you're right! This is the woman whose Lady MacBeth brought even Wexford to tears!"

"And Wexford is a hard nut to crack," Lady Jane said with satisfaction. "He's our nephew-in-law, and a stubborn rakehell to boot. Or he was until he married our niece, Arabella. She's softened him a bit."

"You're a *famous* actress, too." Emma patted Marcail's knee. "I'm glad to meet a woman so capable in her art."

Marcail smiled. "Why, thank you."

Jane sipped her tea. "You're much better than that fat woman—Emma, what's her name?"

"Mrs. Delbert or Mrs. Dantry or Mrs.—"

"Mrs. Dalton?" Marcail ventured, naming one of the grand dames of the theater.

"Yes, that's her! It's such an embarrassment when one is forced to watch someone of one's own sex make a fool of herself."

"And it happens far too often," Emma added, swishing some of her "tea" in her mouth before swallowing it.

"Usually because some fool of a man has talked her into a position for which she's not prepared," Jane added acerbicly. "Based not upon her abilities, but upon how large her breasts may be."

"Oh dear, yes," Emma agreed, taking a swig of her tea and pouring more. "As if having large breasts would make a woman good at acting, or being a governess, or any number of professions."

Marcail choked on her tea.

Emma absently patted Marcail on the back and then added a huge swig of "medicine" to the newly poured tea. "The only profession where large breasts would be an asset would be if one were forced to carry something of weight upon one's back. Then one's breasts might act as counterweights."

"Very good, Emma," Jane agreed, taking a sip of her tea as if discussing breasts was a normal, everyday affair. "I've often thought it was a pity there were not more purpose for breasts other than feeding children, and you just came up with a delightful one. I'm sure we can think of more if we put our minds to it."

"I don't think there are any other useful applications for breasts." Emma took another very long drink of her "tea." "For a woman to be truly liberated, she has to be free of her breasts."

Marcail blinked. "I beg your pardon?"

Jane sighed. "Don't let Emma's wild talking disturb you. She's become a suffragette ever since we went to that speaker at the Ladies' Guild Hall."

"Miss Colton," Emma said, her voice almost reverent. "Have you heard of her?"

"I've read about her in the papers. She's a bit of a radical."

"So she is," Emma said, beaming woozily. "She's a suffera-sulfera-suphragr— That thing that Jane said. That sounds so exciting, doesn't it?"

"Yes, indeed."

Jane snorted. "Well, I don't think it sounds exciting at all. Women shouldn't be allowed to vote. We're too excitable."

"I'm not too excitable," Emma said, blinking owlishly through her glasses.

"Well, I am," Jane stated.

"No, you're not. You're calmer than me. In fact, I don't think I've ever seen you anything but calm. Well, except for when you fell in love with Sir Loughton." Emma leaned toward Marcail. "*That* was a nerve-wracking time, because Jane wagered her *innocence* on a game of cards and lost. Fortunately he wished to marry her, even though he'd already won the right to—"

"Emma!" Jane's face was red. "That is *quite* enough. I'm sure Miss Beauchamp has no desire to learn such intimate details of our lives."

Usually Marcail would have agreed, but she'd spent most of the day alone in a coach. At least Jane and Emma were distracting. "I promise that anything you say in this room will never be repeated. I am most discreet."

"She's an actress, too," Emma added unnecessarily. "They are *always* discreet. They have to be, for they have so many affairs."

Marcail gasped. "I don't."

Jane said, "Perhaps I should have gone onstage. I thought about it when I was younger."

"I don't think Sir Loughton would like it if you did it now," Emma said thoughtfully.

"I think you're right, which is why I *should* do it. It's good to surprise your man now and then. Keeps him on his toes."

Marcail didn't think she'd ever met two stranger or more delightful women.

"We now know why Miss Marcail is here," Emma said. "But she doesn't know why *we're* here. Jane, may I tell her? She's been most discreet and hasn't mentioned any of her affairs. Not a one!"

Jane waved a hand. "You may tell her."

Emma leaned forward, the smell of cognac wafting with her. "You wouldn't know it to look at us, but we're on a *secret mission*."

Jane glanced at the closed door, then added, "We're making a *delivery*."

Emma fished a heavy silver chain from her neck, tugging it over her head. Her mobcap fluttered to her knees and she slapped it back on before handing the chain to Marcail.

At the end was a long vial. "*That* is what we're delivering. It's sheep tonic."

"I beg your pardon—sheep tonic?"

Emma nodded vigorously, making her lace cap

tilt at a rakish angle. "Jane and I make the best sheep tonic in all of Yorkshire."

Jane looked pleased. "We do. Our sheep have more lambs than anyone else's. *Lots* more lambs."

"Of course, our nephew-in-law, the Duke of Wexford, didn't like it when we dosed him up with it and—"

Marcail held up a hand. "Wait. You dosed a duke with *sheep tonic?*"

"Do you know him?" Emma looked delighted at the possibility.

"He has a box at the theater and frequently attends with his wife."

"That's Arabella, our niece," Jane said proudly.

Emma beamed. "She married Wexford and now she's a duchess." She looked at the closed door again before she leaned forward and said in a low voice, "*I* think he married her because of our sheep tonic."

"Emma, don't say such a thing! Wexford married Arabella because he loves her."

"I know he loves her, but our sheep tonic helped him figure *out* that he loved her. He was ill, you know, but wouldn't stay in bed. You can't get out of bed if you take sheep tonic. That made him heal, and he stayed long enough to realize that he loved our niece."

Marcail didn't know how she kept from laughing. "Do you often use your sheep tonic on people?"

Jane shrugged. "Only when necessary."

"And it works?"

"Lud, yes! Wexford didn't rise for weeks."

"*And* he was in love with Arabella." Miss Emma uncapped her flask and added a splash of cognac to her empty teacup. "Don't forget that part! Many people think of sheep tonic as a love tonic, but it's more of an immobilizer. If you dose someone with it, they can't move."

"But they can still talk," Jane added in a reflective voice.

"Oh yes, they become quite chatty. Perhaps that's the part that makes them fall in love—staying in one place long enough to talk things through. People don't do that enough, you know."

Marcail thought wistfully of William. It would be nice if he were in love with her again. She sipped her tea thoughtfully. "Does this sheep tonic work on everyone?"

"I don't know," Jane said. "We haven't tried it on everyone."

Marcail smiled. "I hope you—" In the hallway she distinctly heard William's voice.

Pure happiness flooded through her and she had to fight herself not to jump to her feet and run to the door.

She took a dignified sip, placed her cup on the tray, and stood. "There's my—" She didn't know what to say. He wasn't her friend or her lover—not formally. "My companion has arrived. He's helping me find my cousin."

"Ah, the redhead." Emma stood unsteadily.

"Please sit back down." Marcail helped the older woman back into her chair. "I think you should stay sitting for a little while longer."

Emma beamed. "You are a dear!"

"Thank you. And before I forget, here." Marcail pressed the vial and chain into Emma's hand.

"Oh, no!" Emma handed it back to Marcail. "Take this. You might need it."

"Thank you, but . . . what would I do with this?"

Jane looked surprised. "Don't you own any sheep? Everyone in Yorkshire does."

"No, I live in London." She saw the hurt on their faces and added, "But perhaps now's the time to get one."

"Oh, get *two*," Emma said happily. "With the tonic, you'll need at *least* a pair."

"Two sheep it will be, then." Marcail tucked the vial away. "Thank you both. It was lovely meeting you." She curtsied, listened to the good-byes of her new friends, and then hurried to the door.

William, please tell me you've found her!

Letter from Michael Hurst to his brother Robert, from a barge on the Nile River.

We hope to leave tomorrow, although the weather might once again interfere. The rainy season here is quite unlike the rainy season in England, where one is forced to submit to a constant drizzle alleviated by an occasional mind-numbing deluge, all permeated with a bone-freezing cold. Here it's always warm, and it's either raining buckets or it's not. There's no in between, no lingering, no indecision. Just rain or no rain.

I sometimes wish all of life was like that.

CHAPTER 14

Marcail found William in the foyer, water dripping from his coat and puddling on the floor. On a normal day William was a sight to behold, all tall, dark haired, and broad shouldered, and with that damnably challenging captain's swagger. But now, as he removed his coat to reveal equally wet clothes that clung to his muscular frame, he set her heart to pattering.

She hurried forward. "Did you find her?"

William raked his wet hair from his face. "No, but she can't have gone far in this weather."

"What happened?"

"Poston and I followed Miss Challoner and her men to an inn not far from here. We arrived less than twenty minutes after they did. The innkeeper had seen her and was certain she was in his taproom, but she wasn't there. She wasn't anywhere. Everyone remembered her arrival, for she was apparently in a splendid temper, but no one remembered her leaving. Not the ostlers, the postboys, the chambermaids—no one. It's as if she vanished."

Marcail grimaced. "How does she *do* that?"

"I wish I knew."

"As do I. I warned you she had a tendency to disappear."

"I remember," he said drily. "Unfortunately, being warned about something doesn't always prevent it."

She had to laugh. "I'm sorry. I didn't mean to sound like a know-it-all."

"Good, for I'd hate to disabuse you of that notion."

She lifted her brows. "A challenge, Hurst?"

"Not until I've had something to eat; I'm famished." He grimaced. "Damn it, we were so close! Poston thinks he can identify her now, though."

"Oh?"

"Yes, through one of the horses. One hoof has a shoe that wasn't properly cast. And once this rain stops, there will be plenty of mud to help us find that track."

"That's promising."

He unwound the wet muffler from his neck and tossed it over the overcoat he'd hung on a peg. "Fortunately for us, no one can travel in this weather. As soon as it lets up, four of our men will search the other inns along this stretch of road."

"That's an excellent idea." The firm line of William's mouth told her that he was determined to catch their foe. But that gave her little hope; she knew just how elusive Miss Challoner could be.

She turned away so he wouldn't see her doubts, and her boot hit a puddle caused by William's soaked attire, making her heel skid on the slippery flagstone.

She gasped as her feet flew out from under her, but William's strong arm caught her firmly about the waist and pulled her tight against his broad chest.

"Easy, my sweet." His deep voice rumbled in her ear, his breath warm on her cheek. "I didn't bring you this far for you to break your neck on a slick floor."

Her heart pounded so loudly that her ears rang from it. "It wasn't slick when I got here," she said breathlessly. *But then you arrived, and everything that was safe suddenly became dangerous. Like this.* She leaned her head back against his broad shoulder. "I—I'm quite safe now. You may release me."

He lifted a brow. "You're lucky I was here."

"If you hadn't been here I wouldn't have fallen, for there wouldn't have been any water on the floor," she retorted, though she made no effort to pull away.

The entire front of her gown was sopping wet, but she ignored it. For so much of this trip she and William had been at each other's throats, bitter and suspicious, and she wanted to savor the moment.

Considering all they'd faced in the last few days, they could be excused for some ill temper. They both had so much at stake, they were dealing with their own fears and worries on top of their past history.

She rested her cheek against William's shoulder and briefly closed her eyes. She was wet and cold and tired, the anxious day made all the worse by the unforgiving weather. She wanted nothing more than a hot bath and a clean bed . . . and the warmth of his touch.

She suddenly realized that her relationship with Colchester hadn't just protected her from unwanted advances, but from wanted ones, as well. In fact, over the years she'd managed to isolate herself from practically everyone except Grandmamma.

She would have sworn that she liked her life this way, that peace and quiet were all she desired. But this journey with William had exposed the short-comings. She wasn't just alone; she was *lonely*.

Standing here, with William's massive body

radiating heat through his soaked clothing, his strong arm about her waist, his broad shoulder supporting her completely, she felt protected, and part of something bigger than she was alone.

Her eyes stung, tears clogging her throat. *What is this? I have a perfectly lovely life, with wonderful sisters and a Grandmamma who loves me dearly. And Colchester has always been a friend who cares for me deeply, and who . . .*

She bit her lip. *Who has been living as much of a lie as I.*

When a relationship was based on how deep your twin falsehoods ran, how real could it be? William was right to ask why she hadn't trusted Colchester to help her when she was first blackmailed. She hadn't asked for his help because their relationship couldn't have borne the weight.

It was a difficult truth to face. Colchester wasn't here; a true friend would have been.

She clung to William and buried her face against his wet shoulder. *It would be so easy to get used to this—a strong arm to catch me when I fall, someone to lean on when things get difficult.*

Marcail realized that William was completely still, his arms around her, his chin resting against her head. *He must be wondering what's wrong.*

"I'm sorry. I was just cold and—" She reluctantly stepped clear of his warm arms, goose bumps rising due to her now wet clothing. "Thank you for catching me."

"You'd have landed right on your arse," William agreed in a pleasant tone. "We don't want that to happen." He scooped her up, carried her to the bottom of the stairs, and gently set her down. Then, his amused gaze finding hers, he leaned forward and said softly, "If I were you . . ."

His voice made her shiver, his firm lips so *near*.

She leaned forward as well. "If you were me?" she asked hopefully.

His gaze locked with hers, and the simmer of heat she felt burst into flames. She suddenly wanted him with a fierceness that was almost painful.

"If I were you," he continued, "I'd cover that." His low voice was as intimate as a caress.

"Cover what?" she asked breathlessly.

He looked down at her gown. She did the same, and saw that her cold nipples were clearly outlined by the wet, clinging fabric.

"Oh!" She crossed her arms over her chest, her cheeks burning hotly. "My cloak is on the peg beside yours. Would you please fetch it?"

He did so. "Here you are. Your bags have already been delivered. I will bring my bags in and bespeak us rooms."

"Oh—I already asked and there was only one left. The innkeeper's wife said they were uncommonly busy because of the rain."

Should she invite William to stay in her room?

It would be scandalous, to be sure, but once this wild chase was over, there would be nothing holding them together.

But even as she parted her lips to ask, it dawned on her that inviting him into her room would only make their eventual parting even more difficult. And she feared it would already be hard enough.

So instead of following her heart, she said, "I suppose you could sleep in the stables with Poston and the footmen."

William's smile fled. "I could, I suppose." He raised his brows. "Or, I could join you in—"

"I think the stables will suit very well." Though the sentence cost her dearly, her voice sounded distant and uninterested.

William's jaw tightened. "Fine. I'll find my own accommodations."

She managed a faint air of interest. "Do you expect we will leave early in the morning?"

"Yes, unless the rain continues. Right now the ditches are full, and if we slid off the road—" He shook his head. "We're here for the night, at least."

"I can't say that I'm sorry. I'm looking forward to a warm bath and a clean bed—though I'd give up a year of sleep to be rid of Miss Challoner and her master."

"A soldier to the end." His deep voice was tinged with admiration and—was that disappointment?

Her heart ached. "Thank you for all you've done. You've been remarkably patient about everything."

"I'm quite a bit older than when we knew each other before. A lot of things are different."

That was true; they were both more knowledgeable. And perhaps sadder, too.

She was, anyway.

She realized she was staring at him, her gaze caressing the strong line of his mouth and chin. There was something about this man, so stern and unyielding, that made her want to tease the softer side from him.

William's brows lowered. "What's wrong? Something on my chin?" He swiped his chin with his hand. "It's probably mud. It's as thick as tar out there." He sent her a humorous glance. "The only thing that makes this weather bearable is that our quarry is facing it, too."

"Amen," Marcail said fervently.

He stepped away. "I shall see to the cattle. Perhaps the horse thief of an innkeeper can be convinced to lower the price of hay for our horses."

"I daresay you will prevail." She liked the way he said "our" horses. She was sorry that soon this would be only a memory.

She hugged her cloak tighter. "I should retire since we may be leaving early."

"More than likely." And with that he donned

his cloak and was gone, leaving Marcail alone in the empty hallway.

Having no idea which room was hers, Marcail went in search of Mrs. MacClannahan. She found the woman pouring a bucketful of complaints into her husband's ear. The poor man looked so relieved to see Marcail that she allowed him to escort her to her room.

Once there, she looked around with approval, glad to see her requested bath awaited her. The room was quite pleasant, with a wide bed piled high with large feather pillows, a good-size wardrobe on one wall, and a washstand filling the corner near the fireplace.

She dug into her trunk and portmanteau and removed a night rail and a heavy silk robe, along with a small case that held her lavender soap. Then she undressed and wearily lowered herself into the tub.

The tepid water was cooling even as she sat, so she soaped herself briskly, washing her hair last. When she was done, she dried off in front of the fire, then tugged on her robe and wrapped her hair with the towel.

A little more unpacking revealed her silver-backed brush, and she settled before the fire to dry her hair. It was hard not to think about William while she sat there, brushing her hair, but she tried not to do so. To keep her mind occupied, she recited the lines she could remember from the new play she was supposed to be preparing for, and even tossed in some *Romeo and Juliet* for good measure.

But it seemed that every scene of every play was about one thing and one thing only . . . love or the loss of it. Damn it, when had theater gotten so *maudlin*?

She tried to recite the words of various poems she knew instead, but the same problem plagued her. She finally had to resort to saying the alphabet forward and backward. She made it eight entire minutes before she abruptly stood, tossed her damp hair over her shoulder, and set the brush on the dresser.

The mirror was slightly wavy, making her look taller. Did William prefer a taller woman? He'd surely been with some over the years. And shorter ones, too. Definitely thinner ones and—

She frowned. "This is ridiculous," she informed her reflection, which looked back so expectantly. "You're just making yourself jealous—and you have no right to be."

Her heart sagged as much as her reflection's shoulders did. "You're allowing your pride to ruin tonight. You want to be with him, and soon he'll be gone. As for worrying about it being more difficult to let him go, how can it get any worse than it is now?"

Her reflection nodded in complete agreement.

"Furthermore, we may find Miss Challoner to-morrow, which will mean an abrupt end to ever seeing him again."

A flicker of sadness crossed her reflected face.

"Exactly. So, what are you going to do about it?"

There was only one thing she *could* do. She spun around and removed a chemise and her blue morning gown from her trunk. She quickly changed, loosely pinned her damp hair up, and stuffed her feet into a pair of blue kid half boots. Then she grabbed her cloak and opened the door, slinging her cloak over her shoulders.

As she turned around to lock the door, a large, warm hand took the key.

She knew who it was the second his skin touched hers. Holding her breath, she turned. "William. What are you doing here?"

A letter from William Hurst to his brother Michael, written from the deck of the Agile Witch.

The new information Miss Smythe-Haughton has brought to light about our famous family amulet is most intriguing. I am eager to know what you discover once the papyrus has been translated.

Still, I'm sure it won't intrigue me as much as it will you. Over the last six months, you've been writing more and more about your search for the family amulet and less and less about your other endeavors—the ones that pay your bills and add to your fame as an adventurer. While it's admirable that you wish to return the amulet to our family coffers, you should be cautious not to lose sight of your real purpose, which is to continue adding to your collections. I speak from experience when I say that it's a sad day when you forget your purpose in life. I once was distracted from mine and I rue it to this very day.

CHAPTER 15

William looked into Marcail's violet eyes. He had just been asking himself the same question. He'd made it all the way to the stables before he'd realized that the last place he wanted to be was somewhere Marcail wasn't. He wasn't sure why he'd allowed her to dismiss him, and it annoyed the hell out of him that he had.

What was it about her that turned his thinking so inside out? Whatever it was, he decided then and there to put a stop to it.

He'd just reached her door when he heard the key turn in the lock. He'd stepped quickly out of the way and watched as she came out, her skin flushed, her hair loosely piled upon her head, and smelling faintly of lavender.

Until that moment, William hadn't had a plan of any sort; he'd just wanted to be with her. But the second he saw her blinking up at him in surprise, her long lashes casting shadows over her violet eyes, he knew what he wanted.

He pulled her into her room and locked the door behind them. Then he took off his greatcoat, tossed it over the chair, and loosened his cravat.

Her eyes widened, but she made no move to unlock the door or kick him out. *That's promising.* He removed his outer coat and undid his waistcoat. "Aren't you going to undress, too? It won't be as much fun alone."

Her lips curved into a smile. "I don't know," she said primly, but her hands strayed to her laces as if she were tempted.

He hid a smile, took a chair by the fire, and removed his boots, placing them on the hearth. "I have a motto where lovemaking is concerned."

"Let me guess: 'Often and fervently.'"

He chuckled. "No, but that one would do." He stood and tossed aside his waistcoat and cravat, then tugged his shirt over his head.

Her gaze locked on his chest.

"My motto is 'Before lust goes happiness.' So if this makes us happy, why not?"

She'd managed to undo her ties, but she made no move to tug the laces free.

He slipped his breeches off and tossed them over the chair with his other clothing.

Her gaze traveled slowly down from his shoulders to his stomach to his already bestirred cock. Her eyes widened before she continued her perusal down his thighs and all the way to the floor.

"If you wish me to leave, you have only to say so and I'll go," he said in an innocent voice.

Her gaze flickered to his erection. "You undress and *then* ask if I wish you to leave?"

He grinned, rakish and confident. "I was hoping I could convince you to allow me to stay."

"I can see that."

He shrugged. "The beds in the stables are far too"—he flicked a glance over her fair form—"lumpy."

She burst into laughter, rich and delighted. "So you're here because the bed is more comfortable. That's all?"

"Of course that's not *all*." He grinned. "I have far better reasons to stay." He crossed the room and bent down to brush his scruffy chin over her smooth cheek. "What do you say, Marcail? Shall we share the oh-so-comfortable bed? Or will you send me back out into the rain to sleep in the straw?" He allowed his warm breath to brush her ear. "That would be such a waste, and we've wasted so much time already."

She'd closed her eyes as his chin rubbed against her cheek, but now she took a deep breath, her fingers still toying with her laces. "I have a confession."

He nipped her ear. "Yes, my love?"

"When you arrived, I was just going to see you. We have so little time left and I wanted . . . I wanted *this*."

The words sent a wave of warmth through him. The past didn't matter, or what the future might hold. All that mattered was right now. That was another lesson he'd learned over the years: life was a gift and there wasn't time to argue about the details. He'd faced enough storms, enough dangers, enough illnesses, enough bloodthirsty pirates to realize that every moment was precious and sweet. And for some reason, the moments with Marcail were doubly so. They couldn't afford to lose even these few.

He slipped a hand beneath her hair and pulled her close; she tucked herself against him as if made to be there. He finished undoing her ties and then pushed her gown off her shoulders, bending to kiss each inch of creamy skin as it was exposed.

She gasped as his lips grazed her collarbone, which encouraged him all the more. Accompanied by the crackling fire and the flicker of the flames, he began his seduction in earnest. He nipped and touched as he revealed more and more of her. When her chemise finally fell to the floor, he ran his hands down her silken skin, admiring every curve and shadow. His body ached with the need for her touch.

Marcail had never been so exquisitely tortured and pleasured at the same time. Her skin tingled every place his lips brushed; her body yearned for him. She ran her hands over his broad chest, feeling his muscles ripple beneath her seeking fingers.

He was such a man's man, all hard planes and firm muscles, and she was beset with an urgent desire to touch and taste them all. Her hands slid down his flat stomach to his hips, and then she reached for his erect cock.

He stood stock-still, his breath ragged as she explored his length. It amazed her how his shaft could be so hard and yet the skin was so soft, like velvet over a rock.

She glanced up at his face and saw his eyes were closed, his expression one of tortured ecstasy. Very gently, she encircled his shaft and squeezed.

He gasped and dropped his forehead to hers. "Don't."

"You don't like it?"

His eyes opened and he chuckled, though he was still breathing heavily. "I like it too much. But I like this more—"

And with that, he kissed her—a passionate,

all-possessing kiss, branding her through and through.

As William's hard mouth claimed hers, she could think of nothing but his warm hands molding her to him, of the sensations streaking through her, leaving her gasping and hungry for more. She'd yearned for this for so long; no man had ever captured her the way William had.

He broke the kiss and nuzzled her neck, sending a million shivers dancing up and down her bare skin. As he wrapped her closer, she could feel his cock against her thigh, velvety hard and inviting.

She reeled and clung to him. It was heavenly to be so close, to feel his muscles beneath her seeking fingers, to smell the leather and sandalwood scent of his skin. She was awash in heated desire, all thoughts and cares gone.

William brushed aside the damp hair from her neck and strung delicate kisses down to her shoulder. Shivers rocked her and she clutched his shoulders, her knees weak.

He kept one arm firmly around her waist and his other hand cupped her breast, his thumb flicking against her hardened nipple. She arched against him and moaned, straining toward him, her body reacting to his every touch.

She wanted this, needed it, had dreamed of it— and now he was here, in her arms.

William slid his hand from her breast and boldly pressed it between her thighs, making her gasp again. He'd already aroused her so much that it took only a few strokes before she cried out, wave after wave of passion breaking over her.

William held her tightly, murmuring soft words in her ear.

It took a while before she could even breathe enough for thought to return. When it did, she was encased in his powerful arms, his chin against her temple, his breath warm on her skin.

Outside, the rain beat on the roof and windows, but here, alone in the flickering firelight, their bodies warming each other, Marcail felt as if this was where she belonged—in William's arms.

But that was a dangerous feeling. Even if they found a way to overcome their past, she couldn't imagine William accepting her career, any more than she could imagine leaving London to live on a ship.

He slowly loosened his hold, keeping his arms about her waist. When he saw her expression, the smile in his eyes disappeared. "You look far too serious for a woman who has just been wonderfully pleasured."

She just shook her head.

He regarded her for a long moment. "Before I carry you to bed to pleasure you further, I wish to ask a question."

A tingle ran through her at the thought of further pleasure, and she had to clear her throat before she could speak. "What do you wish to ask?"

"You and Colchester don't share a bed. You never have."

Dear God. What do I do now? I promised never to betray his secret—but I can't lie to William. "That's not a question," she evaded.

"I already know the answer." His brows lowered. "So why is he your lover in name only?"

"William, please don't ask anything more. I can't tell you. I promised to guard Colchester's secrets, just as he's guarded mine."

"His secret is the reason?" William was silent for a few moments, clearly pondering, then his eyebrows rose, a surprised look on his face. "I'll be damned."

"William, you don't know—"

"But I do." He shook his head. "So London's most eligible bachelor isn't madly in love with a woman he can't marry, as most people believe. The truth is that he's not interested in women at all."

"I didn't say that!"

"You didn't need to." Finally, it all made sense. She hadn't turned to Colchester out of love or passion after all. "But how does this relationship benefit you? Why, in the name of God, did you leave me for a man like Colchester?"

"I won't say. I can't—" Marcail tried to pull out of William's arms.

"No," he ground out, scooping her up and carrying her to the bed. He set her on the thick coverlet and joined her, throwing one of his legs over hers to hold her in place. "Explain it to me, Marcail. Explain why you sent me away—"

"This isn't going to help anything. Nothing has changed, and—"

"I get to decide that. Now explain why you sent me away and took Colchester's protection."

"He offered me security. Assistance. A home. His protection—"

"But not his bed."

Her face heated. "No. He never offered that and, to be honest, I didn't want it. I—I cared for someone else."

There was a moment of surprised silence.

"You cared for me." The thought astounded him. All these years he'd believed she'd been fickle, loose with her promises and favors. Now he'd found out something quite different.

She nodded, her eyes bright with tears. "When you left it gave me time to think, and I realized how vulnerable I was—and how dangerous I could be to your career in the navy. You were a very possessive man, and I'm an actress—it would never have worked. *We* would never have worked.

"Though I blamed your possessiveness then, you've made me realize how little of myself I gave to our relationship. It *felt* right, but when it came down to it, we were headed for an ending. If not right then, then soon enough. I hadn't been honest, and you were too possessive—" She shook her head, her thick hair curling about her cheek. "Neither of us were mature enough for the strength of the feelings we had for one another. It would never have worked."

She was right, but that didn't make him like it. "You make our case seem desperate."

"It was. If you'd gone into a rage at the regent, your career and mine would have been over."

"And your sisters depend on you."

She nodded. "I was desperately in love with you, and sending you away was so, so, *so* hard." She closed her eyes and turned her face away. "There were times I wish we'd never met."

His heart ached at her words. William's gaze flickered over her, resting on her throat where her wet hair clung, to her skin still flushed from his touch. With her hair damp and now clinging to her cheeks and neck, she looked far younger than her twenty-seven years. Any man seeing her would think she was a lass of eighteen or so.

Knowing what she'd looked like at that age, he saw how her exotic beauty had bloomed as she'd matured. God, she was a lovely, sensual, devastatingly intelligent woman.

She hadn't been honest with him, but then, he hadn't really allowed her to be. His short temper and quick jealousy had hurt them both.

He turned her face to his and very gently kissed her lips. She opened her eyes, a tear running down her cheek. "William, I—"

He kissed her again. They'd done so many things wrong. There were so many reasons to apologize and never stop.

But right now, with the firelight flickering over the wonder of her naked body, her face tear streaked, her lips swollen from his kisses, he knew only one thing: that this moment was theirs.

And beginning with a tender kiss, he showed her all of that, and more.

A letter from Mary Hurst to her brother William, upon his missing yet another Michaelmas celebration.

It was madness to combine our family celebration with that of the MacLeans. What with Caitlyn and her brood, Triona and Hugh and his three daughters, plus the other three MacLean brothers and a sister and their families, there were so many children and governesses and tutors, I'm queasy just thinking about it.

Yet in the middle of the mayhem, it didn't feel right without having you there. Next year, please make an attempt to come. Family is the only anchor that will hold in a choppy sea.

CHAPTER 16

A rapid knock woke William abruptly. He lifted up on his elbow, seeing Marcail's dark, tousled head on the pillow beside his, her thick lashes resting on her cheeks. Despite the urgent knock on the door, he grinned as he left the bed and yanked on his breeches.

He opened the door, making certain he blocked the view into the room.

Poston stood in the hallway, his expression eager, his hat covered with morning dew. "I'm sorry to wake ye, Cap'n, but this couldn't wait. It stopped raining late last night. I sent the men to each of the local inns to look fer word of the woman."

"You found her in one of those?"

"Nay, Cap'n. I had the coach readied as well, and was checking the traces here in the inn yard when I saw the track. Right there in the mud, in front of this very inn!"

"You found tracks *here*?"

"Aye! She was here, Cap'n. I'm sure of it. The mark on that horse's hoof is distinctive."

"But we questioned everyone; no one saw her." William rubbed his chin. "Perhaps she kept herself hidden. Has anyone left this morning?"

"Several people, but no women."

"Then have the men encircle the inn. Place them on every corner, by every window. Place them by the road, too, in case we miss something."

"Yes, Cap'n."

"I'll dress and be downstairs in a moment. We'll search this place from aft to stern, and find that woman if it's the last thing we do."

Poston nodded and disappeared.

William turned to find Marcail sitting up in bed, rubbing the sleep from her eyes. "You found her?"

"She may be here in the inn somewhere. We're going to search." He crossed the room and added wood to the fire, then stirred it so the air would warm before Marcail rose. "The rain stopped last night and Poston caught sight of the track he was looking for right here in this inn yard."

She slipped out of bed and he was rewarded with

the sight of her long, slender legs as she reached for her robe. "We could recover the onyx box today." Her voice was husky from sleep, but already eager at the thought.

"Yes, we could." He poured water into the basin from the pitcher and quickly washed before gathering his clothing. "We will recover that damned box and discover who has been blackmailing you, too." He pulled on his shirt. "We won't stop until we have defanged that villain. You have my word on it."

Marcail smiled as she pulled a gown from her trunk. "You are very gallant."

"I'm practical. We've chased this woman from Southend into Scotland. I'll be damned if we leave here without having every one of our problems solved."

"That would be heavenly." She tugged on a fresh chemise, aware of a pleasant ache in her nether regions. The feeling made her smile again. Last night had been one of unalloyed passion and her entire body still tingled.

The wind suddenly banged the shutters against the outer wall, making her jump. "Just what we need; more bad weather." She slipped her gown over her head and tugged it into place. "I wish I could send those clouds away and bring us a few hours of sunshine. It would be lovely to be able to control the weather."

"No, it wouldn't." His lips twitched as he tugged on his coat and knotted his cravat, carelessly tucking it into his shirt. "I know some people who are rumored to have that ability, and it's not as pleasant as you might think."

She eyed him uncertainly. He seemed serious, but she could never tell with him. He hid his emotions as carefully as a magician guarded their tricks. "Who are these people?"

"My brothers-in-law, Hugh and Alexander MacLean."

"Ah yes! The supposed MacLean Curse." She pulled clean stockings from her trunk and rolled one up her leg. "There is a play about their family."

"Really? I haven't seen it."

"Neither have I. It's an old one; some say 'twas written by Shakespeare. It's not as well known as his other works because the play has parts for various animals. It's very difficult to find one trained animal, much less three."

"Three?"

"A dog, a horse, and a rabbit."

He flashed a smile as he yanked on his boots. "That must be some play."

"It's quite funny." She eyed William curiously. "It surprises me that you would believe in a curse."

"I don't believe in much, but I do believe in that. I've seen it work, and so have my sisters."

She laughed. "I'm not sure I'd believe it even if I saw it."

He sent her a curious glance. "So cynical, Marcail?"

She slipped her feet into half boots of soft kid leather. "I live in a world where illusions are rewarded with good, hard coins and no one is who they say they are. That would make anyone cynical."

"Perhaps. I never thought of the effect of your career on your soul."

"It's not my soul that's been in danger, but my belief in my fellow man. When you knew me before, I hadn't yet learned the cost of success."

"And what was that cost?"

"Everyone wants to be a part of your life. But not the life of the *real* you, the one that's cranky in the morning and occasionally catches a cold. They want to be a part of the 'you' they see on stage, the one with the glittering costumes and the life that's filled with imaginary adventures. The one who doesn't exist."

She shrugged. "None of those people know me, nor did they ever want to know me."

He crossed the room to sweep her up in his arms. "I know you, Marcail. The real you, not some imaginary stage version. And I—"

Outside, a cry was raised.

William cursed, then set her back on her feet and ran to the window.

She hurried to his side. "That's Poston, isn't it?"

"Yes. I must go." William turned and kissed her hard. "Stay here." And with that he was out the door, his boots loud as he ran down the stairs.

She sniffed. "Stay here? As if I could." She went to collect her cloak, her foot brushing against her gown from the day before. There was a *thunk* as a small vial attached to a gold chain spilled from the pocket.

She picked it up and started to place it on the dresser, but after a second's thought, she slipped the potion into her pocket, grabbed her cloak, and hurried after William.

As she reached the downstairs, she saw the landlord and his wife speaking with William.

"Och, we canno' allow ye to search all of our guests," Mr. MacClannahan protested. The plump man's face was red, his mouth folded with displeasure.

Bleak faced, Mrs. MacClannahan stood at her husband's side, shaking her head no over and over, as if to emphasize his words.

William stood before the two, his arms crossed over his chest, his feet planted as if he were on the deck of a ship in a gale.

"William?" Marcail asked softly.

"Poston found the horse with the marked hoof in the stables."

"Then she's here!"

He nodded. "If these dolts would let me finish searching the guests, I might be able to discover where that woman—"

"What woman?" Mrs. MacClannahan asked.

"A red-haired woman stole an object that belonged to my brother. We've been searching for it and we now know that it might well be on these premises. All we need to do is search—"

"No! Ye canno' do that," the innkeeper said in a staunch voice.

William's jaw firmed. "I wish to recover something that is mine. If your guests are innocent, they'll have no objection to showing me their belongings."

"But they will object," Mrs. MacClannahan said, looking harassed. "Both the nice gentleman from Portsmouth and that Frenchman are already angry that you searched them."

"The 'nice gentleman from Portsmouth' had two of your candlesticks in his bag."

"Aye, and I thanked ye fer returnin' them," Mr. MacClannahan said, blustering and mad. "But I'll no' have ye searching every guest on the premises. The Pelican has a reputation fer bein' a welcomin' place, and I'll no' have it said that we're not."

Marcail noticed that the two old ladies from the night before were peering out of the common room, agog with interest.

Emma wiggled her fingers at Marcail and winked.

"And now, because o' ye," Mrs. MacClannahan said, "we've two gentlemen—"

"One is a thief."

"One gentleman, then," she amended with obvious reluctance, "who is leaving us fer another establishment."

"Aye," Mr. MacClannahan said. "We're losin' two payin' customers because o' yer search."

"And the Frenchman had planned on staying another week or more," Mrs. MacClannahan added, her stance more militant. "When he heard ye wished to search everyone, he yelled something about his rights and stormed out, calling for his horse, vowing not to stay another minute."

As if on cue, from outside came the sound of a very angry Frenchman, his reedy voice pinched with disapproval, though his words were indistinguishable from this distance. Following the outburst was the sound of Poston's soothing reply.

William didn't appear in the least sorry. "I will compensate you for any income you lose, but I cannot allow anyone to leave without searching their bags."

Mrs. MacClannahan plopped her fists on her hips. "But we can't have this and—"

"Perhaps I can assist." Marcail sent William a smile. "Why don't you help Poston while I sort this out? It sounds as if the French brigade might be called if you don't."

He hesitated, but at the growing discord from outside, said, "Thank you. I will honor whatever arrangements you make." He bowed to the innkeepers and left.

Mrs. MacClannahan crossed her arms over her scrawny bosom. "As fer ye, miss, ye told me a falsehood last night. Ye said ye were looking fer yer cousin."

"I didn't wish to upset you that the thief might be among your guests."

"Hmmph. I dinna believe ye."

Marcail had opened her mouth to answer when Emma stepped into the hall. Her spectacles rested slightly askance, and she had apparently dressed in the dark, for she wore a purple gown with a horrible green shawl printed with large blue and red flowers. "Miss MacClannahan," she said, her voice piercing, "my sister and I have been waiting on breakfast for an *hour*. Do we have to march into the kitchen and fetch it ourselves? We're willing to do so, although Lady Loughton's knee is quite sore from falling in *your* entryway."

"Och!" Mrs. MacClannahan's cheeks reddened. "I forgot to fetch yer breakfasts. I'll do so right away, I will."

"Thank you." Emma waited until the innkeeper's wife was gone before she sent a secret wink to Marcail.

"Mr. MacClannahan!" Jane called, wobbling out to the hallway leaning on a cane. Her neat gown was a contrast to Emma's mismatched shawl and skirts. "Do come and add some wood to this fire. It's so cold that I can see my own breath."

"Ye canno' see yer own breath," he protested. "It's no' that cold outside, even."

She lifted her eyebrows and said in a chilling tone, "My good sir, are you calling me a liar?"

"No, no, I jus—" He clamped his mouth together and then said, "I'll be right there." He looked at Marcail. "We're no' done wit' this yet."

"I shall await you right here while you do what you must."

He went into the common room to fix the fire. She heard him grumbling about how the room was warm enough without the added wood, and Jane's sharp retort that when he was her age, he'd understand what cold bones were, but until then she'd thank him to stop complaining and do his job.

Marcail had to bite her lip to keep from giggling aloud. As soon as the innkeeper finished adding the wood, Marcail heard Jane demand that he fetch her shawl from her room so she wouldn't freeze while the newly stirred fire heated the "icy" room. "For you know as well as I that it will take *hours* for the room to warm."

There was no gainsaying such a preemptory command, so Mr. MacClannahan lumbered through the entryway and then took the stairs, grumbling the entire way.

As soon as he was out of sight, Marcail whisked herself into the common room. "Thank you both for your assistance."

Jane's sharp blue gaze glinted. "It seemed as if you were in a bit of a fix."

"Oh, I was."

Emma adjusted her spectacles, leaving them more crooked than before. "I thought you said the red-haired woman was your cousin."

"Yes, but she's not. She's a thief and she stole something."

"Of yours?" Jane asked.

"No. It belonged to Captain Hurst."

Emma clasped her hands together. "I should have *known* he was a captain!"

"As should I," Jane agreed, both of them looking pleased.

"Why?"

"From the way he stood," Jane said. "As if on a ship's deck."

"And he barks orders like a real man," Emma added. "He's very handsome, too."

Jane nodded. "All ships' captains are. We should know, for we're descendants of a captain ourselves."

"I owe you both my deepest gratitude," Marcail said.

"Never fear," Emma said, smiling brightly. "We'll keep Mr. and Mrs. MacClannahan busy for a while longer."

"Yes," agreed Jane. "Mr. MacClannahan will be gone a good ten minutes fetching that shawl, for the one I described to him is here." She lifted the small blanket she'd tossed over her lap and revealed a red-and-gold brocade shawl. She replaced the blanket, her eyes twinkling. "When he doesn't find it in my room, he'll think to appease me and just fetch a different one. But I won't be appeased."

"Jane is very good at not being appeased," Emma added earnestly.

Marcail chuckled. "Thank you both for your assistance. But why are you doing this for me? You've been so kind, yet we just met."

"You remind us of our niece," Emma said.

"Besides, we were talking the other day about how we don't have enough adventures," Jane added. "It's obvious to us that you're on an adventure now—a big one, judging by your search for a mysterious red-haired woman and being accompanied by such a handsome sea captain. That's a very good adventure."

"Very good," Emma agreed. "It could be in a book."

"So we're borrowing a little bit of your adventure so that we can call it ours, too."

"You are more than welcome to join my adventure, but hopefully it will come to an end very soon."

The Frenchman's thin voice could no longer be heard, so Marcail went to the window to see how William had fared. Poston was just stepping back from several men, one of them the Frenchman. He was tall and angular, his expression one of sneering pride. He wore thick face paint and had a black chapeau pinned to his tightly curled black hair.

Emma came to stand beside Marcail. "I hate to say it, but that Frenchman is a royal pain the arse. This morning he wanted more of this and more of that, and didn't like his tea that hot or his water that cold. Such a commotion!"

"Some people just want to be the center of attention," Marcail said absently, watching Poston argue with a footman.

"Lud, yes. That Frenchman was most rude to the help, too. It was almost as if he *wanted* people to pay attention to him," Jane added.

Marcail watched as the Frenchman stood stiffly while Poston searched his bags. Odd, how some people courted even bad attention, as if—

She frowned and leaned forward. The Frenchman had turned his head to say something to one of his men, and his profile itched something in the back of her mind.

On an impulse, she leaned forward and unlatched the window, letting in the voices of the men in the inn yard.

The Frenchman said something to one of his men, his voice loud and clear, and Marcail whirled and ran toward the door.

"Where are you going?" Emma asked, blinking. "What—"

"That's no Frenchman!" Marcail called as she ran out the door.

A letter from William Hurst to his brother Michael as he prepared for his first expedition.

I'm very happy that you're following your dreams. I've discovered that they are fragile things and must be fed if they are to live long enough to turn into reality. There are only two things that will feed a dream: action and honesty. If you are honest enough to face your dream, with all its limitations, and willing to take whatever action is necessary to make up for those limitations, then there is a good chance you will be one of the few to succeed.

CHAPTER 17

William crossed his arms and looked at the woman seated before him. "Miss Challoner, I believe?"

She pressed her lips together and refused to say a word.

When Marcail had come running out of the inn, yelling, "She isn't French!" and pointing at "Monsieur L'Roche," he had sent a shocked gaze at the "Frenchman"—just as she'd whipped a pistol from beneath her coat and pointed it straight at him.

He'd been caught completely off guard. Had it not been for Marcail's quick thinking in grabbing up a loose cobblestone and throwing it at Miss

Challoner, the end of their adventure could have been quite different. But Marcail's aim had been true; the stone had hit the woman's wrist, making her drop her pistol, which had harmlessly gone off when it hit the ground.

All mayhem had broken loose then, for the "Frenchman" wasn't traveling with only one servant, but with all ten of the men Poston had been searching in the courtyard.

It had been a grand fight. Poston was nursing a split lip and a black eye, while William's cheek was bruised and one knuckle was bleeding from having nicked it on someone's tooth. Several of the footmen were nursing sore heads, but they'd all given better than they'd gotten.

Now it was time for some answers.

Miss Challoner languidly crossed one velvet-clad leg over the other, but her eyes snapped green fire. "You may ask me all you wish, but I'm not answering you." Her gaze flickered toward the window and then back.

William caught the quicksilver movement. "If you're thinking of making a run for it, I would suggest that you don't." He nodded toward Marcail, who lifted her pistol threateningly.

They were sitting in the small parlor, the door locked with Marcail sitting beside it.

William had to hold back his grin. He was so

proud of her. Was there nothing she couldn't do? It would be worth it to take the time and find out.

He reluctantly returned his gaze to their prisoner. For now he had other things to see to; regaining possession of the onyx box and discovering who had been so ruthlessly blackmailing Marcail. "Miss Challoner, I would hate to hurt you, but if you run—" He shrugged.

"I wouldn't mind hurting you," Marcail said, "so please feel free to make a dash for it. The door to your right is rather close."

Miss Challoner shot an angry glance at Marcail, but remained in her seat. "I have no choice, do I?" Her voice lilted with a faint Scottish accent.

"No, you don't," William said.

She crossed her arms over her chest and leaned back in the chair. "Would you mind if I take off this wig? It itches."

He shrugged.

She reached for the wig.

Marcail cocked the pistol, the noise loud in the quiet room.

Miss Challoner paused. "I'm not going to pull any tricks; my head really does itch. I would think you know how wigs are."

"I also know how untrustworthy *you* are. If you make a sudden move of any kind, I'll shoot you."

Miss Challoner glared, but removed the black

wig to reveal deep red braids entwined about her head like a crown. She tossed the wig to one side. "So . . . how did you find me?"

It was odd, but even dressed in her masculine attire, the woman was seductively feminine. *Why didn't I see that?* William wondered. "You are very cleverly disguised."

"It served me well in the past, but today . . ." Her gaze flickered toward Marcail. "What gave me away?"

"Your accent," Marcail said. "It's not very French." She shrugged. "French farces are quite popular for the afternoon shows and are often performed by authentic French troupes. I heard your voice and knew instantly that you were many things, but French wasn't one of them."

Miss Challoner nodded thoughtfully. "I'll have to work on that."

"Right now," William said, "you're going to work on telling us where the onyx box is, and who you are delivering it to."

"I suppose I would be wasting time if I pretend I don't know what you're talking about."

"It's over." He crossed his arms over his chest. "Where is the box?"

Her gaze once again flickered past him to the door.

"No one is coming to rescue you; all of your

minions have been disposed of. It's time you told the truth."

She sighed. "I suppose you're right." Her gaze ran over him. "You look like your brother."

William frowned. He certainly hadn't expected that. "Which brother?"

"Robert."

Her gaze dropped to her clasped hands, but not before William caught a light in her eyes. *Oh ho. Is that how it is?* "How do you know Robert?"

She shrugged, the movement elegant and assured. "Our paths have crossed."

William took off his greatcoat and hung it over a chair. "I see." He wasn't sure he did, but when he next saw Robert, he'd make sure he did. "So, Miss Challoner—I believe that's your real name?"

"For now."

Marcail snorted her disbelief, which made William bite his lip. "Well, Miss Challoner, I believe you have something that belongs to me. I will have it now."

"I don't have it. In fact, I'm sorry to say that I already delivered it."

"To whom?" Marcail asked.

William could hear the stress in her husky voice. He caught her gaze and gave her a reassuring wink, and a faint smile curved her lips.

When William turned his gaze back to their prisoner she gave him a smug smile. "Very sweet."

"The box, please."

"You are wasting your time and mine; I'm not telling you anything."

His gaze narrowed. "Things will go easier for you if you cooperate. You are in a lot of trouble. Not only did you steal something—"

"Something that had already been stolen. Will you mention that to the constable?" Her gaze narrowed on Marcail. "Or will I?"

William smoothly interjected, "I have no idea what you're talking about. No one stole anything from me. I gave it to Marcail when she told me she was being blackmailed."

Marcail sent him an astonished glance, then a pleased smile.

"I see you've made your peace," Miss Challoner said.

"That's none of your concern. Who sent you to fetch the box?"

She laughed. "I would be a fool to blurt out all of my secrets. As would you."

Please let me shoot her," Marcail said.

William had to laugh.

"This woman has made my life hell for the last year. I deserve at least one shot."

A flicker of uncertainty crossed their prisoner's face. *So you're not immune to fear, are you?*

William pretended to consider Marcail's request. "I wouldn't want her killed. That would be difficult to explain."

"What if I only shoot her foot? I'm sure I can hit it from here."

The woman whipped around. "Have you *ever* shot a pistol?"

"No." Marcail lifted the muzzle in the general direction of their prisoner's feet. "But it doesn't seem all that difficult. I might hit your leg instead of your foot, but that wouldn't bother me."

The woman's gaze went from the pistol to Marcail. "I don't blame you for being angry. It's been very difficult for me, as well." She leaned forward, her gaze locked with Marcail's. "I haven't had a choice in this, either. I only did what I had to do. Surely you, who've been on your own as long as I have, understand that."

Marcail found that she couldn't disagree. She *did* know what that was like. She lowered the gun the slightest bit. "Be that as it may, I cannot pretend that you're an innocent in all of this. You've stolen thousands of pounds from me, destroyed my peace, caused me untold hours of lost sleep, and now you're not going to blame me if I am angry? How generous of you."

William crossed his arms. "Miss Challoner, if I

were you, I'd tell everything I knew. As you can see, there is very little keeping Miss Beauchamp in her chair."

Miss Challoner's jaw tightened. "I suppose it doesn't matter. I didn't wish to be involved in this from the beginning, but I was being blackmailed as well."

"By whom?" William asked.

"By the same person who is blackmailing Miss Beauchamp."

"What for?"

Miss Challoner's mouth thinned. "I'm not saying."

Marcail stood. "Would you like to select a toe for me to aim for or should I try for the biggest one?"

"I cannot expose the man or he'll—" Miss Challoner's eyes widened as Marcail advanced.

The pistol lowered to Miss Challoner's foot. "Well?" Marcail asked softly. "Is he worth a toe? or perhaps two?"

"I suppose it won't matter, as you're bound to discover it for yourself sooner or later. His name is Aniston," Miss Challoner said in a rush. "George Aniston. He is the cousin of the Duke of Albany and—"

"*What?*" Marcail gasped.

"You know him?" William asked.

"He is Colchester's . . . They are friends. Aniston has been bleeding Colchester dry, and I've done what I could to separate them. I suppose he resented it and so he began to blackmail me." Marcail looked at Miss Challoner. "What are you being blackmailed for?"

She shook her head. "I won't say."

"You'll say that and much more," William said grimly. He took the pistol from Marcail. "Allow me."

"Of course." Marcail took the chair across from their prisoner, eying her thoughtfully. "It isn't pleasant to be blackmailed. How did you fall into Aniston's clutches?"

"I invited him to my house, thinking he might know something of interest I was attempting to find out. Instead, he took the opportunity to go through my things. He took something he shouldn't have; something I must have back at all costs." The woman's expression was stark, and Marcail recognized the deep fear.

She leaned forward. "What did he take that's so valuable to you?"

For a moment, Miss Challoner's expression softened and Marcail thought she might hear the truth, but then the woman shrugged and said, "Aniston is waiting for me in Edinburgh. Once he has the onyx box, he will return my property."

"Do you really think he would have honored that agreement, even if you did return with the onyx box?" Marcail asked gently.

"He must. He keeps saying he will rel—" Miss

Challoner closed her eyes for a moment, finally saying in a weary tone, "Fine. I have your damned box. Aniston has promised to return my—the item to me in exchange. Of course, every time I complete a task, he says there's one more thing to be done."

"Can you go to the Bow Street Runners or—"

"No."

Marcail sighed, feeling more and more sorry for the woman as the minutes passed. She could see that Miss Challoner really was afraid of Aniston. *What sort of a monster is he?*

William spoke from where he stood by the door. "And what will happen if you go to Edinburgh and don't have the box?"

Miss Challoner's shoulders straightened. "I don't know, but he had better not—" Her eyes blazed and Marcail almost shivered at the hard light. Miss Challoner fixed her gaze on William. "All I know is that the second Aniston has returned my possession, I shall enact my revenge—and it will not be pleasant."

A brisk knock sounded on the door and William unlocked it.

Poston stood in the doorway, a small velvet bag in his hand. "I found it, Cap'n! It was sewn into the saddlebag of the horse with the cut hoof. I wonder if perhaps that's why the track was so distinct." He glanced inquiringly at Miss Challoner, seemingly unsurprised to find that the Frenchman had vibrant red hair and was obviously not a man.

Miss Challoner sighed. "We marked the horse's hooves in case it was stolen or ran from us, so we could find it if we had to. Did you use that to track us?"

He nodded. "That's why we were searching everyone from the inn."

William took the case and handed the loaded pistol to Poston. "Guard our prisoner a moment, will you? Miss Beauchamp and I must make arrangements for our return to London."

"What about me?" Miss Challoner asked.

"We will take you with us, and once we arrive in London, you will be sent to the constable. He will decide what to do with you there."

She turned her head to stare out of the window.

William and Marcail crossed the entryway and went into the common room, glad to see that it was empty.

William placed the velvet bag on the long table and removed the onyx box. It caught the late afternoon sun, shimmering as if glad to be free of its dark prison. "Finally."

"It's beautiful." Marcail shook her head. "It's difficult to believe such a simple object could cause so much trouble."

"I know." He looked at her. "So what will you do about Aniston?"

"I shall tell Colchester and Aniston will be so discredited that no one will believe anything he says about me."

"I don't think this was about money at all, but about control. Aniston wished me gone, and this was as good a way as any."

"He would slowly steal your funds—"

"And leave me nervous and alone, worried about the servants and the other people around me—" She hesitated, then added, "I've lately begun to realize that Colchester and I don't have a true friendship. He's . . . he's using me and I'm using him."

In that instant, she seemed so alone that William's heart ached for her. "Marcail, I—"

A voice sounded from the entryway, deep and cultured, with a faint petulant tone to it.

"I know that voice." William went to the door and looked around the corner. "Bloody hell, what are you doing here?"

Robert was removing his greatcoat, turning up his nose at the pegs available to hang it on.

He didn't seem the least surprised to see William, merely saying in a cool voice, "Surely there's a better place to hang a coat than this. It will stretch the collar."

"Bring your damned coat in here. You can spread it on the settee, if you wish."

Robert sighed. "That will do, I suppose." He

followed William into the room, pausing when he caught sight of Marcail. He bowed elegantly. "Miss Beauchamp! Pleased to meet you."

William flicked a hand toward his brother. "My brother Robert. I don't recall if you've met."

"Not until now." She dipped a curtsy. "If you two will excuse me, I should pack and have our trunks brought down."

William watched as she left the room.

Robert waited until she was gone before he flicked a glance at his brother. "She is even more lovely up close. I don't find that the case with most actresses."

William turned back to his brother, noticing the lace cuffs that spilled from Robert's coat sleeves. Good lord, what a dandy. "What are you doing here?"

"I've been chasing you since you left London. I found something that I thought might interest you. It's—" His gaze fell on the onyx box. "Ah. You have the artifact. I feared it might be in the possession of—" Robert's expression closed. "It doesn't matter. I'm just glad you have it back." He reached into his pocket and pulled out something wrapped in red flannel. He unwrapped the object and placed it on the table near the onyx box. "Behold, a match for the first."

William frowned. "There are two boxes?"

"So far."

"Where did you get that?"

"From the private residence of a young lady named Moira McAllen. At least, that was the name she was using at her residence in Edinburgh. She has others."

"Other residences?"

"Yes, and other names, as well. She is a lovely redhead who—"

"Bloody hell. She is the one we were chasing all along. She's a tricky, conniving thief."

"You have no idea," Robert said softly.

William gestured toward the boxes. "One must be a fake."

"No. They are both original." Robert picked up one box and flicked it open, then did the same to the other. With a smooth twist, he undid two more hinges in each until they lay flat upon the table. Then, with a simple nudge, he pushed them together. A soft *click* sounded.

William leaned over. "They connect."

"And make a map."

"Bloody hell! It's . . . Robert, is that a treasure map?"

"Yes. I think that's why so many people have wished to obtain Michael's artifact." Robert traced a thin line. "This is a river of some sort; I'm sure of it by the way it meanders. And these—" He touched a group of upside down V's. "These are mountains, and these—" He ran his thumb over a group of boxes in one corner. "I think these represent a city. All that's missing is the third piece."

"Good God." William looked at the map. "There are three boxes, then."

"Yes. See these markings here? Three lines with a dot between each? That means there are three pieces and that they connect."

"Hmm. I wonder what our prisoner will say to that?"

Robert looked up sharply. "Prisoner? You mean . . . she's still here?"

"Yes. Poston is watching her in the other room."

"Damn it, William, you can't leave him alone with her!" Robert scooped up the onyx boxes and slid them into his coat pocket.

"Poston won't hurt her," William said stiffly.

"*She* might hurt *him*."

"He is armed."

Robert relaxed somewhat. "That's something, at least. Are you certain he's well trained?"

"He was with Wellington on the peninsula."

Robert sighed. "Good. I wouldn't leave her with a novice for a second. She's a master at escaping."

"You said you found this box in the house of this Miss McAllen? How did you know it would be there?"

"I didn't, at first. When I saw the drawing Mary had done, I knew I'd seen the box before. It took me a while to realize where. It was in a collection belonging to a researcher at Edinburgh. I ran into him while there two months ago and he showed me all of his recent finds. He didn't really focus on the box, for as artifacts go it's not really spectacular, but something about it stayed with me. Once I remembered where I'd seen it, I raced to purchase it, but it had already been stolen."

"Let me guess. By a tall redhead."

"Exactly. The researcher was quite besotted, but I knew instantly who it was and I went to her lodgings—"

"You knew where she lived?"

Robert's gaze flickered. "I knew whom to ask. Suffice it to say that I found her residence and repossessed the box."

"Repossessed, eh?" At his brother's bland look, William sighed. "Fine. Don't tell me. Robert, what the hell do you know about this woman?"

Robert's expression shuttered. "Not much. But she'll talk. I'll make certain of that."

"She seems to know you."

"She does—unfortunately for me."

"How well does she know you?"

Robert fidgeted with his cuff.

"Robert?"

He sighed. "I dislike admitting I was a fool. I don't know why it matters, but—" He shrugged. "At one time, Moira and I were married."

William blinked. "I beg your pardon, but—" He shook his head. "I could have sworn you said you were *married*."

Robert gave him a flat stare. "It was a trick. A dirty trick. Years ago, when I first came to London, I was an attaché to the Home Office, as you remember. I met her there and— Well, she is beautiful. You can't deny that."

"No, I can't."

Robert shrugged. "One thing led to another, and I thought myself madly in love. So one night, we were at a masquerade ball and there was a man dressed as a clergyman—I vow that I did not know the man was real. That the license he had in his pocket was the actual thing. That—" Robert's look was black. "I was enamored of her, though I knew her to be a woman of low morals. The silly ceremony seemed to assure that our relationship would progress further."

"You were thinking with your cock."

"True. The little head is always so impulsive, isn't it?"

William sighed. "Yes, it is. But what about the banns?"

"Exactly," Robert said darkly. "Without posting

banns, then the ceremony, even if performed by a clergyman and with my signature on the license, would be false. But someone had indeed posted the banns; I just didn't know it."

William shook his head. "You said you were married to her at one time. So you found a way out of it and aren't married now?"

Robert hesitated. "Technically, we are married, but I don't recognize it."

"I assume a court of law would, though."

"Perhaps. But if they knew of her black heart—" Robert's brow lowered. "She tricked me to discredit me with the Home Office. They almost let me go upon hearing that I'd wed a counteragent."

"*Counteragent?*"

"Yes, the lovely Miss McAllen's family has been very friendly with some of England's greatest enemies. She was once an agent for Bonaparte. They say Bonny himself was madly in love with her, but she would have none of him, so he sent her here, to perform his duties on English soil."

"Why hasn't she been arrested?"

"Who says she hasn't been? And then escaped. Which is why I'm surprised she's still here."

William shook his head. "What a coil."

"There is more to it. She blames me for her arrest, and rightly so. I found evidence of her position—there was no escaping the truth. After she trapped me into marriage, the only way I could win back the trust of the Home Office was to offer her up on a platter." Robert's expression hardened. "Which I did with great delight."

"You know what Father says about vengeance."

"That it's a bitter dish that bites the server as well as the taster."

"Exactly." William eyed his brother. "So what will you do now?"

"I don't know, but I think the lovely Moira knows the location of the third box."

"And Michael?"

"Hopefully he will be free by the time I find the last box. I have an idea about that. Take these boxes to our soon-to-be brother-in-law."

"The Earl of Erroll? What's he have to do with anything?"

"His cousin is reputed to be something of an expert in producing copies of antiquities."

"But that man stole from Erroll."

"Yes, but our tenderhearted sister has arranged for her soon-to-be husband to reconcile with his cousin, so we should have full access to his useful services."

"Very well. I'll do that as soon as I reach London. Once I have the copy, I'll set sail and win Michael's release."

"Excellent. Michael will be very interested in this

map. In fact, once he knows of it, I don't believe he'd want us to trade the boxes for his release."

"I just don't wish him hurt."

"Hurt? His biggest complaint is that he is bored and his assistant has poured out all of his bourbon." Robert shrugged. "Besides, he's—"

A gunshot sounded, followed by the tinkling of broken glass.

Robert was out the door in a trice, William hard on his heels as they yanked open the parlor door.

Poston was seated on the floor holding his arm, blood seeping between his fingers. One of the large front windows was shattered and there was no sign of Miss McAllen.

"What happened?" William demanded as Robert ran to the window and looked out.

"Damn it," Robert swore. "There she goes." They could hear hoofbeats on the cobblestones. "I must go. Take these."

He reached into his pocket, then thrust the two onyx boxes at William. "Guard them carefully. I will contact you."

"I'll guard them with my life, but—"

Marcail hurried into the room, her eyes wide. "What happened?"

"Our captive escaped," William said grimly.

"How?"

Robert scowled. "She has the most damnable

way of making whoever guards her fall in love with her."

Marcail glanced at Poston, who turned a furious red. "She was jus' tellin' me about her family in Wiltshire. Did ye know she came from the same village as I did? In all me years, I've met only one other person from—" The groom blinked as Robert sighed and looked at the ceiling. "She's not from Wiltshire?"

"No, you fool. I doubt she's even been there." Robert swept a bow. "Good-bye. I must fetch her before she wreaks more havoc."

"Wait!" Marcail pulled a vial out of her pocket. "Here, it's a potion of some sort. I've been told that it will keep a person incapacitated for some time. It may also make them think that they're—" She blushed. "Use it sparingly, for I suspect it's very strong. It may help you bring her to London, since she's so difficult to hold prisoner."

Robert took the vial. "Thank you. That could be a great help. William, I will write."

And with that, he was gone. A moment later, the sound of horse's hooves dashing through the courtyard once again filled the crisp spring air.

William helped the groom into a chair. "You should never have let your guard down. I warned you when I left you here."

"I know," the groom said miserably. "She was just so bewitching, Cap'n. Such a loverly woman."

There was a flurry of noise in the entryway and then Emma and Jane stuck their heads in the door, followed shortly by an angry Mrs. MacClannahan who, upon seeing one of her good windows broken to bits, promptly threw herself upon the floor and had a fit.

It took all of Marcail's skill to smooth things over.

An hour later, after enough money had been placed in Mr. MacClannahan's hand to make him all smiles, William gathered up Marcail, said good-bye to the kind old ladies who were still patting Mrs. MacClannahan's hand, installed the bandaged Poston on the coach, and took his entire retinue back on the road to the relative sanity of London.

A letter from Mary Hurst to her brother Michael, on a cold spring evening.

Between William's moping about as if his heart is broken and Robert's secretive behavior, I worry about the Hurst men. They seem to fall in love with the most inappropriate women, and never with the joy one would wish. It would quite put me off the thought of falling in love if I weren't firmly of the opinion that they were both doing it very badly. I trust that you will do better when—and if—you fall in love.

CHAPTER 18

*W*illiam barely waited for the coach door to close before he reached for Marcail. With a huge sigh, he pulled her onto his lap, wrapped his arms about her, and rested his forehead against hers.

Marcail snuggled close. "It's been a difficult morning."

He chuckled, the sound rumbling against her shoulder. "You, my love, have the gift of understatement."

She flattened her hand on his chest. She could feel every breath he drew. Deep and strong, his chest's movement was comforting and steady.

As a young girl, she'd been so driven to succeed in her career and to protect her family, she hadn't appreciated William's steadfastness, his commitment to his family, his trustworthiness.

She wished she could take back the past and start anew, but who didn't wish that for a lost love? The real question was, would it really change anything?

He rubbed his bruised cheek.

"Does it hurt?" she asked.

"A little."

She softly kissed the spot.

He glinted her a smile. "You are very good at taking care of people—your family and even Colchester."

"I did what I had to. I'm certain my sisters would have done the same for me had they been older."

"Your parents are fools."

"They are proud. I've been told it's a family trait."

"There's pride, and then there's prideful. I would never call you prideful."

"We were both too proud for our own good." She toyed with his collar, and he could see she was mulling something over. Finally, she said, "My father says I'm not respectable enough for my sisters' company and he has demanded that I not see them." She grinned unrepentantly. "I do anyway, of course. My father lost the right to tell me what to do when he stopped making responsible decisions for our family."

She spoke as if it hadn't caused her pain, but

William knew better. He couldn't imagine life without his family. His sisters wrote regularly, visited when they could, and spared no energy in trying to organize his life. His brothers shared their dreams and hopes, and expected the same of him. Despite the different directions life had taken them in, they all maintained contact.

Marcail had been left alone.

"Let me get this straight," he said. "You've saved the family house, their lands, their fortune, and your father says you're 'not fit' to visit?"

"I have my grandmother, of course."

One person. The thought nearly broke his heart. She'd sent him away years ago and he'd gone, smoldering and nursing his own wounds without giving any thought to hers.

She smoothed his collar back into place. "Our parents serve one of two purposes in our lives: either they are examples for us to strive toward, or warnings of what we should strive against."

"Well said."

"I've done a lot of thinking about it." She brushed her hair from her forehead, her movements graceful and calm. It was odd. As much as she inflamed him—and he was as randy as a youngster with his first barmaid even now—she also made him feel more . . . peaceful. As if all was right with the world when she was close by.

The thought was ridiculous, but it made him realize her special qualities—something her own parents didn't value as they should, damn them both. "It's amazing you're not bitter about your parents."

"I was angry when I realized Father wasn't going to relent, but I've come to realize that it's for the best. I want my sisters to take their place in society, and that means that they must renounce me publicly. In a way, it was part of the plan."

"I can't believe your mother allowed your father to become such a despot."

"She is cowed by him. I don't know why, for he's not a violent man." A flicker of darkness crossed her eyes. "I believe she fears he'll leave her, which doesn't sound like a horrible fate to me, but perhaps it seems a horrible fate to her. Sometimes relationships can fall into habits and hers is to stay with him no matter what."

"I suppose change can be difficult for some people." He rested his chin on her forehead. "What about you, Marcail? Do you fear change?"

She lifted her head to look up at him. "What sort of change?"

William found that he couldn't speak. Until that moment, he hadn't really thought of what he was going to say, but now, looking into her violet eyes, the words lined up on his tongue, ready to be said for the first time ever. He knew what he wanted. "I'm talking about significant change. About opening your life and allowing someone— me—to enter."

Her eyes widened. "I—I'm not sure what you mean—"

He lifted her hand and kissed it. "Marcail Beauchamp, darling of Drury Lane, unappreciated daughter, passionate lover, and the woman who holds my heart in her hand—will you do me the honor of giving me your hand in marriage?"

"You're . . . you're serious?"

"Totally."

"But . . . I'm an actress."

"And I'm a sea captain. Marcail, we're no longer the children we once were. Neither of us answers to anyone else. It's time we take life by the horns and make it ours."

"I don't want to leave the stage."

"Then don't. I promise not to beat up any of your admirers, even the king, should he be so foolish. But I reserve the right to stand outside your dressing room and look fierce. Furthermore I won't allow my actions to harm you or your career. I'm not that selfish anymore."

Marcail's lips quivered, and tears filled her eyes.

She was filled with a happiness so great that it defied description. "You'll still sail?"

"Yes, but I'll only accept short journeys. I may even buy two or three ships and invest in some ventures."

"I don't wish you to stop doing anything you'll miss—"

"I won't."

"And I don't wish you to feel as if you have to live in London all of the time. I know you enjoy visiting your family at Wythburn and we'll want to go there frequently, which is fine with me."

"If I am overcome with the desire to visit my family, I will do so."

She bit her lip. "Neither one of us owns a house, either. That could be an expense and—"

"For the love of heaven, Marcail, will you stop trying to find reasons to say no?" He captured her face between his warm hands. "Say yes, my love. Say yes to sharing your life, your cares. Say yes to accepting that I love you, and will do everything I can to make our lives better." He dropped his forehead to hers, his voice deepening with an almost desperate plea. "Please, Marcail—say yes to *me.*"

Then she knew in her heart that there was only one answer. Things wouldn't always be easy with her strong-willed, bossy sea captain, but she knew from their adventure that he wasn't one to quit. When the storms came they'd both be ready, and with the lessons they'd learned along the way, they'd weather the storms together. Hand in hand.

And that was how it should be.

She twined her arms about his neck. "Yes."

And they sealed their promise with a kiss.

Letter from the Earl of Erroll to his cousin, Neason Hay.

I received your package yesterday and I must thank you for the excellent facsimiles of those damned onyx boxes that have Mary's family in such an uproar. The facsimiles are so perfectly made that if they had the maps engraved on the inside like the originals, I wouldn't have been able to tell the difference.

Neason, I can't thank you enough for this assistance, and I once more make my plea that you return to New Slains Castle. During the years you spent here, especially those after the death of my first wife, I came to regard you as a brother.

I know you've made some mistakes, but we all have. Living with Mary has shown me how important family is and, come what may, you are my family.

When you receive this letter, pray make haste to New Slains. I should be returning from London within the week and nothing would make me happier than to have you once again residing under our family roof.

$\mathcal{E}$PILOGUE

$\mathcal{A}$s the theater curtain fell closed, the crowd flew to their feet as one. They whistled and stamped, yelled and shouted, and rained coins and flowers upon the stage.

The reaction from the boxes was equally enthusiastic, though more muted. In the largest box to stage left, Mary Hurst wiped her tears and then turned to her brother. "William, she is magnificent."

"Yes, she is." He knew that his grin was probably so wide as to appear ridiculous, but he didn't care. Marcail was now his, and nothing else mattered. They'd wed two days prior in a private ceremony in her grandmamma's garden, attended by

Marcail's four sisters and all of his siblings. Neither of Marcail's parents had come, but both of William's had—a surprise that had made Marcail burst into tears of joy.

Nothing could have cemented her relationship with his family more, and William had felt like a giddy schoolboy ever since.

Tonight was Marcail's final performance for the season, before the theater changed their headline performance to an Italian opera. To William's delight, his bride had almost two free months ahead.

The Earl of Erroll came to stand beside Mary. "I've never seen Lady MacBeth better played. Will Marcail continue to act, now that you're married?"

"Yes, for as long as she wishes." He stood to go. "I must leave. We set sail on the morning tide to win Michael's release." He shook Erroll's hand. "Your cousin did well with the substitutions; they are very well made."

Erroll looked pleased. He and his cousin had had a falling out several months before. William didn't know all of the details, but had gleaned that Neason had been stealing some of the lesser artifacts and selling them on the black market.

"Neason is a good man," Erroll said now. "Just weak."

Mary nodded. "He is to return to New Slains Castle and live with us, as he should." She shot her fiancé an arch look. "We have very big plans for him, don't we?"

"Very. Once Robert returns to London, he's promised to take Neason under his wing and teach him how to successfully—and legitimately—sell the artifacts we don't wish to keep."

William nodded his approval. "That's an excellent idea."

"Have you heard from Robert?" Mary asked.

"Not a word. He must still be on the trail of his elusive redhead."

"Do you think he'll find her?"

"He won't quit until he does. He believes she holds the final piece to our treasure map."

"In the meantime, I suppose all we can do is wait," Mary said in a disgruntled tone. "There are aspects of this affair that have not ended up to my liking." She scowled. "And George Aniston is one of them."

Some of William's happiness faded. Marcail had been right saying that Colchester would set Aniston aside when his dastardly actions were known. William had been determined to have the bastard locked away, but after talking to his solicitor, he realized there was no way to bring charges against

Aniston without dragging Marcail's name through the mud.

William had decided that he'd administer his own form of punishment, but before he could do so, Aniston had packed his belongings and left town. No one knew where the man had gone.

Mary placed her hand on William's arm. "Aniston will get his just desserts. Fate always cleans up her messes. Now go and collect Marcail. I have no doubt she's being mobbed outside her dressing room."

William turned toward the door.

"And William? Promise you'll bring Michael home."

"Of course. Along with the redoubtable Miss Smythe-Haughton. I am most curious about her."

"She sounds like a veritable dragon," Mary said.

"Which makes one wonder." Erroll exchanged an amused look with William.

"Exactly." William left and quickly made his way to the dressing rooms, where Marcail stood surrounded by admirers, looking elegantly beautiful in a white robe.

He watched from the doorway for a while, noting that her expression, though smiling, was cool and distant.

He moved closer, and her eyes found his. A huge smile bloomed over her face and lit her violet eyes, and William needed no more encouragement. He slipped an arm about her waist and gently closed her dressing room door on the crowd.

Once there, with a chair wedged firmly under the doorknob, William tenderly and with great enthusiasm let Mercail know exactly what he thought of her performance by providing her with one of his very own.

Meet the irresistible Hurst sisters!

Sensible Catriona Hurst from
Sleepless in Scotland in the MacLean Curse series,
where it all began

Her lovely twin sister, Caitlin Hurst, from
The Laird Who Loved Me
also in the MacLean Curse series

Fearless Mary Hurst from
One Night in Scotland,
the first Hurst Amulet novel

And in October 2011, look forward to meeting
dashing Robert Hurst in *Seduced in Scotland*!

FROM *Sleepless in Scotland*

"You are no gentleman!" Triona said, her voice trembling furiously.

He chuckled, the sound low and husky in the dark. "I never said I was, and you would be wrong to think I wish to be one."

She clenched her hands into fists. "I am done with this! There has been a horrible mistake."

"If there has, it would be your planning to trick a MacLean into marriage."

She swallowed a flash of temper. The man thought she was Caitlyn, and her sister's brash words and actions were reprehensible.

"My lord, allow me to introduce myself once and for all. I am Caitlyn Hurst's sister, Triona Hurst."

His deep laugh was not pleasant. "Yes, the convenient mystery twin. Really, is that the best story you can come up with?"

"It's the truth. I realize Caitlyn's behavior has

been terrible. I, too, was shocked when I discovered her plan to trick you into—"

He laughed, the sound rolling over her like a dash of cold water. "Come, Miss Hurst, we both know there is no 'sister Triona.'"

"It's the truth," she replied in a waspish tone, clenching her hands. "If you'd light a blasted lamp, you'd see for yourself!"

Still chuckling, he settled into the corner of the rumbling coach. "There's no need for such games, my dear. I am master of this trick now." He yawned. "Because of your silly plan, I had but an hour of sleep last night and was up with the sun. You may entertain me with your faradiddles when I awake."

Triona ground her teeth. The wretch was going to *sleep*? "Look, MacLean, I refuse to just sit here while you—"

"You don't have a choice," he replied, an edge of impatience to his voice.

"I'm *not* going to accept this simply because you—"

"Enough."

His dangerously low, flat voice doused her irritation with cold reason. She was alone in a dark coach with a man she knew very little about, and what she *did* know wasn't promising. Her grandmother's tales about the MacLeans' storm-inducing temper and Aunt Lavinia's warning about the man's pride told her challenging him directly would be a poor decision.

To some extent, she was defenseless—though a woman of intelligence could always find some sort of weapon. She flexed her foot, thinking that her pointed boot could be used to good effect. It wasn't much, but it replenished her sense of calm.

If she wished to escape this little adventure unscathed, she must use her wits. She'd have to make her move when the carriage was still and there might be other people nearby—decent people, she hoped, who would help a woman in distress. "My lord, I suggest we find the nearest inn and repair there to discuss this unfortunate happening."

"There is no inn on this stretch of road, but I plan to stop within the hour. Meanwhile, I've ridden all day and I'm tired, so I am going to sleep." His voice deepened as he added, "Unless, of course, you are offering to entertain me with more than senseless babble?"

"Entertain? How could I—" Realization dawned, along with a flood of heated embarrassment. "I'd rather eat mud!"

He chuckled, the sound as rich as it was unexpected. "Then hush and let me sleep." He shifted deeper into the corner, though his long legs still filled more than his fair half of the space. "Sleep, Caitlyn or Caitriona or whatever you call yourself. Sleep or be silent."

Fuming, Triona hoped the lout would be in a more accommodating mood once he'd slept. She tugged the blankets around her from neck to toe and settled into her own corner.

As soon as they reached someplace with a lantern, MacLean would realize his error and send her home. Meanwhile, all she could do was rest. The mad race to reach London, then the disappointment of failing to find Caitlyn twice over, had exhausted her. Her body ached from the roughness of the ride, too.

She turned toward the plush squabs, slipped her hands beneath her cheek, and willed herself to relax.

Yet she found herself listening to the deep breathing of her captor and wondering dismally where Caitlyn might be. Had her sister changed her mind at the eleventh hour? Or had something befallen her?

Worried for both Caitlyn and herself, Triona shifted, exhausted yet unable to rest. Her knee ached, her body still thrummed from MacLean's kiss, and her lips felt swollen and tender. She lifted a hand to her mouth, shivering at the way it tingled.

No one had ever dared kiss her before. Father's stern presence had protected her from many things, she realized, and in a way, it was rather sad. She was twenty-three years of age and had never been stirred by passion.

Triona frowned, realizing she was sorry for her lack of experience; a moral woman should be scandalized. She couldn't dredge up a bit of outrage, though.

The kiss had been . . . interesting. MacLean had been thorough and expert, a trait even an inexperienced kisser could recognize, and she thought she might enjoy kissing under different circumstances. She might enjoy it a lot, in fact. After all, what harm could come from a simple kiss?

She yawned. The rocking coach and the deep, soft cushions cradled her as they raced through the night, MacLean's deep breathing soothing her. Soon, sleep claimed her and hugged her into blissful nothingness.

Triona awoke, slowly becoming aware of the rocking of the coach, the creak of the straps overhead, and the incredible warmth engulfing her. She stirred, rubbing her fingers against the rough pillow beneath her cheek. She frowned at the roughness; then her fingers grazed something hard. She opened her eyes to find herself in a carriage, enveloped in dim light from a dim lantern, and blinked at the object at her fingertips.

It was a button. A mother-of-pearl button.

On a pillow?

Bemused, her gaze traveled from the button

upward, to another button, to a wide collar and a snowy white cravat, and farther—past a firm chin covered with black stubble, over a sensual mouth, to a pair of amused green eyes. *MacLean!*

Triona gasped and bolted upright, leaving the warmth of the arm that had been tucked about her.

Hugh, who'd been enjoying the many expressions that had flickered over her face, chuckled. "Easy, sweet. You'll hit your head on the ceiling."

His mussed companion hugged herself, her gaze sparkling with anger. With a sniff, she moved to the farthest corner of the coach. "What were you doing on *my* seat?"

He shrugged, enjoying her discomfort. "You began to fall over. I merely gave you something to fall against."

Her brows lowered, her eyes flashing her irritation. Hugh was very glad he'd lit the lamp, though he'd kept it very low so as not to awaken his captive. In the faint, shadowed light, it was a testament to the strength of her expressions that he was able to read them at all.

It was odd, but in the few times he had met Caitlyn Hurst, he'd missed several important things about her—mainly because he'd made a point of not paying her the slightest heed. He hadn't spoken to her, looked directly at her, or even acknowledged her presence. He knew it had piqued her, and he'd enjoyed that immensely. Now he realized what he'd missed by his endeavors.

For one thing, he'd mistakenly thought her a slender, rather pixieish creature, but her face was softer, more curved than his memory had led him to believe, which made him wonder even more about what was under her cloak.

He'd remembered her voice as being higher-pitched, too. He'd certainly never realized that the troublesome chit possessed a voice that dripped over his senses like warm honey.

He also hadn't been aware of the thrum of physical attraction she exuded that made him . . . restless, eager to engage her in some way. Having seen his older brother's reaction to her seductive powers, he should have expected it. Perhaps he'd been immune before because he hadn't been in such close proximity. It was purely an imp of devilment that had made him slip onto her seat and pull her head to his shoulder, and her reaction hadn't disappointed him.

It was his *own* reaction that had astonished him. Having drawn her close, he'd been hard pressed not to touch her in other ways, and only the fact she'd been fast asleep had saved them both. Not that he really needed to worry. Her behavior had been wanton from the beginning, and she'd never squander her attention on a younger son. She'd be as anxious to end this farce as he was, probably more so.

A surprising twist of regret surged through him at the thought.

By Zeus, he needed to tread carefully. This woman was as false as her smiles. He'd suffered the hidden barbs of a woman's wiles before, and he'd not suffer them again.

She'd even attempted to convince him she was an innocent, with her refusal to respond to his kiss. She'd done very well at playing the shocked virgin, he thought grudgingly. Fortunately, he knew just who and what she was, and innocence had nothing to do with it.

Her gaze suddenly focused on the lamp and she turned toward him, looking eager. "Now you can see my face!"

He raised his brows. Was she looking for compliments? "So?"

She said impatiently, "Now you can see I'm not Caitlyn!"

His gaze raked over her honey-gold hair, mussed into curls about a distinctively heart-shaped face. "Still playing me for a fool, Hurst?"

She fisted her hands. "Blast it! You, my lord, have made a mistake."

"Not as much of one as you." The coach slowed and he turned to lift the corner of the curtain. As he did so, she gasped.

He glanced back at her and found her gaze

locked on his hair. She stammered, "Y-y-you're not Alexander MacLean! You're his brother, Hugh!"

She'd seen the streak of white hair that brushed back from one brow, a relic of a dark time that he never dwelled on. "Stop playing the fool; it doesn't become you. You know damned well who I am."

"Oh!" She fisted her hands and pressed them to her eyes for a moment before she dropped them back to her lap. "You are going to drive me mad! You don't believe a word I say and—"

Her lips thinned, her gaze narrowed, and he could almost see the thoughts flickering through her mind. *By Zeus, I've never seen such an expressive face before.*

Her lips relaxed, and then a faint smile curved them as her gaze traced the white hair at his temple.

"There is nothing humorous in this situation."

She lifted her brows, a genuine twinkle in her fine eyes. "Ah, but there is. I thought you were someone else while you now think I'm someone else—" She chuckled, the sound rich as cream. "The situation may be untenable, but the irony is delicious."

But not as delicious as you. He scowled, startled at his own thoughts.

"Stop this nonsense," he said impatiently. "I refuse to—" The coach slowed, then turned a corner. "Ah, the inn. It's about time."

Her eyes, large and dark in the dim light,

sparkled with amusement. "Once we're in the stronger light, you'll see your error." A chuckle broke free, and she regarded him with such lively humor that Hugh was tempted to grin back.

Almost.

Finally he understood why Alexander had pursued her, even though he knew the dangers. There was something incredibly taking about the curve of her cheek, the way her thick lashes shadowed her large eyes, and the fascinating display of emotions across her expressive face.

It was a damned shame she was layered in two cloaks, for he couldn't see her figure. He knew what to expect, yet she seemed more rounded now, and oddly . . . taller, perhaps?

A chill rippled through Hugh.

Good God, had he seen what he wanted to see? What he'd expected to see? Surely he hadn't been so—

The coach rocked to a halt, but Hugh was only distantly aware of the cry of his coachman, the sound of another carriage drawing up beside his.

Then the door flew open and Hugh turned, only to meet a fist as it plowed into his chin.

The blow did little more than stun him for a second. He rubbed his chin and glared at his attacker, a smallish older man wearing a fashionable multi-caped coat. "Lord Galloway," he said curtly.

"You cur!" Galloway's face was a mask of fury.

Hugh's companion lurched into the man's arms. "Uncle Bedford!" she cried. "I am so *glad* to see you!"

"There, there, my dear," Lord Galloway said, fixing a very stern gaze on Hugh. "This ordeal is over, Caitriona."

Caitriona—not Caitlyn. Hugh's heart thudded sickly as he closed his eyes and faced the truth. God help him—he had the wrong woman.

$\mathcal{F}$ROM The Laird Who Loved Me

Viscount Falkland gaped at the doorway, then frantically adjusted his cuffs and smoothed his waistcoat.

Alexander MacLean followed the plump young lord's gaze and found Caitlyn Hurst entering the room arm-in-arm with Miss Ogilvie. They made a pretty picture, and Alexander would wager the family castle that they knew it.

"Good God, she's—" croaked Falkland, turning bright red. "She's an *angel*! A true angel!" He subsided into wide-eyed bliss.

"Easy, fool," Lord Dervishton muttered. "You'll embarrass us all." He stood and flourished a bow. "Good morning! I trust you both slept well."

"I certainly did," Miss Ogilvie said.

"As did I. I slept until almost ten," Miss Hurst added in her rich, melodious voice.

Falkland visibly shivered and it was all Alexander

could do not to chide the fool. The youth was smitten and, judging from the way Dervishton was watching Caitlyn, he was in no better shape.

Good God, did every man except him fall madly in love with the chit? It was damnably annoying.

Falkland leaned forward eagerly. "Miss Hurst, can I carry your plate at the buffet and—"

"Don't even try it." Dervishton slipped his arm through Caitlyn's. "Miss Hurst needs someone with steadier hands to hold her plate."

Falkland stiffened. "I have steady hands, and I can also—"

"For the love of God!" Alexander snapped, unable to take another moment. "Leave the chit alone! She can get her own damned breakfast."

Falkland turned bright red. "I was just—"

"Sausage!" Caitlyn looked past him to the buffet. "There's only one left and I intend to have it. If you will pardon me a moment, please?" She slipped her arm from Dervishton's, whisked around him, and began to fill a plate while exclaiming at the sight of kippers.

"Excuse me!" Falkland scurried off to pester Caitlyn.

Chuckling, Miss Ogilvie followed.

Dervishton returned to his seat. "Well! I've never been dismissed for a plate of sausage before."

Alexander had to hide a reluctant smile. He

should have been irritated, but his sense of humor was too strong to allow it.

He watched Caitlyn chat animatedly to Falkland about the variety of fruit on the buffet as she filled the plate he dutifully held. Last night she'd been equally enthusiastic about their dinner, her reaction immediate and genuine. Their previous relationship had happened so quickly, so fiercely, that he hadn't learned her everyday likes and dislikes. Not that it mattered, he told himself, dispelling a flicker of unease. He knew her character, and that was all he needed to know.

"Falkland is a fool," Dervishton said into the silence. "He is escorting the charming Miss Hurst this way. I'd have taken her to the other end of the table, away from the competition."

Alexander watched as the weak-chinned viscount assisted Caitlyn to a chair down a little and across from Alexander. Caitlyn was chuckling at something the viscount said, while he watched her with an adoring air that made Alexander nauseous.

When Alexander turned to say as much to Dervishton, he realized that the young lord's gaze was locked on Caitlyn, too. "Watch," he murmured to Alexander. "You'll be glad you did."

"Watch what?"

A mesmerized look in his eyes, Dervishton didn't answer.

Muttering an oath, Alexander turned and regarded Caitlyn. The morning sunlight slanted across her, smoothing over her creamy skin and lighting her golden hair. Her long lashes, thick and dark, shadowed her brown eyes and made them appear darker. She looked fresh and lovely, no different than he expected.

Irritated, Alexander shrugged. "So?"

"You're an impatient sort, aren't you?" Dervishton flicked a glance at Alexander and then turned back to Caitlyn. "Wait a moment and you'll see."

Alexander scowled, but as he did so, Caitlyn leaned over her plate and closed her eyes, an expression of deep pleasure on her face. Her expression was like that of a lover, a sensual yearning.

Instantly his throat tightened and his heart thundered an extra beat. "What in the hell is she doing?"

"Smelling the ham, I believe." Dervishton's voice was oddly deep.

Alexander was fairly certain his own voice wouldn't be normal either as he watched Caitlyn savor the scent of her breakfast.

She smiled and lifted her fork and knife . . . and licked her lips.

"Good God," Dervishton whispered hoarsely.

Alexander's body flash heated, and for one wild, crazed moment, he *wanted* that look—wanted to own it, to possess it, for it to be directed at him and no one else.

Caitlyn slipped her fork beneath a small bit of ham and brought it to her lips.

If he had thought her expression rapturous before, he'd been wrong. There was no description for the blatantly sensual expression she wore now. "Has she never had food before?"

Dervishton answered quietly, "I think it's the sophistication of the dishes that she savors."

"Ham and eggs?"

"Seasoned with chives, butter, and a touch of thyme—Roxburge keeps an excellent table. I have seldom—" Caitlyn slipped a forkful of eggs between her lips. "Damn," he breathed as Caitlyn closed her eyes and slowly chewed, her lips moist.

Damn indeed. The woman was talented at garnering attention, but this was beyond enough! Alexander saw that every man in the room was watching her eat—even Roxburge had a greedy expression on his face.

Alexander's jaw tightened. Then he leaned forward and said in a clear voice, "Miss Hurst, I've never seen a woman eat with such relish."

She lowered her fork. "I doubt I enjoy my food any more than anyone else." She turned to Miss Ogilvie, who'd just taken a seat. "Don't you think that's true, Miss Ogilvie?"

"Oh, we all have our weaknesses," Miss Ogilvie said promptly. "For example, no one loves chocolate cake as much as I."

Beside her, the Earl of Caithness grinned. "I've been known to hoard truffles."

"Don't let MacLean fool you," Dervishton added with a wicked twinkle. "He almost fought our host over the last pear."

Caitlyn blinked. "There were *pears*?"

"I have the last one." Alexander cut a piece and made a show of tasting it. "Mmm! Cinnamon. Excellent."

Her gaze narrowed and her lips pressed firmly together, which made the pear taste all the better to Alexander.

Georgiana's sharp voice cut through the moment. "Lord Dervishton, you mentioned last night that you'd enjoy a ride this afternoon."

Dervishton nodded, his gaze drifting back to Caitlyn.

"I shall have the horses readied, then," Georgiana said sharply. She looked at Alexander and her expression softened. "You don't normally ride for pleasure, I recall."

He shrugged. "I ride while attending my lands. I don't normally find it a relaxing pastime."

Lady Kinloss, seated at Georgiana's left, clapped her hands. "A ride would be delightful! Though her grace and some others"—she sent a quick glance at Alexander—"are not much for riding, I'm sure the *rest* of us would enjoy it. Perhaps we could even visit the Snaid."

Miss Ogilvie looked up from a low conversation she was having with Caithness. "The Snaid? Is that a castle?"

Lady Kinloss tittered. "Lud, no! The Snaid is what the locals call Inversnaid. It's a very small village, but there's an inn there with exceptionally good fare and some astounding views of the Ben, which is quite a lovely mountain. We could ride to the Snaid this afternoon, have tea, and return in plenty of time to get ready for dinner."

"Miss Hurst, do you ride?" Dervishton asked.

"Somewhat. I was learning in London when—" Her gaze slipped to Alexander and then, catching his hard look, she colored. "Of course I can ride."

He lifted his brows, amused at her pink-stained cheeks. Though she was talking about their rides in the park, she was *thinking* about the kisses that had followed. As was he.

Glad to know that those memories still caused her some flustered moments, he allowed his gaze to flicker over her mouth. "Miss Hurst is an excellent . . . *rider*."

She flushed a deeper pink, her gaze flying

to meet his. "Thank you, Lord MacLean, but I wouldn't classify myself as excellent."

"Oh, come now. Don't be so shy about your talents."

All eyes turned toward Caitlyn. She flicked him a cold glance before offering a breathless laugh. "While I can ride, I don't know the horses in her grace's stables and—"

Alexander drawled, "You are worried they wouldn't be up to your standards, of course. Having seen you ride, I can certainly understand your concern."

Dervishton raised his brows. "You have ridden together before?"

"I had the privilege of teaching Miss Hurst when she was in London last season."

There was a distinct pause in the conversation.

Caitlyn's cheeks couldn't be brighter. "Fortunately, I've had more instruction since."

Alexander's humor disappeared. What in the hell did she mean by *that*? Was she talking about riding, or kissing? Dammit, she'd been ensconced in the countryside for the last three months! Had some country bumpkin dared touch her?

Alexander's blood boiled at the thought of Caitlyn's pink and white perfection in the hands of a rough farmer.

Georgiana said, "Miss Hurst, I'm sure we'll find a mount that will match your ability."

"Thank you, your grace," Caitlyn purred, smiling as if she knew the irritation she'd managed to cause him.

"Your grace," Miss Ogilvie interjected, "I'm afraid my riding skills are quite negligible. I will need a gentle mount."

Georgiana seemed amused by this artless confession. "Don't worry, Miss Ogilvie. I have quite a number of smaller, gentler mounts in the stables for just such a reason."

Miss Ogilvie sighed in relief. "Thank you, your grace!"

"Of course." Georgiana sent a look at Alexander from under her lashes and said in a lazy voice, "While most of you are enjoying a ride, I will stay here and attend to some correspondence. That should be a lovely way to spend the afternoon."

Alexander wished she'd try for a little subtlety, but he supposed it was beyond her. To show his disinterest, he turned back to his plate to enjoy his pear. But as he raised his fork, he realized it was gone.

Across from him, Caitlyn lifted the last piece of pear with her fork. She'd stolen *his* pear from *his* plate, the wench!

She smiled at him as she slid the pear between

her lips and chewed it with obvious relish. Her eyes twinkled mischievously and an answering spark of amusement lifted one corner of his mouth, but he staunched it immediately.

For a dangerous moment, he'd almost forgotten why she was here. Dammit, he had to be on guard that she didn't beguile him the way she'd already enslaved the majority of men here. He had a plan for the delectable Miss Caitlyn Hurst that had nothing to do with stolen cinnamon pears or genteel rides through the picturesque countryside. His plan was for revenge, cold and sweet. He owed her a humiliation or two, and before this house party was over, he'd see to it that she got what she so richly deserved—and more.

From One Night in Scotland

Mary Hurst glanced at the clock. If she were a wagering sort, she'd say the earl would burst into their room in approximately five more minutes.

She tilted the chair higher the next time, then slammed it down with all of her might. *Yes, that's quite a bit more—*

The door slammed open, causing Abigail to drop her chair and squeak while Mary froze in place.

The earl was framed by the doorway, his broad shoulders almost filling the space, his head barely clearing the door frame. His dark hair was mussed about his stern visage, his lips pressed in fury, a neck cloth knotted about his throat.

He stalked into the room, a man the size of a great black bear, yet with a firm jaw and flashing pale green eyes.

A delicious shiver ran down Mary's spine. *He arrives like the hero in a play, ready to fight a villain.*

Only, *he* was the villain. Still, she had to admit that the man possessed an unconscious theatrical flair. No one could be immune to the way he moved, all athletic grace and restrained power; the second he walked into a room, he dominated the space and the people without even trying. Added to that was his penchant to dress all in black, and the scarf that covered his jaw and hid a rumored scar . . . Who could blame her for shivering whenever he was near?

His icy gaze locked on her now.

She dipped a quick curtsy. "My lord, how kind of you to join us."

"I will not have this racket in my house."

"And I will not be locked in a room like a mad dog."

His mouth thinned, his hands fisted at his side. The tension in the room grew so thick that Mary thought that she could walk upon it. She stood behind her chair, ready to resume her noise warfare at a second's notice.

But Abigail was not so sternly made. She swallowed noisily, looking from her mistress to the earl and back, her eyes wide, her breath swift.

Erroll turned suddenly, his gaze now locked upon the maid. "*You.*"

Abigail let the chair she was holding drop back and dipped a jerky curtsy, her face pale. "Y-y-yes, m-m-me lord?"

"Out." The earl didn't even glance at Abigail's heaving chest before turning back to Mary.

He wasn't an easily distracted man, she'd give him that, for the maid was difficult to ignore.

"Aye, m-m-my lord, but I—I—" Abigail gulped and shot an uncertain glance at Mary.

"It's quite all right," Mary said despite her own racing heart. "I wish to have a word with his lordship and this will be the perfect opportunity."

Abigail needed no more encouragement and she scuttled toward the door.

"Close it," the earl ordered, his gaze locked on Mary.

With a final, worried backward glance at Mary, Abigail closed the door behind her.

The earl crossed his arms over his broad chest and scowled. "I don't appreciate being awakened in such a fashion."

Mary realized that the earl must have dressed in extreme haste, for his waistcoat was hanging open and his shirt was half tucked. His coat, too, was slightly askew, as if he'd pulled it on while walking.

That was odd. One of the servants must have rushed to his apartments and awoken him with a complaint about the noise, which had obviously made him furiously toss on his clothes and race here. But how had he gotten here so fast? His bedchamber was in the opposite wing; Muir had let that fact slip as he escorted her here last night.

Well, however it happened, her ploy had worked, for here he was.

She folded her hands primly before her and smiled. "I can see that we awakened you and it's put you in an ill mood. I'm not being unreasonable, for I *did* ask to be allowed out, but we were refused."

"On my orders."

"Exactly. Therefore, I was forced to more extreme measures. If you'll unlock the door and leave it unlocked, I promise the noise won't happen again."

"No."

Her calm smile slipped. No explanation, no appreciation of her logic, just "no" in a deadly cold voice. She lifted her chin. "Fine. Then I'll continue with my concert." She grasped the chair, rocked it forward on its front legs, then slammed it down onto the floor.

"Stop that."

"Not until you release me from this room."

A low rumble remarkably like a growl emanated from the earl. "Do not push me in this manner. You will regret it."

"Do not push *me,* my lord. I won't accept such rude treatment."

His lips were almost white as he attempted to

hold back God only knew what sort of improper retort.

Mary's heart thudded rapidly and she had to quell a childish desire to hike her skirts and run. She'd wanted to ignite him to action, and she had his attention now. *Don't get rattled. Face your enemy and do not flinch.*

She cleared her throat. "This is an intolerable situation. I'm not happy being locked away."

"I'm not happy that you're making so much noise that I cannot even think in peace."

"Then allow me out. I promise to behave myself. I shall be a perfect guest while we wait to hear from Mr. Young."

"No. I won't have you traipsing around, looking for that damned artifact every time my back is turned."

She frowned, tapping one foot in impatience.

He lifted a brow. "I don't hear you offering to refrain from such a search."

"I suppose I could, but it wouldn't be honest," she replied regretfully. "However much I wish for my freedom, it would be useless to pretend I'm not desperate to place my hands on that artifact."

"You are doing your purpose a grave disservice with that announcement."

"It's the truth." She gripped the back of the chair tighter and leaned forward. "Erroll, my brother's life hangs in the balance. I *must* have that artifact."

His gaze narrowed. "You are almost convincing. . . ."

She closed her eyes and counted to ten. "You will see how mistaken you are when Mr. Young confirms my identity."

"*If* that happens, then the artifact is yours. But until then, you will remain in this room and cease this noise."

"Erroll, I cannot—"

"No. That's my final word. There is no more to be said." He turned and strode back toward the door.

"No."

He paused, one hand on the knob before he shot her a dark look over his shoulder. "*What?*"

"I said no. It's not in my nature to sit tamely by and acquiesce to such barbaric behavior."

His green gaze flickered over her. "You will do as you are told and that's that." He reached for the knob and turned it.

Meanwhile, she gripped the chair again, lifted it, and dropped it to the ground. *THUNK!*

She did it again. And again. And—

The earl spun on his heel, curses snapping from his lips as he strode across the room toward her, his green gaze furious.

Mary instinctively stepped away, which was fortuitous, as the earl snatched up her chair and strode to the window. To Mary's shock, he threw open the window, glanced down to the courtyard, and then tossed the chair over the ledge.

With a splintering crash, the chair smashed on the cobblestones below.

Mary blinked.

Erroll turned away from the window, a faint smile touching his mouth. "There."

"That was—" She couldn't find the words, couldn't believe he'd done such a thing.

"Now, you will behave yourself and remain quietly in your room as you've been told. I shall see to it that some books are brought for your amusement. Hopefully we'll hear from Mr. Young in a week or so—"

"A *week?*"

The earl frowned. "I asked Mr. Young to return here and identify you in person, just so there can be no misunderstanding. So it will be a week, at least."

A *week?* A *whole* week?

Mary clenched her fists at her sides. She was so angry she could have stomped her foot, but she refused to give him the satisfaction. "My lord, I don't think you understand. I must deliver that artifact to my—"

"To your brother William. You informed me of that fact last night. As far as I'm concerned, your brother can wait; I will not release the artifact until I am completely certain you are who you say you are. I owe Michael Hurst my caution, if nothing else."

She lifted her chin. "He doesn't need your caution; he needs your *help*, which you could grant if you'd just give me that artifact and release me so that I can deliver it!"

He scowled, his hands opening and closing at his sides. "You will not be reasonable."

"If you mean will I accept your bullying, then the answer is *no*."

"Fine." He crossed to another chair, swooped it up, and tossed it out the window as well. He did it again, and yet again. The cool outside air began to wash over the room as it emptied, stirring the curtains and making Mary shiver as wood splintered upon the courtyard below.

As Erroll reached for the final chair, this one a lovely cushioned one covered with embroidered tapestry, she could bear no more. "Oh, stop! It's a horrid waste. Those are beautiful chairs."

He shrugged. "If I wish to replace them, I'll order more." And with that, that last chair joined its fellows on the cobblestones below.

Mary rubbed her forehead. When she was growing up in the vicarage, a chair—especially one as finely made as these—was a treasure to be enjoyed and savored, not something to be tossed away like a broken dish. The wastefulness banished her fear as nothing else could have.

Had Erroll been one of her brothers, she'd have

set him to rights with a few well-chosen words. But he was her enemy sworn, so she held her anger like a shield, using her scorn as her bolster in the coming confrontation.

Mary didn't know what Michael would do in this situation, and suddenly she didn't care. She'd handle this her own way. *If the furnishings mean so little to him, then let him toss all of them.*

She eyed the remaining furniture, then pointed to a small stool. "I could make noise with that."

His brows snapped down. "You challenge me, woman."

"Someone needs to."

Scowling as blackly as a pirate, he strode to the stool, snatched it up, and tossed it out the window.

She waited until she heard the crash from the courtyard before she pointed to the tapestry-covered seat to the dressing table. "And that."

Seconds later, it joined the others.

She pointed to the fire poker set. "And those, of course. You wouldn't believe the noise I could make with iron."

Without a second's delay, they joined the tumbled, splintered pile in the courtyard.

"Anything else?" he asked grimly.

"Oh, I'm sure I'll find something." She gave him a brilliantly smug smile, her anger hidden behind her teeth. "I don't cry quit simply because someone else cannot keep their temper."

For one second, she feared she'd gone too far, for his mouth thinned in a most ominous way. Instead, he turned on his heel and emptied out the remainder of movable furniture, tossing each item one at a time out the window. When he was done, nothing was left in the room other than a large wardrobe, the massive bed, and the heavy, marble-topped dressing table.

Mary looked about the nearly empty room. "That was certainly dramatic."

His gaze narrowed, as she shrugged. "It may be a bit late to mention this, but I suppose you couldn't have had the furniture removed and stored, rather than destroying it?"

"I could, but it wouldn't have made my point."

"Your point being that you've a horrid temper and can act like a complete and utter ass? Yes, I'd say you've made your point quite well."

He was across the room so quickly that she didn't have time to do more than suck in her breath. He glared down at her, his broad shoulders blocking all of the light from the windows, and she was once again astounded at his size.

His deep voice roiled across her like the hot lick of flames. "Listen to me well: I will not brook insolence. You *will* do as you're told. Until Mr. Young confirms your identity, you will remain here, in this room, and behave yourself. If you don't, then you won't have even the luxuries you have now. Am I understood?"

She straightened her shoulders and tilted her head back to stare up into his haughty face. "Even if you take *all* of the furnishings *and* toss them out the window *and* remove me from this room *and* lock me away in the—the—the stables, I will do what I must to make certain you are every bit as miserable as I. Am *I* understood?"

Angus had never been so furious in his entire life. This woman, this impostor, who'd dared come to *his* home to steal an object entrusted to him by one of the few men he deemed a friend, did not deserve even the kindnesses he had bestowed upon her—a luxurious bedchamber with her maid in attendance. Why, he'd even left his own comfortable bedchamber for the smaller one adjacent to this to make certain she was safe!

Yet the chit showed no gratitude and actively attempted to irk him. Well, she'd succeeded.

He knew some of his anger had to do with being awakened from a rare, deep sleep, but more of it was because she refused to be bent to his will. He wasn't used to that, and he'd be damned if he'd start now.

Even now she glared up at him as if unafraid and unmoved by his fury. Yet she lied, and he knew it.

Her modestly covered chest—temptingly generous—rose and fell quickly, straining at her pale blue gown. Her sherry-colored eyes were slightly dilated, her lips parted, her creamy skin flushed.

Every word she uttered was a deliberate challenge. Well, the chit was about to get what she so desperately desired: an answer for her impertinence.

He grasped her to him, lifted her off her feet, and pulled her curvaceous figure against him. He had intended to simply hold her there until she begged to be released, but once he felt her warm skin beneath his hands, the pressure of her generous breasts upon his chest, the excited gasp from her parted lips, suddenly holding her wasn't nearly enough.

He bent his head and kissed her, pouring all of his discontent, fury, and heated desire into it.

The instant his mouth closed over hers, he realized his mistake. His anger fled before an onslaught of pure, red-hot lust. He forgot why he was mad, why she was locked here in this room, forgot everything but the blinding sensuality of her soft curves pressed against him while her lavender scent engulfed him like a velvet prison.

She froze for a second, then she, too, was lost in the heat that flared between them. He could feel the thunder of her heart as it merged with his, the desperation of her hands as they grasped his coat.

He cupped her to him, lifting her higher until her

arms wrapped about his neck. She moaned against his mouth, opening her lips beneath his, desperately seeking.

He was vaguely surprised at her boldness, yet her response answered his own passion so clearly that he didn't question it, but welcomed and encouraged it. He teased her lips farther apart and deepened the kiss, holding her firmly to him, no longer thinking—just feeling, enjoying, tasting and touching and stroking. His hands never stilled, but molded her to him, cupping her rounded ass, sliding up her sides to find her generous breasts and—

A shout rose through the open window as a servant found the pile of broken furniture. Recalled to his senses, Angus reluctantly broke the kiss and slid Mary to the floor.

Her eyes were still closed, her lips still parted as she panted, her hands bunched about his lapels as if she might fall if she released them.

The sight relaxed him. He might be flushed with passion, but she was utterly overcome.

The thought soothed his irritation as nothing else had, and he felt a sense of self-satisfaction as he gently released his hold.

Her eyes fluttered open and she gazed up at him in bemused amazement, her mouth temptingly swollen from his kiss. For a wild, impulsive moment he considered kissing her again, but reason returned.

He stepped away and her hands fell from his lapels. "There." He had to clear his throat from the husky passion that still gripped him. "Let that be a lesson to you not to try my temper."

She blinked and opened her mouth as if to say something, but no words tumbled from her parted lips.

Ha! He might have a husky voice, but she was rendered speechless by a mere kiss.

Smirking, he went to the window and closed it. Then he strode to the door, pausing to look back.

She still stood in the center of the almost-empty room. As he watched, she pressed a hand to her lips as if they still tingled from his kiss. Even more interesting, she made no move to argue with him—not a single word or look turned his way.

That was more like it. Though the kiss had affected him more than he'd wished, he was no slave to it as she was. He, therefore, was stronger than she.

Now I know how to stop her. He gave her a mocking bow. "Good day, Miss Hurst. I shall send your maid to you. If you maintain your decorum for the rest of the day, I shall send in a chair with your dinner so that you may have some comfort, though it will be removed once you finish. In the meantime, I believe I shall go for my morning ride."

Satisfied and feeling magnanimous, he left, closing the door behind him.

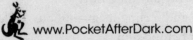